CPITAL
WIVES

OCT 2011

CH

AA

ROCHELLE ALERS

CAPITAL WIVES

Recycling programs
for this product may
not exist in your area.

CAPITAL WIVES

ISBN-13: 978-0-373-22997-0

www.kimanipress.com

Printed in U.S.A.

A worthy wife is the crown of her husband,
but a disgraceful one is like rot in his bones.
— *Proverbs* 12:4

Bethany Paxton

Chapter One

Bethany Paxton went completely still, holding her breath when she felt the whisper of her husband's warm, mint-scented breath brush her cheek, then the press of his mouth.

"Feel better, baby."

She wanted to tell him there was no way she would ever feel better—not when she had been forced to play stepmother to a teenager who had to have been the devil's spawn. Her ultraconservative Bible belt parents had lectured her over and over about using the word *hate,* but she could truly say that she hated her husband's fifteen-year-old daughter. The bitch-in-training went out of her way to work Bethany into a frenzy wherein she'd seriously considered murdering the girl.

One time when she was slicing fruit for a salad, she'd gripped the handle of the knife and had been ready to plunge it into Paige's heart. The thought was so shocking that Bethany called her twin brother, telling him of her wicked thoughts, and he was able to talk her off the proverbial ledge.

Later that night, Bethany downed a bottle of wine, went to sleep and didn't wake up until her children roused her, crying that if she didn't get up they were going to be late for school. Now when she drank herself into a stupor it didn't matter whether she got out of bed or not. That's what live-in housekeepers were for. As hired help, the woman got up early and made certain her son and daughter were washed, dressed and fed breakfast before she walked them to the corner to wait for the school bus.

At first Damon had balked at hiring a housekeeper when a cleaning service came in twice a week to clean, dust, vacuum and do the laundry, but Bethany did what she hadn't done since she'd first laid eyes on Damon Paxton sitting at a table in an upscale D.C. restaurant more than ten years ago. She had seduced him.

Twenty years his junior, Bethany offered Damon the best sex he'd ever had in his life. It hadn't mattered that he'd been married with a young child. She'd wanted Damon, and after a torrid affair and an uncontested divorce wherein Damon had given his wife a sizable settlement, Bethany had married her prince.

Opening one eye, she squinted at the clock on the bedside table. It was almost eight, and that meant in another hour she would be alone—alone to think about the turn her life had taken. She was only thirty-five but felt years older. She was drinking much too much, and the result was she'd gained weight and the skin under her eyes was puffy.

As Mrs. Damon Paxton she'd found herself isolated, snubbed by the wives of her husband's business associates, which initially led Bethany to doubt her attractiveness and femininity. However, when rumors surfaced that she was a tramp and home wrecker she realized it had been retribution. The first Mrs. Paxton was D.C. royalty, and Bethany was a former beauty queen who had grown up in an Alabama trailer park. Only within the privacy of her bedroom did she feel confident enough to ensure her marriage was on solid footing.

Turning over and staring up at the gossamer fabric draping the antique canopy bed, Bethany knew she couldn't continue the pretense that she had the perfect life and the perfect marriage. If she were truly honest, she would admit that both were in the toilet.

Something had to change; something had to give; she had to change or she would end up like her mother, who'd looked seventy at forty, was depressed, broken and had been dead a week before her body was discovered when a neighbor called the police after she'd noticed a strange odor coming from the adjoining apartment.

Her parents had moved out of the trailer and into a one-bedroom apartment once all their children had left home. Her dad had gone to West Virginia to visit his sister, who'd been hospitalized with a terminal illness, when he was notified that his wife had died from natural causes. It had been the last time Bethany had visited Parkers Corner.

Bethany sat up, opened the drawer to the bedside table and removed a cloth-covered journal and pen. Flipping to a blank page, she jotted down a list of things she needed to do: Diet. Call dermatologist about Botox. Contact personal trainer. She closed the book, picked up her cell phone, scrolled through her directory and tapped the button for her dermatologist, leaving a voice-mail message for someone to return her call. Minutes later she confirmed a session with her longtime personal trainer.

Dieting was easy. All she had to do was drink more water, increase daily portions of fruits and vegetables and limit eating red meat to twice a week. She would give herself two weeks of dieting and exercise before emerging from what had become a period of self-isolation. Damon's social secretary had called her with an update of his calendar and Bethany would call Caroline and let her know to which of the events she would accompany her husband.

Swinging her legs over the side of the bed, she walked from the bedroom to her en suite bath. One thing she had insisted on when she and Damon had gone house hunting: she had to have her own bathroom. Living in a double-wide with six other people and one bathroom had scarred Bethany for life. She could never linger more than three minutes because someone was always knocking on the door. What family members didn't know was the bathroom had become her sanctuary—a place that in her imagination had become a magical place where she as a princess waited for her prince to come and rescue her from the squalor, poverty and the ridicule of other kids who constantly reminded Bethany that she was wearing her older sister's hand-me-downs.

But that all changed as her body filled out. Boys had begun to notice her long legs, natural wavy flaxen hair, luminous violet eyes framed by long charcoal-gray lashes and her seductive smile that never failed to elicit gasps from the opposite sex. It had taken hours of practicing in front of the bathroom mirror before Bethany was able to lower her eyelids, tilt her head at an angle and peer up at a man through her lashes to get him to do whatever she wanted.

Her smile, body and face had been her ticket out of the tiny mill town and into the spotlight as beauty queen, soap opera actress and news correspondent. When she was assigned to cover a newly elected representative from her home state, her life had changed forever. It was her first visit to the nation's capital and the first time she came face-to-face with Damon Paxton. As one of D.C.'s most influential lobbyists, Damon was purported to be as powerful as any man, past or present, who'd occupied the Oval Office.

Bethany stared at her reflection in the mirrors above the counter that created an illusion of infinite space. Pale ash cabinetry and a raised one-step from the vanity area functioned as a dressing room; a water closet and low tub were screened by sliding ash doors fitted with light-filtering frosted glass.

Her bathroom had become her retreat when she closed and locked the door, shutting out the constant bickering between her son and daughter and Damon when he went on incessantly about up-and-coming politicos and veteran elected officials whom he'd sought to bring into his sphere of influence.

It was no wonder she'd begun drinking. It was either booze or drugs. Even when her college friends were smoking marijuana and/or snorting cocaine, Bethany had never been one to experiment, because she feared becoming addicted like her father, who had become hooked on painkillers after he'd broken his back when he'd slipped on a wet floor at the garage where he'd worked as a mechanic. He'd tried suing the owner, but lost his case because he'd neglected to wipe up the oil that had been leaking from the car he'd been working on. Her father was forced to retire and wound up on welfare with a Medicaid card and food stamps.

And she didn't need a therapist to tell her why she had begun drinking more than usual. It was because of Damon's daughter Paige. It was as if the girl existed solely to disrupt her father's marriage and to make their lives a living hell. Beth knew the girl blamed her for breaking up her father and mother's marriage. What Paige hadn't known was that her parents' marriage had been over for years.

Opening a drawer under the counter, Bethany took out a jar of cleansing cream her dermatologist had recommended to offset the dry, red patches that occurred whenever she used soap on her face. Going through her morning ritual, she washed her face, brushed her teeth, followed by a liberal amount of mouthwash, then showered and shampooed her hair. The clock on a table in the dressing room chimed the hour. It was nine o'clock, and that meant she had the house to herself. Abigail and Connor were probably boarding their bus that would take them to a private school, while Paige was settling into her second-period class at a nearby high school.

After slathering her body with a scented moisturizer, Bethany walked back into her bedroom to get dressed. She didn't have to think about what she would wear, because it was always the same: a matching set of underwear, white T, fitted jeans and running shoes. There had been a time before she'd married Damon that jeans and running shoes were relegated to weekends. But that was when she'd worked as a news correspondent.

She wasn't complaining, because she'd traded her career for marriage and motherhood, but Bethany couldn't have predicted she would become a stepmother to a surly, impudent teenage girl. Walking out of the bedroom, she made her way down the carpeted hallway to the back staircase that provided direct access to the gourmet kitchen, pantry and the housekeeper's one-bedroom apartment. Mrs. Rodgers had become an invaluable addition to the family, because her presence allowed Bethany the freedom to make and keep appointments that coincided with her children getting off the bus at the end of a school day.

There were two things Damon had insisted on: she would become a stay-at-home mother and she had to be home in time to meet their children's school bus. She was still a stay-at-home mom, but Mrs. Rodgers filled in for her whenever she wasn't there when her children came home from school.

Entering the kitchen, Bethany went completely still when

she saw Paige sitting at the table in the breakfast nook flipping the pages of a magazine. "What are you still doing here?" The question had come out harsher than Bethany wanted it to.

Paige Paxton's head popped up, her cold blue gaze raking her stepmother's too-perfect face like a bird's talons. Even with no makeup, wet hair, jeans and a T her father's trophy wife was stunning.

The teenager's thin upper lip curled into a sneer. "If you'd put my school calendar up like you do Connor's and Abigail's, you would've known that I don't have classes today. The teachers have staff development today and tomorrow."

"I would have put it up if you'd given it to me," Bethany countered, walking into the kitchen and over to the coffeemaker. She turned it on and placed a pod into the well.

Paige made a clucking sound with her tongue. "Whateva," she drawled.

Resting a hip against the counter, Bethany crossed her arms under her breasts. "Are you or aren't you going to give me your calendar?"

"I'll think about it."

Spots of color dotted Bethany's cheeks. "What's there to think about, Paige?"

Paige's gaze went back to the magazines with photos of models wearing incredible clothes—clothes the girls at her school wore when they didn't have to wear the regulation uniform of a charcoal-gray pleated skirt, matching knee socks, white blouse with a red tie and navy blazer. "I think I want to be homeschooled."

Bethany froze for the second time in a matter of minutes. "Where is this coming from, Paige? I thought you liked your school."

"I'm surprised you even think. I was under the impression the only thing you know how to do is *fuck!*"

An audible gasp escaped Bethany's parted lips as she took a step and then stopped herself before she could launch herself across the space separating her from the girl. Her hands curled into tight fists. "If you ever utter that word in my presence again I'll make certain you'll never spend another night under this roof."

Paige's eyes narrowed as she pushed to her feet. "I don't think so. This is my father's house."

"Wrong, Paige. This is also my house, and don't forget I did you a favor when I told your father you could come and live here because you didn't want to move to Idaho. Disrespect me again and you're outta here."

A wave of color suffused Paige's face, which appeared more pale than it actually was because of the inky-black hair she'd inherited from her mother. "I don't have to talk to you."

"Then don't," Bethany retorted as she struggled to control her rising temper. Connor and Abigail had never argued or fought with each other until their older sister had come to live with them. Now the bickering was nonstop. "If you don't want to live here, then I'll talk to your father about sending you back to your mother."

"I don't want to live with her."

"You don't want to live with her, and you don't want to live with me. I suggest you make up your mind, because right now I can't see you celebrating your sweet sixteen here."

Rolling her eyes, Paige flopped back down to the cushioned bench seat. "What do you want from me?"

"An apology will do," Bethany said.

"You want me to tell you I'm sorry even when I don't mean it?"

Resting her hands at her waist, Bethany stared at Damon's eldest child. "Maybe I just need to hear it even if you'll never mean it."

There came a beat. "Okay…I'm sorry. There. I've said it," Paige spat out.

"Apology accepted." Bethany decided to extend the olive branch because going toe-to-toe with the child was wearing her down. "I was going to make breakfast for myself. Would you like me to fix something for you?"

"Do I look like I need to eat?" Paige snapped.

"If you think you're going to lose weight by not eating, then you're taking the wrong approach," she told Paige as she opened the built-in refrigerator and took out a carton of eggs.

She knew some of the girl's hostility was because of body image. Paige had stopped growing after hitting a height of five-three. Although her parents were both tall and slim, she had yet to lose what one would refer to as baby fat. Her best features were her eyes and hair. And except for an occasional breakout, her skin was as clear as bone china. Bethany had overheard Paige asking Damon if she could get a nose job and liposuction. He'd promised her she could get her nose fixed for her sixteenth birthday but had drawn the line at liposuction. His comeback was that if she exercised more then she would not only lose weight but also keep it off.

"FYI…I lost two pounds last week eating salads."

"What kind of salads?"

"Lettuce."

"Lettuce and what?" Bethany asked.

"Just lettuce with light Italian dressing."

Opening the refrigerator again, Bethany took out the ingredients for a veggie omelet. "What about fruit, vegetables or protein?"

"What about them?"

"You need them for a balanced diet."

"Meat makes me fat."

Bethany diced an onion, pepper and several mushrooms.

"You're not fat, Paige. What you need to do is tone your body. You can come with me when I work out with my trainer."

"I'll think about it," Paige mumbled. She wasn't about to give Bethany the satisfaction of agreeing with her. She would never have her stepmother's tall, willowy body, but knew she would look better without the additional twenty pounds she'd put on after her mother told her she was going to marry the man who'd once been her landscaper before he'd become her lover. What had frightened Paige was that the man had made sexual innuendos to his employer's daughter the year she turned twelve. At first she'd believed she'd imagined his intent, but the one time he walked into her bedroom while she was getting dressed confirmed her suspicions that he was a predator. There was no way she was going to live with her mother, even if she still blamed Bethany for breaking up her parents' marriage.

"Are you certain you don't want an omelet?" Bethany asked, breaking into Paige's musing.

"Is it fattening?"

Bethany smiled. "No. I doubt if it's more than fifty calories. And that includes cooking it with a nonstick butter-flavored cooking spray."

"Okay. I'll have one."

Not wanting to believe she'd scaled a small hurdle, Bethany cut up enough vegetables for two omelets. She squeezed oranges for juice and toasted two slices of all-grain bread. She wasn't certain if Paige would eat the bread, but she decided to offer it to her anyway. She'd been where Paige was now—yo-yo dieting that had compromised her health when she experienced horrific headaches and fainting spells. A nutritionist taught her what to eat to lose and then maintain her weight, while a personal trainer put her through an exercise regimen that toned and reconfigured her body until she looked as if she'd been nipped and tucked—even after two children.

Bethany was aware that she was a trophy wife, and she planned to look the part for as long as she could. The wives of Damon's associates had not accepted her, but she wasn't going to give the jealous women the satisfaction of knowing how much their rejection had affected her. The few times she'd found herself in their presence she'd made certain to look her best. The saying was that revenge was best served cold, but for Bethany it was looking hot. So hot that their husbands couldn't stop staring at her. And if she had been the bitch everyone thought she was, then she would have slept with each of the men, then reported back to their wives on their performances—or lack thereof.

Bethany and Paige ate without talking, only the sound of music coming from a stereo unit on the counter breaking the uncomfortable silence. There was so much she wanted to talk about with Paige, but she decided to enjoy their unexpected and no doubt temporary truce. She was only twenty years older than the girl and had wanted to relate to her not as a mother but as an older sister.

Bethany had never been on good terms with her two sisters because they'd always resented her ambition to escape the predictable existence if she'd remained in the tiny town where everyone knew one another. Alice and Mary-Beth stayed, married local boys and continued the cycle of working for the mill or in the newly constructed Walmart. Her younger brother did get out when he joined the Marines as a reservist, but after two tours in Iraq had moved to Alaska where he'd married and fathered three children in five years. It had been more than four years since Bethany had gotten a letter from him. Her letters to him had been returned with a stamp indicating addressee unknown.

Her parents had stopped talking to her when she told them she couldn't send them any more money, so that left just her and her twin. Jack was kind, gentle, but easily misled. He'd been arrested so many times for petty crimes that the local sheriff would lock him up for his own safety. Although Jack hadn't been able to stay out of trouble he had become Bethany's voice of reason. Whenever she needed someone to listen without passing judgment, Jack was there. Whenever she felt as if she was at her wit's end, Jack was able to give her another perspective. When he'd told her that nothing or no one was worth her losing her freedom she'd thought about what he had gone through whenever he was locked up. The one time he'd admitted that another prisoner had sexually abused him, Bethany had cried for days. Then she'd called the sheriff to tell him if he had to lock up her brother, to please not put him in a cell with another prisoner. If the sheriff had been anyone but the boy who'd been homecoming king while she was his homecoming queen he would've hung up on her. She and Lenny Mortimer had dated during their last year in high school, and although many thought they would eventually marry Bethany knew differently. She'd sworn an oath when she'd received notification that she had been granted an academic scholarship to attend the University of Virginia that she would never return to Parkers Corner to live.

"Are you serious about wanting to be homeschooled?" she asked Paige, who'd eaten half her omelet before setting down her fork.

"Yeah."

"Have you spoken to your father about it?" Paige nodded. "What did he say?" Bethany asked, continuing with her questioning.

"He said I would have to talk to you."

Pale eyebrows lifted a fraction. "Why me?"

A hint of smile played at the corners of Paige's mouth. "Because you would have to be my teacher."

Bethany's mouth opened and closed several times. "You're kidding."

"Nope. Who else did you think would teach me?"

"I'm not a teacher, Paige."

"But you did graduate college, didn't you?"

"Yes, I did. But that still doesn't mean I would be the best candidate to teach you chemistry, algebra and trigonometry."

Paige smiled. "That's what teachers' guides are for."

"That's where you're wrong, Paige. I have enough to do when I check and help Abby and Connor with their home-work. There's no way I'm going to spend five hours a day teaching and tutoring you."

"What the hell else do you have to do all day?" Paige shouted. "You have someone come in twice a week to clean the house and do laundry. Miss Rodgers does everything else. So why can't you become my teacher?"

"Because I am *not* a teacher." Bethany had punctuated each word. "I majored in English and communications, not math and science."

"Maybe I should tell Daddy that you don't want to home-school me because I'm not your daughter."

"I don't give a damn what you tell him. I'm not going to homeschool you when you're enrolled in one of the best private schools in Virginia and—"

Paige put up her hand, stopping Bethany's tirade. "Daddy told me he's going to talk to you about it."

Rising to her feet, Bethany glared down at the manipula-tive girl. There was nothing to talk about. She had no in-tention of homeschooling Paige when Damon spent what amounted to a small fortune for her tuition. If Paige had planned to come between her and Damon, then she was fighting hard to make it a reality. As much as she loved her husband, Bethany had made up her mind to risk her marriage rather than be manipulated by a malcontent, rebellious and jealous adolescent.

Leaning closer, she narrowed her eyes. "There is nothing to talk about."

Reaching over, Bethany picked up Paige's plate and emptied the contents in the trash. She left the dishes in the sink for Mrs. Rodgers to put in the dishwasher, then went to get her coat, purse and car keys. She had to get out of the house before she did or said something she would later regret.

Bethany did not glance up from the book she was reading when Damon walked into the bedroom, closing and locking the door behind him. He'd called earlier to let her know he would not join the family for dinner. He'd had a dinner meeting with the junior senator from Wisconsin.

"Hey, baby."

She looked up and smiled. At fifty-four, Damon Pennington Paxton had movie-star looks. His close-cropped light brown hair was sprinkled with silver, and he had tiny, attractive lines around large, deep-set dark blue eyes that were mesmerizing whenever he smiled. Damon held a powerful position in D.C., and whenever elected officials were told Damon was on the phone, his call was promptly answered.

"Hey, yourself," she said. Rising off the window seat, Bethany approached him. Wrapping her arms around his waist, she pressed her breasts to his chest. "How was your day?" It was the same thing she asked him every day.

"It could've been better," he said, his soft Southern drawl caressing her ear.

"What's wrong, sweetheart?" she crooned, her hand massaging her husband's back over his shirt.

"Paige called me at the office, crying that you won't home-school her because you hate her."

Easing back, Bethany met Damon's eyes. "That's not true, and you know it, Damon. If I hated her, then I never would've agreed to have her come here to live. When I spoke to Jean about Paige coming here to live with us, she was up-set because she didn't want to lose her daughter. I reassured her I would treat Paige no differently than I would Abby or Connor, but it hasn't been easy. She fights with me about everything." Bethany then informed him that Paige had dis-rupted what had been a peaceful household to one where the younger children were now fighting with each other.

"Why didn't you tell me about this before?"

Bethany closed her eyes, and when she opened them she saw something in her husband's eyes that hadn't been there before—anger. "I thought I'd be able to deal with her."

"There's no way you could deal with her, Beth! She's my daughter, not yours, so it's my responsibility to deal with her. You don't need to be involved when it concerns my child."

The frustration that had been building inside Bethany for the past four months felt like gall in her mouth; she dropped her arms and took a step backward. "So, it's going to be your child and my children!" she screamed. "What do I do, Damon? Let her verbally abuse me, then say wait until your father gets home? I'm sorry, but it's not going to go down that way. I'm tired of being nice to her out of respect for you. You better tell your daughter that she'd better take her ass to that fancy school you pay twenty gees for, because I wouldn't help her add two and two."

Turning on her heel, Bethany walked out of the bedroom and into one of the guest suites. Falling across the bed, she did what she hadn't done in years. She cried. She cried until her sobs became hiccuping sounds before she slept from emotional exhaustion. It would be the first night since she had seduced Damon Paxton that they would sleep under the same roof, but not in the same bed.

Deanna Tyson

Chapter Two

Deanna Tyson sat in her client's solarium going over the seating arrangements for an intimate dinner party for the following evening. It was the fourth time Mrs. Otis Charles had changed her mind as to where she wanted her guests to sit.

Crossing one long, slender leg over the opposite knee, Deanna gave the older woman a steely look. "I have to know tonight where everyone is going to sit because when I come here tomorrow I'll be too busy with the catering staff to begin rearranging seating."

Hannah Charles exhaled an audible breath at the same time as she shook her head. "You just can't imagine the dilemma I'm going through with my sorors. A couple of them have been at each other's throats for the past two months. And it's not as if I can uninvite them."

Deanna stared at the wife of one of the ranking House members. Hannah had married Illinois Representative Otis Charles, chairman of the Ways and Means Committee three months after his wife of twenty-six years had passed away.

There were rumors that Hannah had been sleeping with the elder statesman even before the late Mrs. Charles was diagnosed with an aggressive form of cancer. Hannah was fairly attractive, and what most people found shocking was that she was more than a decade older than her fiftysomething husband. And her silver hair complemented a flawless complexion that reminded Deanna of golden honey.

"You don't have to uninvite them. Seat them at opposite ends of the table," she suggested. "And I'd like to believe they wouldn't disrespect you, your husband or your home with a confrontation."

Hannah patted her ample bosom over a white silk blouse. "I would like to believe that, but I'm beginning to believe what my other sorority sisters are saying about Andrea. Since she lost her husband she hasn't been the same."

"Perhaps you can ask your husband if he has a male friend who can come. I know it's short notice, but it will give Andrea someone to talk to."

Hannah's large eyes became even larger when she contemplated the event planner's suggestion. "I'm certain Otis can find someone. Will you excuse me while I call his office?"

Deanna forced a polite smile. "Of course."

She wanted to tell her client that she wanted to conclude her business and go home. It seemed like a month when it was actually two weeks since she and Spencer had had dinner together. She and Spencer had recently celebrated their eighth wedding anniversary, but Deanna still felt like a newlywed. Maybe it was because she and her husband didn't get to see that much of each other, and when they did it was cause for a minor celebration.

Deanna wasn't one of those complaining wives who bemoaned that she didn't get to see enough of her husband because both were overly ambitious. As a D.C.-based litigator, there were occasions when Spencer spent more time at his office than he did at their Alexandria, Virginia, home. When Deanna set up her event-planning enterprise she hadn't expected it to take off so quickly. One influential client became two, and soon she had made a name for herself as a preeminent D.C. event planner. Her client list included former presidents, vice-presidents and members of the house and senate and diplomatic corps.

She was very discriminating about with whom she contracted because she worked alone. Deanna designed the invitations and response cards and made recommendations as to seating, music, flowers and menus. She'd planned one wedding with eight hundred and fifty guests, and that was for the daughter of a former ambassador to France. Her specialty was dinner parties.

Running a hand over the back of her neck, she lifted the braided twists she had secured with an elastic band. Deanna had experimented with styling her hair with twists three years ago, and they were now shoulder-length. The hairstyle suited her lifestyle, in which she found herself with less and less time to devote to standing hair and nail appointments. Every Sunday evening she washed her hair and went through the ritual of repairing the twists until they were smooth and smelling of the special coconut-scented hairdressing she'd purchased from a local D.C. street vendor.

She stared at the fronds of a potted palm in a corner of the solarium, wondering how Hannah could move into a house that had belonged to another woman and not insist she make some changes. Everything in the house was exactly the same as the first Mrs. Charles had left it. Deanna sat up straight when Hannah returned.

"Otis had one of his aides call his widowed father, and thankfully the man said yes."

Deanna nodded as she uncapped her pen. "What's the gentleman's name?"

"Langdon White."

She wrote down the name on the seating chart next to Andrea Wells, then recapped the pen with a solid gold nib that had been a gift from one of her clients. She closed the planner, slipped it into her tote and stood up. "I'll be here around three, so make certain the cleaning service finishes up before I arrive."

Hannah pressed her palms together. "This is my first dinner party, so I want it to be perfect."

"And it will be," Deanna reassured her.

She wanted to tell the woman that a catered sit-down dinner for twelve was as relaxed as a stroll in the park. It was when an affair resembled a White House state dinner that everything had to be exact, from the wording of the printed invitations to the correct spelling and addresses of the invitees. Seating preferences became a priority, as well as synchronizing when each dish would be served and picked up, along with the accompanying wines. Deanna had a number of caterers and waitstaff companies on speed dial that she'd used over and over with astonishing results.

Those were the affairs when she would arrive early and stay late, all the while standing on her feet. Then she would go home and collapse, sleeping undisturbed for hours. Deanna was paid quite well for her services, but now at thirty-three she'd begun to wonder if it was worth the sacrifice of not having a family.

She and Spencer had decided to wait until their tenth anniversary before starting a family, but Deanna knew she was quickly approaching the age where each year her chance of conceiving decreased appreciably. In another two years she would be considered high risk. That was something she did *not* want to think about.

Deanna followed Hannah out of the solarium to the spacious entryway where a young woman handed Deanna her coat. Washington, D.C., like most of the northeast, had experienced one of the snowiest winters on record. It had snowed at least once or twice a week since Thanksgiving, and every time she tuned in to the Weather Channel it was with the hope that daytime temperatures would rise above freezing. It was mid-February, and winter still hadn't loosened its fierce grip on the region.

Turning the collar of her mohair-and-cashmere-blend coat up around her neck, she walked briskly to where she had parked her car at the end of the block with its stately town houses. Depressing a button on the key fob, she started up the late-model BMW with the remote device, and by the time she was seated behind the wheel, Deanna felt heat flowing from the sedan's vents. She waited a full minute before maneuvering away from the curb and headed for her home in Alexandria.

The house was ablaze with lights when she drove into the two-car garage and entered through a door in the garage. It was a rare occasion when her car and Spencer's classic Jaguar were parked side by side before nine at night.

Her husband had shocked her earlier that afternoon when he'd called her cell to ask her for a date. Giggling like a teenager, Deanna had accepted. Her shock was exacerbated when Spencer offered to cook. Her brilliant and very talented husband had worked as a part-time short-order cook while he'd attended law school. His parents had deposited money into a checking account for him every month, but for Spencer it wasn't enough. What the elder Tysons failed to realize was that they'd exposed their only child to the finer things in life, and taking his date to a local neighborhood hangout spot wouldn't do for Spencer. For him it had to be upscale restaurants whenever he entertained a woman.

His love for the finer things in life was reflected in their three-story Tudor house, choice of cars and those in their social circle. Deanna's client list was a D.C. who's who, and the clients at the firm where Spencer was now partner had some of the country's most prestigious companies on retainer.

She placed her tote on a high stool and hung up her coat on a hook in an area between the pantry and the kitchen, from which wafted the most delicious smells. She took several steps, leaning against the entrance leading into the gourmet kitchen. A smile parted Deanna's lips as she watched Spencer whisk a salad dressing, stopping to test its thickness.

He'd exchanged his tailored suit, custom-made shirt, silk tie and imported footwear for a white T, jeans and a pair of thick white cotton socks. Light from the high hats and track lights reflected off the red in his coarse cropped hair. Deanna couldn't remember the last time Spencer had allowed his hair to grow more than half an inch. He'd told her how he hated being a black man with red hair, but when she reminded him that El-Hajj Malik El-Shabazz, also known as Malcolm X, had red hair, Spencer never mentioned it again. She found his red hair and freckles cute—something she wouldn't say openly, but she wondered if whether they did have a child if he or she would inherit their father's and paternal grand-mother's titian strands.

"There's something very sexy about a man in a kitchen."

Spencer Tyson's head popped up when he heard his wife's sultry voice. He smiled, his light brown eyes twinkling like newly minted pennies. "What's even sexier is having his woman in the kitchen with him," he said, his Midwest drawl still evident despite having lived more than half his life in the South.

Deanna stood up straight. A platter with thinly sliced steak and chicken and a bowl of water with bamboo skewers indicated Spencer intended to grill the meat on the stove top and probably serve them with accompanying sauces. He knew she loved Thai cuisine, and there was no doubt he would concoct a spicy peanut sauce for the chicken.

"Do you need some help?"

Spencer shook his head. "No, but I could use some company."

"Do I have time to shower and change into something more comfortable?"

"Of course. It's going to be at least half an hour before everything is ready."

Deanna blew him a kiss, then turned and walked down the hallway to the staircase that led to the second-floor bedrooms. Two years ago she and Spencer had made a decision to turn the third floor into space for entertaining family and friends, but they had yet to use it. However, Spencer wanted to upgrade the space and had a contractor install an elevator. Standing five-eight in bare feet and tipping the scales at one hundred forty-two pounds when stripped down to bare skin Deanna preferred walking the staircase to riding the elevator.

There were times when Spencer was preparing for a trial that he and his team stayed over in a downtown D.C. hotel, but whenever he came home after she'd gone to sleep he would usually bed down in one of the other bedrooms so not to disturb her. Deanna was fixated about getting at least seven hours of sleep or she would find herself out of sorts.

Her home had become a showplace thanks to Marisol Rivera–McDonald, who had become the go-to interior designer for Washington's elite. Deanna had been introduced to Marisol at a soirée several years before, and they had hit it off immediately. There weren't too many women in the D.C. area she would think of as a friend, but Marisol was the exception. They talked often and got together at least twice each month—whenever their busy schedules permitted.

Deanna expected to see Marisol and her political-consultant husband Bryce McDonald at the National Museum of Women in the Arts for the American Red Cross Annual Oscar Night fundraiser the first weekend in March. Spencer had bought a table for ten, and it would give Deanna a chance to reconnect with his law partners, their wives and the McDonalds.

She undressed, leaving her clothes in a large wicker hamper in the laundry room at the end of the hall. She'd had the laundry room moved from the first to the second floor because she'd tired of carrying baskets up the stairs. Although someone came in once a week to clean, Deanna felt uncomfortable with strangers handling her underwear. The phobia had come from her overly superstitious grandmother's warning never to let anyone get a hold of her underwear because they could use it to cast an evil spell. Of all of her nana's warnings, this was the only one that she'd adhered to.

Covering her hair with a large plastic shower cap, Deanna stepped into the shower stall. Punching several buttons, she programmed the water temperature before turning it on. She sighed as the warm water sluiced over her face and body. Usually she ended her day with a warm soak in the tub, but tonight it was a shower because she wanted to spend as much time as she could with Spencer before they went to bed.

After lathering her body with her favorite scented bath gel, Deanna rinsed off the bubbles and stepped out of the stall, reaching for a towel on the heated rack. Fifteen minutes later she skipped down the staircase in a pair of white sweatpants, matching tank top and fluffy slippers. She'd removed the elastic band from her hair and a profusion of twists framed her face while brushing her bare shoulders.

She walked up behind Spencer, wrapping her arms around his slim waist. For a man who spent hours sitting behind a desk he was incredibly physically fit. She knew there was a gym at the firm but doubted Spencer found the time to work out there.

"You keep pushing up on me like that and I'm going to have you as the appetizer."

Deanna smiled as she pressed her cheek to his muscled shoulder. "I didn't realize you were serving appetizers."

Spencer glanced at his wife over his shoulder, finding her stunningly exotic. Her oval, flawless, medium-brown face with large almond-shaped light brown eyes was hypnotic. It had been her eyes and lush mouth that had caught his attention when he saw her at a party she'd planned in a private room at a D.C. restaurant. He'd asked for her business card, then called her the following week, not to contract for her services but for a date. One date led to a second one, and less than a year later they were husband and wife.

"I hadn't planned to serve any. But if you want to be the appetizer, then we can wait for the entrée."

Deanna pressed a kiss to his spine. "Oo-oo! I love it when my baby talks nasty."

"Wrong. Your baby is hungry for his woman."

She sobered. "How long has it been since we last made love?"

"Too long."

Deanna knew Spencer was right. She was thirty-three and he thirty-seven, and they had to schedule time to make love with each other. When, she mused, had they become so involved in their careers that they had neglected each other? Would it continue after they became parents?

She closed her eyes. "I want you to promise me that we'll make more time for each other, Spencer."

His hands stilled. "You know I can't do that, Deanna."

"Why not?"

"Because every case is different. Some we're able to settle and others we take to trial."

"Can't you let some of the other associates fill in for you?"

Spencer went back to peeling and chopping a shallot. "It depends on the case."

"What's going to happen when we have children, Spencer? Will I have to call and ask your secretary to schedule a time when you can see your son or daughter?"

Reaching for the arms around his waist, Spencer unclasped his wife's hands and turned to face her. Vertical lines appeared between his eyes when he frowned. "That's a cruel thing to say."

Deanna refused back down. "Cruel or true?"

His frown deepened. "You damn well know it's not going to be that way."

"I don't know how it's going to be. All I have to go on is what's happening in our lives right now. You just wrapped up a case, so you call to let me know that you're going be home earlier than usual. How often does that happen?" Deanna asked. "When you get home I'm already asleep and when I get up in the morning you're gone. If I don't call you or if you don't call me, then I wouldn't know if you're alive or dead. I married you because I'm in love with you, Spencer, but if I'd known what I know now—"

"Don't say it," Spencer interrupted. "Please don't say you wouldn't have married me, because we both know that's not true. We married for all the right reasons. It's just that we're caught up with our careers. I've worked hard to make junior partner—"

"And you'll work even harder to become a senior partner," Deanna said, cutting him off. "How many more years will I have to put my life on hold?"

"What are you talking about?"

"A baby, Spencer. I want a child, but I'm not going to bring a baby into a situation where he or she will have to deal with a part-time father."

"Aren't you being a little premature?" he asked.

"About what?"

Cradling Deanna's face in his hands, Spencer kissed her forehead. "We have another two years before we start trying for a baby."

"I don't want to wait two years, Spencer. In two years I'll be thirty-five and high risk. And my chances of having a baby with Down syndrome also increases with age."

"There are tests to confirm that, and if it is then you'll just abort it."

Deanna felt as if someone had plunged a dagger into her chest, then twisted it until she found it impossible to draw a normal breath. "Abort!" she screamed. "Do you know how you sound? You're talking about a human life, not an apple that when you bite into it and discover that the insides are rotted you throw it away."

"I didn't mean it that way, Dee."

"Please explain, because right now I'm thoroughly confused. When you talk about aborting a child it is not only my child but yours." Her voice was soft, almost conciliatory. "I love you, Spencer. I want your children and I want to spend the rest of my life with you. But we can't continue living the way we have. We have to make time for each other."

Lowering his head, Spencer buried his face in the sweet-smelling twists. "You're right, Dee. Starting tomorrow I'm going to meet with some of the associates and have them handle the cases that don't require my immediate supervision."

"Don't make promises you can't keep."

"I'm not promising anything. I said I'm going to *try* and lighten my caseload."

"Thank you for meeting me halfway."

Deanna didn't want to tell Spencer that there were a few events she'd turned down because they were either on the West Coast or out of the country. The ones in California would require that she spend more than a week with her client to plan the event, then return several times to make certain all the vendors were on board. The ones in the Caribbean were more convenient because they were in the same time zone and she could hop a flight at a moment's notice.

She'd made sacrifices to preserve her marriage, while her husband thought nothing of spending days at his office or in a hotel when working on a case. The one time she'd mentioned that she was going to stop by the hotel to surprise Spencer he had accused her of not trusting him. What he didn't know was that she *did* trust him, because it was something they'd talked about before exchanging vows. Both had promised that if they found someone else they wouldn't sneak around but be forthcoming. Spencer trusted her and she trusted him.

Spencer brushed his mouth over Deanna's. "I need you to set the table and uncork the wine. As soon as I grill the steak and chicken we can eat."

It had become a running joke between them that although Spencer could cook he was all thumbs when it came to uncorking a bottle of wine. When they'd begun dating Deanna didn't know why he always served wine with a twist-off cap until he finally admitted that most times the cork ended up inside the bottle. Much to her chagrin, she realized they'd seen more of each and had more fun when they were struggling to make ends meet because both had refused to accept handouts from their parents.

Spencer had moved from his studio apartment and into her one-bedroom apartment after they were married. They worked hard and saved like misers before they were able to buy a house in a less-than-desirable D.C. neighborhood. Everything changed when Spencer's grandmother died and he'd inherited her entire estate, which included more than a dozen apartment buildings in a gentrified Chicago neighborhood. He sold the properties for a sizable profit, bought the house he'd coveted in Alexandria, then invested the balance in tax-free municipal bonds for their children's education. They had come a long way in eight years, but it was the next eight and many more eights that Deanna looked forward to.

"What do you say we host a little something for our friends?" Spencer said as she finished rearranging the place settings.

Deanna gave him a sidelong glance, wondering what had prompted that suggestion. "When?"

"Sometime next month."

"Remember, we have the Red Cross function the beginning of March," she reminded him.

"Then let's make it the end of March or the beginning of April. Hopefully the weather will be warmer by that time."

Deanna suddenly warmed to the idea. It had been too long since they'd entertained as a couple. "How many people do you want to invite?"

Spencer cocked his head at an angle. "No more than twenty."

"Buffet or sit-down?"

"That depends on you, Dee. If it's formal, then sit-down. Otherwise I'm not opposed to buffet-style."

"Buffet is more casual and relaxed."

Spencer smiled. "Then buffet it is. Friday or Saturday?"

"Let me get my BlackBerry and I'll let you know what I have available in April." Deanna retrieved her cell phone from her handbag and scrolled through her calendar. "All of my Saturdays are booked, but I have the second and fourth Fridays free. Which one is better for you?"

Spencer lifted his shoulders. "It doesn't matter."

"Give me one," Deanna insisted.

"The second Friday."

"Okay. You'll have to let me know who you want to invite before I make up the invitations. We can have happy hour from five to seven and a buffet dinner starting at eight. That will allow time for those who want to go home and change."

"Who are you going to get to cater it?" Spencer asked.

Deanna chewed her lip. "I'm not certain. It's a toss-up between Jimmy Snell and Dominique Lambert." She had a listing of caterers and restaurants she used exclusively, but had her favorites. The two she'd mentioned were at the top of her list of favorites.

"Are you going to invite your sister and brother?"

"I will if they can get babysitters, otherwise they'll probably decline." Deanna's sister and brother had six children between them—all under the age of ten.

"Knowing your sister, she'll probably bring her kids with her."

Deanna rolled her eyes at her husband. "Not to a grown-folks gathering."

"Well, she did when we first moved here."

"I know you don't like my sister—"

"Did I say I didn't like your sister, Deanna?"

"You don't have to say it, Spencer. You don't like her because she called you pompous."

"That's not all she called me," he countered.

"What did she call you?"

"Something I will not repeat."

"I'll admit Neva has a sharp tongue, but—"

"Don't try and defend her, Dee. She is who she is and I'm willing to accept that. Just tell her that I'm not going to tolerate her disrespecting me in my home."

"Can we please drop the subject and enjoy our time together without talking about other folks?"

Spencer's lids came down as he stared at Deanna. He knew she hated confrontation, but confrontation and debate came as easily to him as breathing. It was how he earned his living. "Okay, baby."

Minutes later the kitchen was filled with the aroma of grilling meat, and he turned on the commercial exhaust that quickly got rid of the smell. Spencer knew Deanna was right about their not spending enough time together, but what he couldn't tell her was that it wasn't just work that kept him at the office. It was another distraction.

The chilled rosé was the perfect complement to the grilled steak and chicken with rice pilaf and a Greek salad with cherry tomatoes. Deanna drank two glasses of wine to offset the piquant taste of the spicy peanut sauce. Her eyelids were drooping when Spencer suggested she go to bed while he clean up the kitchen. She went upstairs, brushed her teeth, got into bed and within minutes was asleep.

Spencer waited twenty minutes after Deanna left the kitchen to tap several buttons on his cell. His call was answered after the second ring. "What are you doing?" he whispered into the mouthpiece.

"I've been waiting for you to call me."

"I couldn't call before."

"Where is she?"

"She's in bed."

"Are you going to make love to her, Spence?"

A rush of blood darkened Spencer's face, concealing the freckles sprinkled across the bridge of his nose and cheeks. "I told you before that what goes on between me and my wife is none of your business."

"It is my business, Spence, when you tell me you love me. Is it really possible for you to love two women?"

"Yes, it is. I didn't call you to talk about love, but to ask if you can meet me tomorrow."

There was a moment of silence. "Where?"

"I'll pick you up at Union Station."

"At what time?"

"Make it ten. That way we can spend most of the day together. I promised Dee that I would take her out to dinner," Spencer lied smoothly.

There came another beat before the feminine voice said, "Okay."

Spencer ended the call with the tap of a key. It wasn't easy living a double life, but there was something about Jenah he couldn't resist. She was like a narcotic. Sleeping with her was addictive.

Marisol Rivera-McDonald

Chapter Three

"Are you certain this fabric is good for the settee?"

Marisol Rivera-McDonald gave the nervous woman a reassuring smile. "I am very certain, Mrs. Wardlaw. What you want is much too heavy for the settee's frame."

The widowed socialite stroked the gaudy brooch pinned to the lapel of her Chanel suit jacket. Marisol wanted to tell the woman that the suit alone spoke volumes. The proceeds from the sale of the ruby brooch and the enormous diamond solitaire on her left hand could feed a family of four for months—if they were conservative food shoppers.

Marisol had met more quirky people than she could count on both hands and feet since she'd become a D.C.-based interior designer. Most of her clients had more money than they knew what do with it, so they called her regularly to ask whether they should buy a new rug, change a chandelier or give away all the furniture in their home to a charitable organization just to fill it up again. She found it wasn't so much their permanent residences that prompted them to start over but their vacation properties.

Sylvia Wardlaw had come from old, old money. Upon the advice of her financial planner, Mrs. Wardlaw had sold her home in McLean, Virginia, and had purchased a suite of rooms on the top floor of the Beaumont Hotel overlooking DuPont Circle.

The attractive and mentally sharp octogenarian had buried three husbands and was seriously contemplating marrying a fourth, but discovered he wasn't as wealthy as he had purported. She'd told Marisol in confidence that she'd had him investigated because at thirty years her junior she suspected he was after her money. Marisol had shaken her head, while calling him an unscrupulous scoundrel, which had endeared her to the woman.

Sylvia nodded. "You know I trust you to always give me good advice."

She wanted to tell the woman her reputation was based on good advice and honesty. It didn't matter if her clients were wealthy, Marisol wanted them to be pleased with her services.

"Covering the settee with cream-colored silk instead of brocade will not detract from the fluid design typical of Chippendale." The double-chair-back settee was an authentic reproduction of the high-quality colonial of American Chippendale furniture, circa 1880.

"You know I don't want my furniture removed from the premises," Sylvia reminded Marisol.

"The work can be done here. After I get in touch with the upholsterer I'll call to let you know the dates and times he's available. It shouldn't take him more than two days to complete the job. Is there anything else you'd like me to help you with?" Marisol asked her best client.

Sylvia pursed her vermilion-colored lips as she appeared

to be deep in thought. "I don't believe so, but if I think of something I'll have Alyssa call you." She smiled, and a network of minute lines fanned out around her cool gray eyes. "I want to thank you for recommending her as my personal assistant. I don't know how I've gotten along all these years without someone like her."

Marisol smiled. "I'm glad I could find someone to make life easier for you." Alyssa had been the personal assistant for a woman who'd fired her when she suspected her husband had more than a passing interest in her employee.

Alyssa had asked Marisol if she knew of someone who needed a live-in gofer, and she had asked Sylvia, who had to have control of every phase of her day-to-day existence, if she wanted to hire a personal assistant/social secretary. It wasn't easy for Sylvia to relinquish control of answering the telephone, reading her mail, accepting and declining invitations to various fundraisers and social events, but Alyssa had miraculously gained the woman's confidence and in turn protected her from those who sought to take advantage of her employer's generosity.

"She's my guardian angel."

Marisol closed the large leather-bound catalogue filled with swatches of fabric, praying Sylvia was right about Alyssa. Marisol had insisted Alyssa submit to a background check before she recommended her to her client, because she hadn't wanted to be responsible for someone whose main focus was to work for wealthy people because of an ulterior motive. When she saw Alyssa's boyfriend she had warned her that he was never for any reason to come to Mrs. Wardlaw's apartment. One glance at the chronically unemployed young man spoke volumes. He wanted money, but didn't want to work for it.

She picked up her handbag and stood up. "Please don't

bother to get up, Mrs. Wardlaw. Alyssa will show me out." Marisol met the young woman as she walked out of the living room. Conservatively dressed in a white blouse and a pair of black slacks, Alyssa Jenkins nodded. Her braided extensions were pulled into a ponytail.

"I had to call Mrs. Wardlaw's doctor this morning," she said sotto voce.

Marisol came to a stop in the expansive entryway. "Is she all right?"

"She'd complained that she was feeling dizzy. The doctor said her blood pressure was slightly elevated. I guess it came from the popcorn we had last night when we were watching a movie."

"You have to watch her sodium intake," Marisol whispered.

"I know that now."

"I'll probably call tomorrow to let you know when someone is going to come to replace the seat on the settee in the living room."

Alyssa smiled, her dark eyes sparkling in an equally dark face. "Okay." She opened the door for Marisol, waited until she walked into the elevator, then closed and locked the door.

Marisol flagged down a taxi, giving him her Georgetown address. She hadn't taken her car because she hadn't wanted to waste time trying to find a place to park. DuPont Circle wasn't that far from Georgetown, so getting around by taxi was faster and easier.

She barely had time to settle back in the rear seat when the driver maneuvered up in front of the three-story town house she owned with her political-consultant husband. She and Bryce used the first floor for their professional offices and the second and third as their personal residence. Marisol paid the driver, requested a receipt and exited the cab.

She had barely put the key in the lock when the door swung open and she came face-to-face with someone she hadn't expected to see. "Mami, what are you doing here?"

The smile on Pilar Rivera's face vanished quickly, replaced by a scowl. "Is that any way to greet your mother?"

Leaning forward, Marisol pressed her cheek to her mother's. "I didn't expect to find you here. Why didn't you tell me you were coming?" She dropped the catalogue and her handbag on a chair in the entryway and closed the door.

Pilar stared at her daughter, seeing things only a mother would see when Marisol took off her black cashmere swing coat and hung it on a coatrack. She was dressed entirely in black: sweater, pencil skirt, stockings and suede pumps. It was as if the thirty-two-year-old interior designer with her profusion of shiny black curls framing her round face like a cameo was in mourning. Even without makeup Marisol was stunning. Her olive coloring, large dark brown eyes and delicate features conjured up one word: *exotic*.

"If I'd told you I was coming then it wouldn't have been a surprise."

Marisol smiled. "You're right, Mami." She hugged and kissed her mother. "How long are you staying?"

"Not too long. I had some time coming to me, so I decided to take the train down to see you."

"Did your decision to take the train down have anything to do with you talking with my husband?"

Pilar shook her head, salt-and-pepper curls moving with the motion. "Not really, *m'ija*. When I called the house this morning Bryce answered. I told him that I had a taken a few days off from my job and he invited me to come and spend a few days with you." Her eyes narrowed suspiciously. "What aren't you telling me, *m'ija*?"

Marisol ran her fingers through her hair, pushing a profusion of curls off her forehead. "Nothing."

"Are you pregnant?"

"No."

"What's the matter?"

Closing her eyes, Marisol exhaled an audible sigh. "Nothing, Mami. I'm just a little tired."

"You're as skinny as a stick. And wearing black makes you look *flaca.*"

"I've never been *gorda,*" Marisol countered, mixing her English with Spanish. What did her mother expect? She was five-three and her weight fluctuated between one hundred eight and twelve.

"You're still too skinny."

"*Sí, sí, sí,* Mami," she intoned.

"Don't *yes* me, Marisol Pilar Rivera-McDonald," Pilar shot back. "Bryce said he was going to take us out for dinner, but I've just decided I'd rather stay home. Go upstairs and relax while I fix you a good Puerto Rican home-cooked meal. I already checked out your refrigerator, so you don't have the excuse that you have nothing in the house."

Marisol closed her eyes and gently massaged her forehead "How do you just come to my house and take over?"

"Easy. It's because I'm your mother and I'm worried about you. I know you're still having those headaches because you're rubbing your forehead. You work too hard, don't eat enough and the result is you're a bag of bones. Remember, *m'ija.* No man wants a bag of bones in his bed."

"Bryce has never complained about my weight."

"That's because he loves you."

Movement caught Marisol's eye over her mother's shoulder. The topic of their discussion had come out of his office. Her gaze softened when her eyes met a pair that were a shocking baby-blue. Bryce McDonald was the epitome of preppie, from his conservative haircut to his button-down shirt, cuffed slacks and wingtips. During the summer months he spent hours on the water aboard his parents' yacht. The hot sun turned him into a golden statue with his sun-streaked light brown hair and slim, toned body.

Marisol lifted her chin for her husband's kiss. "How's it going?" she asked.

Bryce smiled, revealing a set of straight white teeth. "Pretty good. I hope you don't mind that I invited your mother to hang out with us for the weekend."

Marisol placed a hand on Bryce's back. "Of course not."

"I'm going to call the Equinox and see if I can get a reservation for three."

"Make it for tomorrow," Pilar said. "I'm going to cook tonight."

Bryce stared at his mother-in-law. "Are you sure?"

Pilar smiled. It had been six years since she'd become mother of the bride and Pilar was still shocked that her little girl had managed to marry one of Washington's most eligible bachelors. "Very sure. Go and relax with your wife and I'll call you when it's time to eat."

Reaching for Marisol's hand, Bryce led her into his office while Pilar walked up the staircase to the second floor. As soon as he closed the door, she rounded on him. "Why didn't you call me to let me know my mother was coming down?"

Cradling her face, he touched his mouth to hers. "I wanted it to be a surprise."

Marisol's fingers went around his wrists. "It was more like a shock than a surprise. You know I didn't schedule anything for this weekend because I wanted to be alone with you." What she hadn't told Bryce was that she was ovulating and if they were lucky, then they could look forward to becoming parents before the end of the year.

Bending slightly, Bryce picked her up and carried her over to the leather sofa. He sat, bringing her down to his lap. "We'll have many more weekends to spend together after she leaves."

Resting her head on his shoulder, Marisol inhaled the lingering scent of her husband's aftershave on his lean jaw. Although he worked from home, Bryce got up every morning to shave and shower as if he were going into a traditional office, because he never knew when he would have to leave at a moment's notice to meet with a client and/or candidate who needed his political expertise. Some men in Washington sold influence, while Bryce McDonald sold advice and strategy. His family was as entrenched in politics as some families were in banking and finance. His father, grandfather and great-grandfather had earned a reputation and amassed their wealth as power brokers.

Marisol's dilemma wasn't that she didn't love her husband, but his reluctance to go to a fertility specialist to determine if her inability to get pregnant was the result of a low sperm count. She'd tried to assure Bryce that she wasn't attacking his virility, but if they had to resort to other measures then she wanted him to consider other options.

His comeback was if they couldn't have a child through the normal intercourse route, then maybe they were destined not to become parents. He followed his tirade with the statement of adoption not even being a remote possibility. It was the first time since she'd become Mrs. Bryce McDonald that Marisol had thought about seeing a divorce attorney. A two-week stay in Jamaica redesigning a client's vacation retreat had saved her marriage. When she returned she realized she'd married Bryce because she loved him, and if they never became parents, then she would still love him.

"The next time you invite her, please call to give me prior warning," she crooned, placing light kisses along his jaw. "I always need to gear up before dealing with my mother."

Bryce's hand was busy searching under Marisol's sweater. He gave her breast a gentle squeeze. "Your mother is a pussycat compared to mine."

"My mom is pushy."

He laughed softly. "That's because you're all she has. My mother has three other children to annoy."

Marisol knew Bryce was right. Pilar Rivera was only seventeen when she'd found herself pregnant with a married man's child. Her parents sent her to Puerto Rico to have the baby, and when she returned Pilar moved in with her grandmother before she finally got her own apartment in an East Harlem public housing development. Pilar went to beauty school, graduated and worked in a local hair salon for years. She had finally saved enough money to open her own salon, but six months later a fire in an adjacent restaurant destroyed her shop and half the stores and apartments on the block.

Pilar had returned to school, this time to become a medical technician, where she'd learned to take blood pressure readings and draw blood. She applied for a position at a local medical clinic and twenty years later she was now their office manager.

Marisol knew it hadn't been easy for Pilar, and she struggled not to repeat her mother's life as an unwed mother living in public housing. Unlike her mother, she didn't have her first serious relationship until after she'd graduated college. It was when she met Bryce McDonald at a Washington Redskins football game that she knew she had met her soul mate. Their six-month I–95 courtship ended when Bryce asked her to relocate from New York to D.C.—as his wife.

What Marisol had planned as a small gathering quickly became an extravaganza when Bryce's parents invited politicians, elected officials and several heads of state. Her family was definitely outnumbered, and she sought to even the odds when she invited many of her Puerto Rican relatives—some of whom had never left the island—to her nuptials. The highlight of the reception was when the Latin band began playing salsa, mambo, meringue and samba. Her relatives had put on a dancing exhibition that was still talked about when Marisol and Bryce returned from their two-week Mediterranean honeymoon.

"What are you doing?" Marisol whispered when Bryce shifted her off his lap and pressed her down to the sofa.

"I'm going to make love to my wife."

She tried to sit up, but he pushed her back. "No! My mother will hear us."

Bryce left Marisol staring at him as he stood up, locked the door and turned on a radio, increasing the volume until the thumping baseline beat reverberated off the walls. She was still staring with wide eyes when he began to undress. This was a side of her husband she had never seen before, but she wasn't going to complain if their lovemaking resulted in her becoming pregnant.

Smiling, she beckoned him closer. *"Venga aquí, Papi."* Speaking Spanish to Bryce, although he didn't understand the language, turned him on.

Marisol took off her sweater, dropping it to the floor. Her shoes, skirt and stockings followed. Bryce was naked and fully aroused when she unhooked her bra and added it to the pile of clothing. Going to her knees, she slid her hands down her waist to her hips, pushing the narrow elastic waistband off her hips and down her thighs. By the time the panties joined the discarded clothing Bryce was between her legs, pushing inside her.

There was no foreplay, no whispered words of affection as Bryce made love to her like a man possessed. His heavy breathing, grunts and groans aroused Marisol until she felt as if she was coming out of her skin. Raising her legs, she looped them around Bryce's waist, allowing for deeper penetration. Her whole body shuddered as passion made her its captive and pleasure, pure and explosive, ripped through the area between her thighs. She was on fire! Bryce was on fire as an inferno engulfed them both in flames that would only be quenched when they climaxed simultaneously.

"Harder, harder," she gasped when she felt the beginnings of an orgasm. "Harder, dammit!"

Grasping her buttocks, Bryce gripped the firm flesh as he went to his knees and thrust over and over into her moist warmth. Every time he made love to Marisol it was like the first time. He'd slept with a lot of women, yet collectively they couldn't compare to the woman he planned to spend the rest of his life with. He felt the tightening in his scrotum that indicated he was about to ejaculate. His fingers dug into her flesh as he pulled back one last time and then plunged into her vagina, holding her fast as he felt the rush of semen that stopped his heart for several seconds as he experienced *le petit mort*.

Completely spent, Bryce collapsed on Marisol's writhing body, smiling as her gasps of fulfillment echoed in his ear. Yes, making love to her was just like the first time—exciting and fulfilling. And he would always remember the first time he saw her sitting in the stadium screaming at the top of her lungs because the Redskins were beating her favored New York Giants. Her hair was longer, a mass of raven curls falling around a doll-like face with expressive dark eyes. Physically, she was the complete opposite of the girls he'd dated, but there was something about the petite exotic beauty that had made him want to know her better. They'd programmed each other's numbers into their cell phones and he waited a week before calling her.

What had begun as a telephone courtship segued to driving to New York City to take her out. Although she'd shared an apartment with another woman, she wouldn't permit him to sleep over, nor would she sleep with him at his hotel.

The one time he'd invited her to D.C. for a black-tie event, he'd arranged for a car to pick her up and bring her to a Washington day spa for a total beauty makeover. When she'd checked into their hotel room Bryce had surprised her when the owner of a boutique arrived with racks of dresses, shoes and accessories from which to choose for the event. With her shorter coiffed hair, professional makeup and a requisite little black dress that hugged every curve of her petite body, Marisol had managed to charm every man he'd introduced her to. And that included his father.

His parents invited her to come down the following weekend to hang out at their vacation home on the Chesapeake, and when Bryce drove her back to New York he knew he had fallen in love with her. It wasn't until after he'd slipped the three-carat, emerald-cut diamond on her finger with a promise to love her forever that he'd experienced what it was to make love to the woman who was to become his wife.

Being in her arms, lying between her scented thighs, made him regret all the women he'd ever slept with. Especially Odette. She'd given him chlamydia and gonorrhea, all the while swearing he was the only man she'd slept with. He finally ended their relationship, but it was too late. Repeated bouts of STDs had left him sterile. Marisol wanted a baby, and unless there was a procedure to reverse his infertility he would never father a child.

"I'll never look at this sofa again without remembering what we did here," he whispered in her ear.

"Thankfully it can be cleaned," Marisol whispered back. "We have to get up and shower. This place smells like sex."

"I love the smell of sex in the morning," Bryce intoned like Robert Duvall in *Apocalypse Now*.

Marisol landed a soft punch to his shoulder. "He said napalm, and it's not morning. Please, let me up so I can wash up."

"What happened to keeping your legs up so the sperm can swim upstream?"

"I'll leave them up until they start getting numb."

"Mari?"

"Sí, Papi."

Bryce chose his words carefully. "If we don't make a baby before the end of the year, then I'm willing to consider other alternatives."

Marisol blinked back tears. "You're not kidding, are you?"

He kissed her nose and wrapped a curl around his finger. "No, sweetheart. I'm not kidding. If you don't want to go through the whole artificial insemination scene, then I'm more than willing to adopt. I know lawyers who can speed up the process and get us a newborn in less than six months."

It was a full minute before Marisol said, "Even if I do become pregnant, I would still like to adopt. It doesn't have to be a newborn."

"You'd want an older child?"

"Why not, Bryce? They are the ones who languish in foster care because everyone wants a newborn."

"I don't mind an older child as long as they're not too old."

"What made you change your mind when you were so against adoption?"

"I had the TV on earlier this morning and there was a segment about adoption with testimonials from adoptive parents and kids still waiting to be adopted. I suppose you can say it got to me."

"I'm glad it did, *m'ijo*. You're going to be an incredible father."

"We'll see."

"What's there to see, Bryce?"

"I just don't want to become one of those overindulgent fathers whose so-called good kid has the family attorney on speed dial."

"Never happen," Marisol said confidently. "I will never let our kids forget that their mother grew up in El Barrio and she can roll with the best of them."

"Boo-hoo, I'm scared of you."

"Don't let my size fool you. I'm one tough *chica*." Lowering her legs, she moaned softly. "You're going to have to massage my legs. They feel like someone is sticking them with pins."

Bryce pulled out, slid down the sofa and pressed his face to the neatly trimmed fuzz covering Marisol's mound. He inhaled, held his breath, then let it out slowly. "I love the way you smell after we make love."

A dreamy smile parted her lips when his hands moved over her calves, working their magic.

Life was better than good for Marisol.

It was perfect.

Bryce had told his wife what he knew she'd wanted to hear. He had no intention of subjecting himself to a fertility test when he knew what the results would be. How could he explain to Marisol that he'd slept with a woman who let him do whatever he wanted to her and in the end had contracted a

STD that left him unable to father a child? And he definitely had no intention of adopting some woman's cast-off or stray. If it wasn't his seed, then he didn't want it.

Capital Wives

Chapter Four

Marisol and Deanna exchanged puzzled glances in the mirror of the powder room at the National Museum of Women in the Arts. "Is that someone crying?" Deanna whispered.

Marisol nodded. "I think so." Soft sobs were coming from behind the door of one of the stalls.

Deanna bent down to find a pair of pale feet in a pair of designer heels. "Block the door and do *not* let anyone in," she told Marisol. "I'm going to try and get her to come out." She knocked softly on the stall door while Marisol walked to the outer door. "Hello? Are you all right in there?"

"Leave me alone."

"I'm not going to leave you alone until you open the door to let me see that you're okay."

"Use another bathroom," Marisol called out to someone knocking on the door. "Someone just threw up in here."

"Good girl," Deanna crooned, replying to her friend's quick thinking. She knocked softly on the stall again. "Open the door or I'll get the museum's security to do it."

What she didn't want was to read about an incident that someone had been found dead or unconscious in the restroom during a fundraiser and she had done nothing because she was minding her business.

"Just open it a little bit," Deanna continued, this time in a softer tone. She heard the distinctive sound of the sliding latch and then the door opened a fraction. "A little more so I can see your face." The crack widened and she saw the pale, mascara-streaked face with red, puffy eyes. "You know you can't go back to the ballroom looking like a hot mess." The blonde woman nodded. "Where's your purse?"

"It's...it's back at my table."

"Who are you here with?"

"My husband."

"Don't move," Deanna ordered. Walking back to the counter, she pulled several tissues from a dispenser, pushing the wad through the slight opening. "Blow your nose."

"Hey, Dee. I'm not going to be able to keep them out indefinitely."

"Give me a few more minutes," she said to Marisol. "Who's your husband?"

There came a moment of silence. "Damon Paxton."

Deanna whistled softly. She knew there was something familiar about the woman, but hadn't been able to recall her name. The tabloids had had a field day when Damon Paxton divorced his wife to marry a woman young enough to be his daughter. The fact that Jean Paxton had come from an old D.C. moneyed family hadn't endeared Bethany to those who had labeled her as a home wrecker, along with a few other four- and five-letter words that were whispered but not printed.

"Close the door. I'm going to get your purse, so you can clean up your face before you go back to your table. I'm certain you don't want to give the old cows the satisfaction of seeing you upset."

"You know who I am?"

"Yes, I do. Now, close and lock the door. Marisol, come here," she called out when the lock to the stall slid into place.

Marisol McDonald strutted over in a pair of five-inches strappy stilettos. Instead of the requisite full-length gown, she had worn a short fitted black dress with a scooped neckline and bared back. Her inky-black curls, piled atop her head, added several inches to her diminutive frame.

"What's up, Dee?"

"She's Damon Paxton's wife," Deanna whispered. "I need you to go and get her purse so she can fix her face. If her husband asks, just tell him that she's not feeling well. Meanwhile, I'm going to try to keep her calm."

Deanna studied her face in the mirror while she waited for Marisol to return. She opened her evening purse and touched up her makeup. It had taken her more than two weeks to find a dress for the affair. After trying on the umpteenth dress she had decided on a strapless satin sheath gown in a becoming claret-red with a generous front slit. Fortunately, she'd found a pair of stilettos in the same shade with satin ties that flattered her slender ankles.

"Mrs. Paxton?"

"Yes?" came a soft voice in the stall.

"What's your first name?"

"Bethany."

"How are you doing, Bethany?"

"Just say I've been better."

Deanna smiled. "You sound like a Southern girl. Where your folks from?" she asked, lapsing into dialect.

"Alabama."

"Hey-y-y. A blonde sister-girl from my granddaddy's home state."

"Where was he from?"

"Mobile. Your people?"

"They're from a little mill town in the northeast corner of the state known as Parkers Corner."

"Are your folks okay?"

"Last I heard they were," Bethany replied.

"What about your kids?"

"They're good."

Deanna knew she had to keep Bethany talking until Marisol returned. "What about your husband?"

"Damon's good—except when it comes to…" Her words trailed off. "What's your name?"

"It's Deanna. Deanna Tyson."

"Are you the party planner?"

"I'm an event planner," she corrected. "Keep talking," Deanna whispered when voices floated through the powder room door.

"I've read about some of the parties—I mean events— you've put together," Bethany said in a normal tone. "Do you do weddings?"

Deanna nodded to two women who'd just come in to fluff up their hair and reapply lipstick. "I don't think I've planned more than four or five. What I mean is I try to avoid them, because I don't have the temperament to deal with young women who thrive on acting out."

"What about small dinner parties?"

"That's my specialty. Are you thinking of hosting one?"

"Maybe."

"I'm going to give you my business card whenever you're finished in there." Deanna removed a card from a sterling card case and placed it on the counter. "Have fun, ladies," she said to the two women who'd washed their hands and dried their hands.

"You, too," they chorused.

"I'm back," chanted Marisol as she walked into the space with a beaded evening bag. "Her husband is outside waiting for her."

Deanna knocked on the stall door. "Come on out, Bethany, and make yourself presentable. Your husband is waiting for you."

The door opened and Bethany walked out. She was stunning in a black fitted slip dress that clung to her slim body like a second skin. "What did you tell him?"

Marisol met Deanna's eyes before she stared at Bethany. "I told him you had probably eaten something that didn't agree with you, so you were in here hurling your guts out."

Deanna gave the interior designer an incredulous look. "Did you have to be so melodramatic?"

Marisol rolled her head. "Look at Barbie. She's a dog's mess."

"Don't you mean hot mess?" Bethany drawled.

"No," Marisol spat out. "I said what I meant, and I meant what I said. You look like something the dogs dumped on." She waved a hand. "Get some tissues and clean up that mascara. You look like a raccoon."

Bethany rolled her head on her neck. "Well, thank you."

"You're welcome, Barbie."

"I have a name."

"What is it?" Marisol asked.

"Bethany."

"Beth or Barb. They're both the same."

Bethany extended her hand. "May I please have my bag?"

Marisol gave her the small bag that had probably set Bethany's husband back by at least five figures. "Everything's in there."

A becoming flush suffused the blonde's face. "I know you're not a thief."

"How would you know that?" Marisol asked.

"You have enough bling on your hand and ears to choke a horse."

Marisol touched the studs in her ear. They had been a wedding gift from Bryce. "Fix your face before your husband comes barging in here." Turning on her heels, Marisol walked out of the powder room, leaving Bethany and Deanna staring at her back.

Deanna closed her purse. "Marisol is right."

Bethany nodded. "Thank you, Deanna. May I call you?"

"Isn't that why I gave you my card? You may call me even if you're not planning a party. Good luck." Deanna gave Bethany a tender smile and walked out the powder room.

Chapter Five

Deanna saw Damon Paxton pacing back and forth. "Mr. Paxton?" He stopped pacing, turned and stared at her. "Your wife is feeling better and should be out shortly."

Damon stopped pacing; his eyes grew wider when he recognized the woman who'd earned the reputation of hosting the best parties in the Capitol District. He extended his hand. "Deanna Tyson?"

Deanna stared at the large, well-groomed hand, then took it. "Yes, it is. Have we met before?"

"Not really. But I have attended some of your functions. The one you planned for Senator Rosenthal's sixtieth birthday was exceptional."

She smiled. "I'm glad you enjoyed it."

"What the hell is going on here?"

Deanna snatched her hand from Damon's loose grip when she heard Spencer's accusatory tone. "There's nothing going on except that Damon and I were talking."

"Dial it down, son. Your wife and I were just talking business."

Spencer hand went around Deanna's upper arm. "I think you have your bastards mixed up, Paxton. Sorry, but I am not your son."

"Spencer!" Deanna gasped.

He tightened his grip on her arm. "Let's go, Dee, before I'm cuffed for kicking an old man's ass."

Spencer literally pulled Deanna across the floor when she rounded on her husband. "Have you lost your mind?"

"Have you?" Spencer countered. "The man was drooling on your breasts."

"What are you snorting or smoking, Spencer? I work with men all the time and you've never displayed one iota of jealousy. What has Damon Paxton done to you to come at him like a rabid dog?"

Spencer released Deanna's arm and ran a hand over his face. "I'm sorry, Dee. I don't know what got into me."

"What you're going to do is go over there and apologize or..."

"Or what?"

"Or our marriage is in some serious trouble. I rely on people like Damon Paxton for my business. All I need is for him to put the word out that I'm persona non grata and I won't be able to get a job in any cathouse in the lower forty-eight. In case you've forgotten, I sell hospitality, not intimidation. And I'm dead serious about you apologizing, Spencer." She and her husband engaged in what had become a stare-down. Deanna loved him, but not enough to jeopardize everything that she'd worked so hard to achieve. "We're done," she whispered.

"Okay," Spencer said quickly. "I'll apologize."

"Do it now," she said between clenched teeth.

She watched as Spencer approached Damon, extended his

hand before the older man grasped it. She couldn't hear what they were saying but saw Damon reach into the breast pocket of his tuxedo and hand Spencer a business card, who reciprocated giving him his card. The two men shared a few words again before shaking hands.

"Is that better?" Spencer asked when he returned to where Deanna had waited for him. He took her hand, cradling it in the bend of his elbow.

"Much better. Why couldn't you have done that the first time?"

"I guess you could say it was a little male posturing. Paxton said he understood and probably would've reacted the same way if I had been mauling his wife."

Deanna gave Spencer a sidelong glance. She had to admit he looked incredibly handsome in formal attire. "He wasn't mauling me."

"He was the one who said *maul,* not me. We're going to meet for drinks one day next week."

Shaking her head, Deanna didn't want to think about what had just gone down. It was the first time since she'd known Spencer that he had displayed a modicum of possessiveness. In one breath he'd threatened to kick a man's ass, then minutes later they were talking about getting together for cocktails.

If there was one thing she knew about the man she'd married it was that he was an overachiever and had rather predictable behavior. Somehow jealousy was not one of his personality traits. Something was bothering him, and she decided to watch and wait for whatever it was to manifest. Sooner or later he would have to show his hand. They returned to the ballroom and their table. Marisol, who had changed seats with Bryce, pressed her shoulder to Deanna's.

"When Spencer asked why you hadn't come back with me I told him you were coming," Marisol whispered.

Deanna tapped Spencer's arm to get his attention. "Could you please get me something from the bar?"

"What do you want?"

"A glass of red wine." She waited until he walked away to get her drink, then leaned closer to Marisol and told her what had transpired with Bethany's husband.

Marisol's mouth formed a perfect O. "That's some crazy shit."

Deanna made a sucking noise with her tongue and teeth. "It has to be a full moon. Why were you so nasty to Bethany?"

It was Marisol's turn to suck her teeth. "Please don't get me started, Dee. I have very little sympathy for hood ornaments."

"You may not be a hood ornament, but you're definitely Bryce's *muñeca*. A doll by another name is still a doll, chica."

"Very funny…" Marisol's eyes narrowed when she noticed a woman sitting at a nearby table, staring at them. "Don't look now, but do you know the woman in red sitting at the table to our left?"

Surreptitiously, Deanna glanced at the table, her gaze lingering briefly on a young woman with highlighted blunt-cut hair covering one eye. The bodice of her dress was so revealing that she should have been arrested for indecency. Each time she exhaled her breasts shimmied like gelatin.

"No. It could be she recognizes me—" Her explanation was preempted when Spencer returned with Deanna's glass of wine. "Thank you," she said when he sat down beside her and draped his right arm over the back of her chair.

Spencer stared at his wife's profile. His reaction when he saw Damon Paxton holding her hand wasn't generated by jealousy but fear and frustration. He hadn't expected Jenah to attend the gathering, and to have her seated at a table only a few feet from where he sat with his wife was risky and indefensible. There was no reason why she would attend an event without his knowledge when she knew Deanna would be in attendance. It was as if Jenah wanted to openly flaunt their affair.

She wasn't the first woman he'd slept with during his eight-year marriage, but she was the youngest and most difficult to control. Spencer realized he'd made a serious faux pas. He'd told his mistress he loved her in the throes of passion; the truth was he loved what Jenah was willing to do to please him.

He spent the rest of evening avoiding eye contact with Jenah while interacting with those at his table. Sometime between when the monitors were darkened and instrumental music played while the evening's raffle was announced, Jenah slipped out and didn't return. He must have emitted an audible sigh, because Deanna turned to stare at him.

"Bored?"

"A little."

Though only four years old, Oscar Night was quickly becoming one of Washington's signature's black-tie charity events. However, Spencer found it hard to distinguish one from the other, because they were supported by the same people.

Deanna rested her hand on his thigh under the tablecloth. "I'm ready to leave whenever you are."

Spencer rose and pulled back Deanna's chair as she stood up. "We're going to call it a night."

Deanna hugged and kissed Marisol, waved to the others and walked with Spencer to retrieve their coats. She was still disturbed by his outburst, wondering if perhaps he was experiencing a meltdown because he'd been working too hard. What she didn't want to acknowledge was that he could be undergoing a premature midlife crises.

Chapter Six

Spencer was sitting up, his back supported by a pile of pillows, when Deanna walked into the bedroom and got into bed beside him. She was surprised to find that he'd waited up for her.

The drive home from the museum had been spent in complete silence. Usually that was when she and Spencer talked—about anything. Even after he'd parked his car in the garage and they'd come into the house the silence had continued. Deanna knew instinctively that something was wrong, that their marriage was in trouble and if she and Spencer didn't talk about it then they wouldn't stay together long enough to celebrate their tenth anniversary. Reaching over, she flicked off the lamp on her side of the bed, plunging the bedroom in darkness.

She adjusted the pillows under her shoulders and lay with her back to her husband. "Do you want to talk about it?" Her voice was low, coaxing.

"There's nothing to talk about."

Deanna held her breath, counting slowly to ten. "Please don't insult my intelligence, Spencer. I've lived with you long enough to know when something is bothering you. Maybe you don't have to give me all the intimate details, but I'm not going to allow you to shut me out."

"It's work-related."

"Is it something you can talk about?" she asked.

There came a pregnant silence before Spencer said, "I can't talk about it without mentioning names, and that would breach client–attorney confidentiality."

"You're representing someone who works at your firm?"

"Yes. I didn't want to accept his case, but I couldn't in good conscience stand by and let him go to jail for something he didn't do."

"Are you telling me the man is innocent?"

"Of course he's innocent, Dee. I'd never risk my reputation defending a guilty client."

"That's not true, Spencer. I remember you taking on the case of that woman who'd admitted to murdering her husband because he'd discovered she was sleeping with his chauffeur."

"I didn't defend her personally. The firm did. And we normally don't handle cases that involve murder, but we did because she was the granddaughter of a prominent judge and one of the partners owed him a favor."

"She'd confessed to murder, yet the jury found her not guilty of all charges."

"That's because we could prove that her husband had planned to kill her. It's not often the self-defense theory works, but that time it did."

"This case you're handling for a coworker, does it involve murder?" Deanna asked.

"No."

"Have you thought that maybe you should let another attorney handle it?"

"Why would you say that, Dee?"

"Because it's affecting you," she countered. "I saw a side of you tonight that frightened me. I've never seen you act like a street thug."

"I'm a street thug because I thought a man was trying to get into my wife's panties? Don't forget I spent the first ten years of my life on the South Side."

Deanna ignored Spencer's reference to his Chicago roots. "Damon Paxton wasn't trying to get into my panties, so get your mind out of the gutter, Spencer."

"Don't be so naive, Dee."

"What does that mean?"

"It's exactly what I said. Don't be naive. Damon is no Boy Scout."

"I could say the same thing about a lot of the men I do business with, but that doesn't mean I'm going to sleep with them because they may smile at me or hold my hand."

"Have you ever cheated on me?"

Deanna went completely still, unable to believe what her husband had just asked her. "I can't believe you just asked me that," she said, voicing her thoughts aloud.

"Just answer the question, Dee."

Her temper flared. "I'm not on trial, so I'm not going to answer anything."

"Not answering can be construed as an omission of guilt."

Deanna popped up like a jack-in-the-box and turned on the lamp. "I'm not your client, so don't try and relate to me like one. We had this conversation before we got married, and I remember telling you that if I met someone I wanted to sleep or be with I'd be forthcoming and tell you, Spencer, because I don't do subterfuge. And the fact that in eight years

I've never told you that I want a divorce or a separation means I've never cheated on you. Or better yet. Do you want me to cheat on you, so it would make it easier for you to cheat?"

"I've never cheated on you," Spencer lied smoothly.

"So you say."

He sat up. "You don't believe me?"

"Let's say I believe you until I find out differently. The truth is like cream. It always rises to the top."

"Maybe it's a good thing we decided to wait ten years before starting a family, because bringing a child into marriage where trust is an issue—"

"Trust is not an issue," Deanna interrupted. "You're making it an issue. If I didn't trust you, Spencer, then I never would've married you. If I didn't trust you, then I would have hired someone to follow you when you claim you're working late or you're not coming home because you're stuck in some hotel suite preparing for trial. I'm not so insecure that I need you in my face 24/7, so you're going to have to come up with another excuse as to why our marriage may be in trouble."

"Our marriage isn't in trouble."

"What is it, Spencer?"

"I don't know."

"Well, I know," Deanna countered quickly. "Our marriage is in a rut. When was the last time we went on vacation together? I can't remember the last time you called to tell me to meet you in a hotel where we would act like married lovers and fuck our brains out. I used to get so excited thinking about what I wanted you to do to me that I had to change my panties a couple of times before I left the house. I miss our date nights, the impromptu rendezvous, and just my waking up with you beside me."

"Aren't you the one who complains if I come in late and wake you because you need your sleep?"

"Why can't you come home earlier?"

"I can't because I'm working."

"Why do you make it sound as if you're the only one who's working?" Deanna asked. "I usually don't plan daytime events. There are plenty of nights when I don't get home until three or four in the morning, but there are nights when I don't have an event and I'm home alone. You're well aware of my schedule because it's on the board in the kitchen and in the upstairs office. And there is never a time when you ring my phone that I don't answer. Let me assure you that if I did have a man between my legs not only wouldn't I answer the phone, but I'd turn it off."

"I can't answer my phone when I'm in the middle of—"

"You *don't* answer your phone, Spencer," she corrected. "Whenever I call your office either the receptionist answers or it goes to your secretary. And I don't call your BlackBerry because you claim you use it exclusively for business."

"I *do* use it exclusively for business."

"Who are you trying to convince?"

"What's up with you, Deanna? It's as if you're looking for an excuse to argue."

"I'm not looking for an excuse. I just need clarification."

"About what?"

"If our marriage is worth saving."

"We don't have to save it, because there's nothing wrong with our marriage," Spencer said confidently. "We have very demanding careers. And don't forget what attracted us to each other is our ambition to be the best. It takes hard work and sacrifice to be the best. What you have to decide, Dee, is what are you willing to sacrifice when it comes time to start a family?"

"Becoming a mother doesn't mean I'll have to give up my business. I'll hire an assistant, or maybe more than one, and delegate. And once the child is school-aged, then I'll resume a more active role."

"And I'll rearrange my schedule to come home and eat dinner with my wife and baby, even if I have to bring work home."

Deanna smiled. "That sounds like a plan."

Spencer returned her smile. "See, baby. It's not impossible when we talk it out. Maybe we do need a date night." Shifting slightly, he angled his head and kissed Deanna, pulling her lower lip between his teeth. He gently suckled her. "If my gorgeous, sexy wife doesn't have anything on her schedule for tomorrow I'd like to take her on a mini road trip where we can stop and check into a quaint inn and fuck our brains out."

Resting a hand on his cheek, Deanna deepened the kiss. "My calendar doesn't have a thing on it but the date. Shall I pencil you in?"

"Yeah. With a permanent marker." Reaching over her body, Spencer turned off the lamp, then his hand began a slow exploration of his wife's body under the silk nightgown.

Within minutes everything they'd talked about was forgotten when he guided his blood-engorged penis inside Deanna. Making love to her was always a reminder of why he'd married her. She completed him.

Chapter Seven

Damon Paxton stood by the entrance to Bethany's bathroom, watching as she dotted moisturizer on her face and neck before going through a ritual of massaging her forehead, cheeks and throat.

He didn't know why she found the need to buy and use so many creams and lotions, but he signed the checks payable to her dermatologist because it made her happy. And there wasn't anything he wouldn't do to keep Bethany happy.

When he'd been told that she was in the museum's bathroom throwing up his first thought was Bethany was pregnant—again. At fifty-four he didn't need another child, yet he hadn't taken the necessary steps to make certain he would never father another. When Bethany reassured him she'd eaten something that hadn't agreed with her Damon was finally able to relax. He had his daughters, and he also had a son to carry on the Paxton name.

"Are you certain Mrs. Rodgers can't bring you a cup of tea to settle your stomach?"

Bethany met his gaze in the mirror's reflection. "I'm good."

She turned to walk out of the bathroom, but Damon blocked her retreat. "Not tonight, Beth."

Her luminous violet eyes darkened. "What are you talking about?"

His hands went to her shoulders, tightening slightly when she attempted to escape him. "You've spent the past two weeks sleeping in the guest bedroom. It stops tonight."

"Why tonight, Damon? What makes tonight so different from the others?"

He closed his eyes for several seconds. "When Marisol McDonald told me you were in the bathroom throwing up I thought you were pregnant again."

"Would that have been so horrible?"

Damon smiled. "No. At least not for you."

Bethany's pale eyebrows lifted. "And it would be for you?"

"Do you realize how old I am?"

"I know how old you are, Daddy."

His smile widened. Bethany always called him *Daddy* when talking to their children, but there were times when making love she did call him daddy. "I love my children, but at fifty-four I can't see myself with a newborn."

"You know I'm on the Pill, so that should alleviate your worry that I'll become pregnant again."

"I'm not worried, Beth. The only birth control that is guaranteed is sterilization, and if you were to get pregnant again you know I'll be here with you." With each of her pregnancies, Damon had rearranged his schedule to accompany her to every appointment and test. He'd been her La-maze coach and sat with her when she'd opted for natural childbirth.

"I know that, Damon." Taking a step, Bethany buried

her face between his neck and shoulder. "I don't need any more children. We have a son and a daughter, so I'm totally fulfilled."

Damon's arms came down and he looped them around her waist. "I love you, Beth. I love you more than I could have imagined loving any woman. I've never made it a secret that I married Jean because she was pregnant with Paige. When I look back I realize it was a piss-poor reason to marry, but I wanted to do the right thing."

Curving her arms under Damon's shoulders, Bethany molded her breasts to his solid chest. "Never apologize for doing the right thing."

"I know it hasn't been easy for you because everyone believes you broke up my marriage to Jean, but it was over before it had a chance to begin. I'm not one to kiss and tell, but I don't think we made love a dozen times during the time we stayed together."

Bethany pulled back, staring up at Damon staring back at her. "What did you do?"

"I slept with a lot of women, including you."

Her eyelids fluttered wildly. "But…but you told me you never cheated on me."

"And I haven't. From the first time we slept together I've never looked at another woman, because I don't have to." He ran a hand through her thick hair. "You're everything I want. You're beautiful, smart, sexy and a good mother."

"I want to be a good wife, too."

He kissed her nose. "You are a good wife."

"The wives of your business associates don't think so. They hate me because they blame me for breaking up your marriage."

"They're not worth talking about."

"They are," Bethany insisted. "Not one of them sitting at the table tonight looked at me or uttered a word."

"They were jealous."

"They are heifers."

"I agree," Damon said, smiling. "They don't have to like you, but the moment I hear that they've said something that's out of line their husbands will pay the price."

"I don't need you to fight my battles."

"You don't understand, Beth. It's about taking care of what belongs to me. It's my responsibility to protect you the same way I protect Paige, Abby and Connor."

Bethany wanted to talk to Damon about Paige, but knew it would end in a row or stalemate. Her meltdown at the fundraiser was the result of Paige sabotaging the chili she'd made for Abigail and Connor. Her children loved her to cook for them, and she did at least five days each week. It was apparent Paige had emptied an inordinate amount of salt into the pot when she wasn't looking. And when she'd questioned the girl about it she'd turned the tables, claiming Bethany wanted to get her in trouble with her father.

After dumping the pot of chili into the garbage, she had Mrs. Rodgers drive the children to a local restaurant for dinner. Paige continued to taunt Bethany when she'd used a tube of her favorite lipstick and wrote the word *chili* on her bathroom mirror.

Bethany was tempted to leave it for Damon to see, but decided ignoring Paige would be more effective than giving her the negative attention she craved. It was when a woman at the table had asked Damon about Paige and he began to sing her praises that Bethany had suddenly felt physically ill. She knew if she hadn't left the table she would've not only embarrassed herself but also Damon. And she knew within a matter of hours the rumors would've been swirling around

D.C. that Mrs. Bethany Damon had had an emotional melt-down at a VIP fundraiser.

And she had Deanna Tyson to thank for rescuing her. Despite her emotional state, Bethany knew she'd found an ally in Deanna when she told her not to give the old cows the satisfaction of seeing her upset. That single sentence had the same impact of being doused with icy-cold water, being shocked by a volt of electricity or slapped violently across the face.

Bethany had continued to give herself a pep talk on the drive back to Falls Church, reminding herself that she had managed to rise above poverty to become a successful actress and journalist. It had taken focus and determination to leave Parkers Corners, a town with fewer than six hundred residents, for Charlottesville, Virginia—a city with a population of more than forty thousand. She'd been called country, white trash, trailer trash and the derogatory honkey. But she had sucked it up and survived to graduate with honors. Most times she attributed the hostility and rejection to envy and jealousy. She had what men wanted and what women didn't have. But most of all she'd had an overabundance of confidence, something she'd lost when she married Damon.

"It feels good to know that someone wants to protect me," Bethany said after a prolonged silence.

"Not someone, Beth. Me."

Going on tiptoe, she pressed light kisses at the corner of Damon's mouth. "What do you say we go to bed—together?"

Damon's eyes darkened until all traces of blue disappeared. "I'd like that."

Chapter Eight

Deanna sat at the computer, designing the invitation for her dinner party. She'd wanted engraved invitations, but when she'd called the printer he told her she would have a six-week wait. The problem was she didn't have six but only four weeks. She had to allow for a two-week turnaround for the return of phone calls and/or response cards. Her cell phone buzzed and she tapped the speaker feature when she saw the name on the display.

"Thanks for getting back to me, Esther."

"What's up, Dee?"

"Do you have time to do thirty invitations for me?"

"How soon do you need them?"

"Two weeks," she told the calligrapher.

"Done. Just email me everything and I'll have them back to you in a week. I just hired an assistant who does Asian calligraphy, so whenever you want an Asian theme I'll give her the job."

Deanna removed her reading glasses. "You've just given me an idea."

"Talk to me, girl."

She smiled although Esther couldn't see her. "Maybe I'll use an Asian theme for the dinner. I'll buy silk fans for the ladies and splits of champagne with personalized labels with their names in English and Chinese for the men."

"That's a nice touch, Dee. I'll have Carley do something with red and gold that will look nice. Do you want to see a sample before we complete the job?"

"No. I want to be surprised."

"Don't you mean shocked?"

"If it's shocked as in good, then so be it."

"You're my homegirl, Deanna. You know I'll always hook you up, because if it hadn't been for you steering business my way I would've closed up a long time ago."

"What do they say about it takes a village? If we don't help out one another, then none of us will survive."

"You do more than help," Esther said, her voice filling with emotion. "You're always looking out for other folks."

"Cast your bread upon the water—"

"Don't you dare go to church on me, Deanna Tyson," Esther warned.

Deanna laughed. Esther's father had been a preacher and she had been required to read the Bible every day. Even at forty she could quote chapter and verse. "When was the last time you went to church?"

"I'm not going to answer that because it might tend to incriminate me. Send me what you want and I'll have it back to you in a week."

Putting on her glasses, Deanna saved what she'd typed. Then she went online and downloaded the files to Esther. "You know your name is on the list."

"Can I bring my partner?"

"Of course."

She ended the call, her head filled with ideas now that she'd decided to change from a traditional theme to one with an Asian flare. That meant the menu would also change. There was a restaurant along Woodley Road that served Chinese, Japanese and Thai dishes. Deanna would also order the ubiquitious American hors d'oeuvres and entrées from her favorite caterer and wine and liquors from a wholesale distributor.

The phone buzzed again and she picked it up. "Tyson Planners, Deanna speaking."

"Hi, Deanna. This is Bethany Paxton. I don't know if you remember me, but I was the hot mess in the bathroom at the museum."

"I remember you, Bethany. How are you?"

"I'm well. In fact, I'm real good. Thanks to you and your friend—"

"Marisol. Her name is Marisol Rivera-McDonald."

"Is she married to Bryce McDonald?"

"Yes. Why?"

"I thought I saw him at your table when I came back from the bathroom. I'm calling because I would like to treat you to lunch or dinner to thank you for helping me to get my head together. And I'd also like your opinion about a party."

Deanna stared at the calendar she had put up on a board over the desk with her computer. "Are you available today?"

"Do you mean now?"

"No, not right now. How about one-thirty? If that's too late for you because you have to pick up your children—"

"My housekeeper picks up my children," Bethany interrupted. "One-thirty is fine. Where do you want to meet?"

"Where do you live?"

"Falls Church. Where do you live, Deanna?"

"Alexandria."

"I love Alexandria. Why don't you pick the restaurant and I'll meet you there at one-thirty. And don't forget it's my treat. Oh—do you think it's possible for Marisol to join us?"

"I don't know. I'll have to call her and see," Deanna said. She knew Marisol wasn't really into Bethany, but would call and feel her out. "Your number came up on my ID, so I'll call you back after I talk to Marisol and make the reservation."

"You're a doll, Deanna. I'll wait for your call."

Deanna wanted to tell Bethany she was the Barbie doll. All made up and coiffed for her Ken. And she had to admit that Damon Paxton was the perfect male counterpart to his wife, with his tanned face, patrician features, tall, slender physique and expertly barbered hair. Although middle-aged, Damon was still an extremely attractive man. And from what Spencer had implied, he was quite the ladies' man.

"Do you have a food preference?" she asked before Bethany hung up.

"I love seafood."

"How about red meat?"

"I only eat red meat twice a week, so if I eat it today, then I'm good."

"I'm anemic, so I have to have red meat at least four times a week. There's Morton's of Chicago in downtown D.C. They also serve lobster and grilled fish."

"It sounds good."

Deanna hung up and hit speed dial for Marisol. Judging from her slurred response, she figured she had awoken the interior designer. "Do you want me to call you back?"

"No," Marisol said alertly. "I was watching a movie and had dozed off. What's up?"

She told Marisol about Bethany's call. "She wants you to

come along. I thought Morton's would be a good place to eat."

"I don't know what it is about this chick, Dee, but something about her is not sitting right with me. Maybe I have some *sangre de la bruja* like *mi abuela,* but I don't know about Bethany Paxton."

Deanna shuddered when a cold shiver swept over her body. "You know I don't like it when you talk about witch's blood and spells."

"You don't like it because you know they exist."

"Can we go back to the subject? Are you coming?"

"Why not? It's not as if I was doing anything but catching up on watching the movies I've missed."

"Where's Bryce?"

"He's in Denver."

"What's or should I ask who's there?"

"Some millionaire looking to unseat the incumbent governor. Bryce says the man's delusional if he believes he can defeat that state's most popular governor in more than half a century, but if he wants to pay Bryce the big bucks as a consultant then who is he to tell him he's wrong?"

"Bryce is right."

"Where are we meeting?" Marisol asked.

"Morton's on Connecticut."

"Isn't that close to the Mayflower?"

"It's a block from the hotel."

"I think I'm going to take a taxi and leave my car here. Can you drop me off when we're finished?"

"I can come and pick you up if you want."

"That's not necessary. What time are we meeting Miss Bethany?"

Deanna rolled her eyes upward. When she'd first met Marisol it had taken her a while to get used to her sarcasm, but under her friend's tough girl exterior beat a heart of gold. "One-thirty. I'll see you later, chica."

"*¡Adiós!*"

Chapter Nine

It was a very different Bethany Paxton who smiled at the two women who had literally saved her reputation two weeks before. Her gaze swept over Deanna, who looked incredibly chic in a black wool gabardine pantsuit, white silk blouse and Prada pumps. The single strand of pearls around her long, graceful neck matched the studs in her ears.

Marisol was equally conservatively dressed in a navy wool pencil skirt, white turtleneck and red bolero jacket. Sheer navy hose and matching suede pumps pulled her winning look together. She'd replaced the large diamond studs she usually wore with pearls.

Bethany had changed twice before deciding on a pair of charcoal-gray slacks, a cashmere twinset in a robin's-egg-blue and a pair of Gucci slip-ons. A plain gold wedding band and small gold hoops completed what she considered her on-air professional look—a look she'd perfected when she was a news reporter.

Bethany hugged and affected air kisses when Marisol and Deanna stood up. "Thanks again for meeting me."

Deanna stared at the narrow blue velvet headband holding Bethany's flaxen hair off her face. "You're looking well." The color of her twinset accentuated the color of her eyes, which at first appeared dark blue but were actually violet.

"You do look a lot better than you did the last time we saw you," Marisol quipped flippantly.

Bethany's smile did not falter. "Thankfully I feel a lot better than I did the last time you saw me."

"Ladies, your table is ready."

Deanna turned and nodded to the hostess. "Thank you."

She led the way into the dining room, the others following. The lunch crowd was thinning out and they were given a table in a corner that provided a modicum of privacy. They studied the menu, deciding what they wanted to eat. All had opted for sparkling water in lieu of a cocktail.

Bethany raised her goblet in a toast. "To the ladies who helped me to see what I can be."

Deanna touched her glass to Bethany's, but Marisol was slower in acknowledging the toast. "Here, here," they chorused in unison.

Marisol took a sip, set down her glass and then leaned forward. "If you don't mind my asking, what was up with the waterworks at the museum?"

Bethany touched her napkin to the corners of her mouth. "I don't mind you asking. You probably know that I'm not Damon's first wife." Deanna and Marisol nodded. "He has a daughter from his first marriage, and she wakes up every morning to make my life a living hell. I won't go into detail about what she's done and said to me, but the straw that broke the proverbial camel's back was when I made a pot of chili for my son and daughter, who'd been pestering me for a week to make it for them. That was the night of the fundraiser.

"When I served it to my children they claimed they couldn't eat it because it was too salty. When I tasted it I realized someone must have dumped at least a cup of salt into the pot."

"Did you ask your stepdaughter?" Deanna asked.

Bethany rolled her eyes and sucked her teeth. "You know I did, but she denied it, saying I must have done it to get her into trouble with her father. Damon usually defends her, but if she does anything to Connor or Abby, then he's on her like white on rice."

Marisol shook her head. "Did you tell Damon?"

"No. I think that's what she wanted me to do. I had the housekeeper take the kids out to a restaurant, but the look of disappointment on their faces haunted me until I finally went into the bathroom and lost it."

Deanna gave Bethany a long, penetrating stare. "Why isn't she living with her mother?"

"She doesn't want to live with her."

"Why?" Marisol and Deanna asked in unison.

Bethany closed her eyes, and when she opened them they were shimmering with moisture. "Her mother has remarried and moved to Idaho. She didn't want to go with her."

"Damn," Marisol drawled. "That's a long way from here. She probably didn't want to leave her friends."

"She doesn't have any friends," Bethany said. "I know it sounds strange, but at fifteen she should have at least one friend."

Leaning back in her chair, Deanna crossed her arms under breasts. "She doesn't want to live with her mother, she disrespects you and disrupts your entire household. It sounds as if the girl needs to be in therapy."

Bethany nodded in agreement. "When I told Damon that, he said she's just going through a phase. And I told him I wasn't allowed to go through a phase. Either I did as my parents said or I knew which road to take to get out of town."

"My mother used to say it was either her way or the highway," Deanna intoned.

"I hear you," Marisol crooned. "Mami would say, 'I brought you into this world, please don't make me take you out.'" Conversation halted when the waiter set plates of salad at each place setting.

"What do you do during the day, Bethany?" Deanna asked after she'd swallowed a forkful of radicchio and red-leaf lettuce delicately seasoned with vinaigrette.

"I'm a stay-at-home mom."

Marisol gave her an incredulous look. "Why do you say that as if you just won the lottery?"

Bethany frowned. "I don't understand."

"What's not to understand?" Marisol had answered her with a question. "You're a young woman who went to college in order to have a career. You marry a man, push out a couple of kids and then sit down and watch soaps and game shows."

Bethany sat up straight. "Don't knock the soaps, Marisol. I had a recurring role in one for a couple of years that paid the bills and served as a stepping-stone to a career as a television journalist."

Marisol glared at the superficial woman whose life was a disaster because she didn't know how to get out of her own way. "Why aren't you working as a journalist?"

"I can't."

"Why not?" she asked.

"Because I have children."

"Didn't you say you have a housekeeper?" Bethany nodded. "Is she part-time?"

Marisol held up a hand. "I think I can answer that for Ms. Paxton. Her housekeeper is not only full-time, but probably live-in. Right or wrong, Beth?"

Bethany flushed a becoming pink shade. "You're right."

Marisol flipped back a curl that had fallen over her forehead with a toss of her head. "Herein lies your problem. You're a thirtysomething woman trying to be something you're not. And that is the socialite wife of a wealthy man. You're a wife, but that's all. You talk about your husband, children and stepdaughter, but not about Bethany. Why aren't you on the board of some nonprofit organization? Why aren't you on the PTA or volunteering as class mom at your children's school? Do you even get up in time to see your kids off to school?"

"You don't like me, do you, Marisol?"

It was Marisol's turn for her face to darken as she compressed her lips tightly. "I don't know you enough *not* to like you. What I don't like is you making excuses as to why your life is so screwed up."

"I didn't say my life was screwed up," Bethany retorted.

"You think not?" Marisol questioned. "You're bored, Beth. Bored and frustrated because you thought marrying Damon was the answer to all your dreams. But you didn't count on becoming a stepmother. I saw those women sitting at your table when I came to tell Damon what had happened to you. If they live to a hundred and you to a hundred and one they will *never* accept you."

"Is that what happened when you married Bryce McDonald?" Bethany spat out.

Marisol wagged at finger at Bethany. "No, *puta*. Don't even go there. I'm not going to lie and say that some of Bryce's family didn't like the fact that he'd fallen in love and married a Latina, but the difference is I didn't give a shit. And because I didn't, they tried everything to win me over. Some I forgave. Others I'll never forgive. I know who I am. More importantly, I like who I am. Bryce may have been born into money, but I don't need his money because I make enough to buy what I need *and* also what I want. That's the difference between *you* and *me*." She punctuated the pronouns, pointing a finger at Bethany, then tapping her own chest.

Deanna patted Bethany's arm. "Marisol's right. You need to get involved in something that doesn't include Damon, your kids or your stepdaughter. I've never watched soap operas, so I can't judge your acting ability. But I do remember seeing you reporting the news. You were professional *and* memorable. Why don't you volunteer to supervise interns at one of the local networks? I'm certain they would love to have you."

Bethany's expression brightened. "That's a good idea."

Marisol gave Bethany a facetious grin. "It's a wonderful idea, but only if you follow through."

Reaching into her handbag, Bethany took out her cell phone. "I still have a contact at the station. To show you I'm serious I'll call him now." She asked for the man who'd been her mentor at the station, but he no longer worked there. "Do you know how I can get in touch with him?" she asked the woman in human resources. "This is Bethany...Collins. I used to work there." She reached into her bag for a pen. It took less than three minutes to get the information she needed to contact her former mentor.

She flashed a Cheshire cat grin. "I did it. I have the contact information I need. The next time we get together I will definitely have a job."

Deanna and Marisol shared a wink. "Speaking of getting together, I need your address. I'm having a dinner party at my home next month on the sixteenth. If you and Damon are free, Spencer and I would love for you to join us."

Picking up a paper napkin, Bethany jotted down her address and phone number, handing it to Deanna. "Whatever Damon has planned can be postponed. We'll be there."

Two servers approached the table carrying their entrées, followed by the sommelier carrying champagne. "It's a gift from the gentleman over there." He pointed to a table where a well-dressed man affected a snappy salute.

"Who's that?" Marisol whispered.

Deanna returned the salute, smiling. "He's a friend of the French ambassador. We met when I coordinated an engagement party for his daughter."

Peering over her shoulder, Bethany smiled at the elegant man. "You must meet a lot of important people in your line of work."

Deanna nodded. "More than I care to know."

"I'd like to contract your services."

"For what?"

"Damon will celebrate his fifty-fifth birthday in August, and because it's a milestone birthday I'd like to throw a little something for him."

"We'll talk about it later," Deanna said, not wanting to talk business.

Flutes were filled with the premium wine and raised for a second toast. This time it was for old and new friendships.

Chapter Ten

Damon walked into the lobby of the Victoria, a charming residential boutique hotel nestled in a block of Victorian row houses. Smiling, he nodded to the doorman. "Good afternoon. I'm here to meet Mr. Spencer Tyson."

The man in the dark gray livery returned the smile. "Your name, sir."

"Damon Paxton."

"Mr. Tyson is expecting you. He's in the bar area." He pointed to his left. "Go down that hallway and turn left."

"Thank you." Spencer had called him a week after their confrontation at the museum to set up an appointment to have drinks. Damon had been available, but had decided to make him wait because of his unprovoked threat. It was another week before he'd called the lawyer back to arrange a meeting.

He saw Spencer sitting at a round table for two in the rosewood-paneled bar reading a newspaper. There were half a dozen couples sitting at tables, talking quietly to one another.

Recessed light bathed Deanna Tyson's husband in a halo of gold, highlighting the red in his cropped hair.

"Tyson."

Spencer's head popped up and he came to his feet, extending his hand. "Paxton. Thanks for coming. Please sit down." Damon shook his hand, then sat opposite him. "What's your poison?"

"Extra dry gin martini with a splash of Dubonnet and a twist."

Raising his hand, Spencer caught the attention of the waitress, giving her Damon's drink order. "I took the initiative to order a few appetizers. I'm scheduled to work late tonight, so I need to have a clear head."

Unbuttoning his suit jacket, Damon crossed one leg over the opposite knee. "I never knew this hotel existed. It's nice and off the beaten track."

Spencer ran a hand over his dark gray tie. "I found it completely by accident."

"How convenient. It's the perfect place for a liaison."

"I wouldn't know about that. I come here for the bar."

"Are you saying the drinks are *that* good?"

"Good drinks and service."

Tiny lines fanned out around Damon's eyes when he smiled. "It's the same at the Four Seasons, Ritz-Carlton Georgetown and the Hays-Adams Hotel."

"You're right," Spencer agreed. "Maybe I should've added discretion to the list."

Damon grinned broadly. "Now you're talking."

He stared at the wide gold band on the large left hand wrapped around a double old-fashioned glass half-filled with ice and an amber liquid, wondering if the brilliant litigator thought he was that naive. Those familiar with the Victoria knew it was where men hid their mistresses, because Damon had been one of those men when he was married to Jean. One of his friends had referred to the hotel as a "safe house." Everyone associated with the establishment, from its owner, doorman, chef and housekeeping personified discretion.

"Are you saying you cheat on your wife?"

Damon's smile faded. "That's not what I'm saying, Tyson. What I meant is *if* I did think of cheating this would be the perfect spot. Now, tell me why you wanted to have drinks." He had decided to cut directly to the chase. Over the years he'd played enough mind games with elected officials to last several lifetimes. The people who paid him the big bucks to influence their interests didn't care how he conducted business. And they continued to throw money his way until he gave them what they wanted.

Spencer rolled his head from side to side, then took a deep swallow of Scotch on the rocks. "I wanted to apologize to you."

"You already did that." Damon paused when the waitress placed a glass coaster on the table before setting down his glass. Rising slightly, he reached into the pocket of his trousers to give her a tip, but Spencer reached over and caught his wrist.

"I'll take care of her."

He nodded, acquiescing. "Thanks." Picking up the glass, he took a swallow, savoring the taste of the expertly prepared martini. "That's real nice."

Spencer was grinning as if he'd personally mixed the cocktail. "I told you the drinks are excellent."

Damon took another sip, enjoying the iciness in the back of his throat, then the burst of warmth settling in his chest and belly. He was anxious to get back to why he was sitting in a hotel with a man who was as brilliant as he was a liar. "I'd like you to answer one question for me, Spencer."

the House it shattered the glass ceiling. It told everyone that politics was no longer the private club of old white men. Obama becoming president signaled another change, because now there was a man of color in the Oval Office. Even the Supreme Court had to come into the new millennium with three women justices on the bench. If you're going to make a name for yourself it won't be as a senior partner. Your wife is an influential event planner with a client list of who's who, while you're slaving your ass off sixty to eighty hours a week to make partner. It's not adding up, Spencer."

"What's in this for you?"

"Nothing. I work for a group of people just like you do. They pay me to give them what they want, and right now they want you. Enough talk. Let's eat."

Damon picked up a plate, filling it with dim sum, sushi, steak tartar and caviar on tiny crackers, handing it to Spencer. "Eat up."

Forty-five minutes later Damon walked out of the Victoria and slipped into the rear of the car parked at the curb. He'd promised Spencer Tyson a judgeship, knowing it would never happen. There was no way the man could pass a background investigation.

He'd duped the arrogant attorney to stop him from cheating on Deanna. Bethany had come clean, telling him about her meltdown in the bathroom and how Deanna Tyson and Marisol McDonald had helped her. She also told him of her luncheon date with the two women.

Deanna had saved his wife's reputation and that meant he owed her; he'd done what he did to ensure she would never know about her husband's after-work escapades. He just prayed Spencer would take his advice and get rid of his

"What's that?"

"What led you to believe that I was coming on to your wife?"

Lifting broad shoulders under his tailored suit jacket, Spencer feigned an expression of innocence. "I really don't know. I suppose I'd had too much to drink that night and when I saw you holding Dee's hand I kind of lost it."

"You did more than lose it. You threatened to kick an old man's ass."

"Well, you did call me *son*," Spencer shot back. It was an expression he hated almost as much as *boy*.

"And you took *that* the wrong way, too."

"I told you I was a little drunk."

Damon leaned over the small space separating them. "You weren't as drunk as you were scared. It's not easy to remain in control when your whore shows up unexpectedly." It was hard for him to keep a straight face when Spencer looked as if he was going to fall off his chair. "You're smart, Tyson, but I just happen to be a little smarter than you, *son*. I would've let you off the hook that night and chalked your reaction to me holding Deanna's hand as a jealous husband protecting his woman. But you made a serious, a very serious faux pas when you threatened me.

"The reason I didn't have drinks with you last week was because the man I had checking into your background still hadn't given me his final report. I know all about you, Spencer James Tyson. I know the day, hour and minute you were born, the address of the house where you spent the first ten years of your life on Chicago's South Side and the names of the women you've screwed after you married your beautiful wife." He held up a hand to stop Spencer when he opened his mouth. "I know what you're going to say. How can I accuse you of being unfaithful when I cheated on my first wife? I'll admit I did, but I had what I consider a very good reason. If you don't get it at home, then you have to get it elsewhere."

"I don't know what the hell you're talking about," Spencer said when Damon paused to sip his drink.

A sardonic smile parted Damon's firm mouth. "You're so wrong. You know exactly what I'm talking about, but you're going to play the innocent. Man the *fuck* up, Tyson!" he snarled between clenched teeth. "Just come out and say, yeah, I fuck around on my wife."

The tight rein on Spencer's temper loosened. "And so what if I do?" he said recklessly. "I do it, you did it and so do a million men every day and every hour." Rage roiled through him with the force of a twister. "What are you going to do now? Go back and tell Deanna that I'm cheating on her?"

Damon swirled the clear, icy liquid around in the glass, his gaze fixed on the lemon peel. "No." His gaze shifted to the man who looked as if he was going to burst into tears at any second. "No," he repeated. "I'm not into breaking up marriages. What I want to do is help you save yours."

Spencer's prominent Adam's apple moved up and down like a bobblehead doll. "My marriage isn't in trouble."

Damon's eyebrows inched up a fraction. "You think not? What do you think will happen if your wife finds out that you're sleeping with another woman? I can assure you she won't be that forgiving." He paused. "What do you want?"

"What do you mean?"

"What do you want for your future?"

The sweep hand on Spencer's watch made a full revolution as he appeared deep in thought. It was the same question one of the senior partners at the firm had asked him during a breakfast interview. He'd been so nervous that he'd forgotten to eat—something he rarely did. Now the emotion was back, holding him an unwilling captive.

"I want to become senior partner."

Damon smiled at the waitress when she returned to the table with a tray of hot and cold appetizers, china and silver and a stack of linen napkins with the hotel's logo. Quickly and expertly, she set the table and left as quietly as she'd come.

"You're too ambitious to aim so low," Damon said as if there hadn't been a lull in the conversation.

"That's where *you* are wrong, Paxton." Spencer's bravado had returned. "Becoming senior partner at one of the top law firms in D.C. is definitely not aiming low."

"What about a judgeship?"

Spencer's expression did not change. "What about it?"

"How does Judge Tyson sound to you?"

The younger man smiled. "It sounds real good."

"I can make it happen for you, Spencer, but first you have to do something for me. I'm going to make you an offer I'd like you to consider. You don't have to give me an answer now. In fact, sleep on it for a couple of weeks, then get back to me."

"What?"

"Jenah Morris is a liability. I want you to get rid of her."

"That's not going to be easy."

"I'm going to give you thirty…no make that sixty days to make her disappear. After her, there can't be any more outside women. I know people who can clean up your past as easily as erasing a chalkboard. But that's not going to happen if you continue to cheat on your wife."

Resting his elbows on his knees, Spencer glared at Damon. "Is this about me or *my* wife?"

"You've been in Washington long enough to know it's never about the husband or the wife, but the couple."

"Why me? Why us?" Spencer asked, totally confused.

"When Nancy Pelosi became the first female Speaker of

mistress. If not, then Spencer Tyson would have to learn the hard way that his climb to the top of the legal ladder would end in complete ruin.

Chapter Eleven

Spencer hadn't moved from where he'd sat waiting for Damon Paxton, talking and sharing cocktails and hors d'oeuvres with the man. He knew Jenah was upstairs waiting for him, but for a reason he couldn't fathom he found it impossible to go to her.

He replayed everything that had gone down with him and Damon, his denial and the lobbyist's accusations. They weren't accusations but the truth. But who was Damon Paxton to lecture him about morality when he'd had a reputation for screwing any woman who smiled at him? However, he had to agree with Damon when he said he'd aimed too low.

Spencer had achieved his boyhood dream of becoming a lawyer, but he'd never aspired to the bench because he eschewed politics. He hadn't wanted to be beholden to anyone but himself for his successes. If he worked hard, then he would attain his goals, not because he owed some power broker.

It was apparent someone recognized something in him that

he'd refused to acknowledge: the ability to sit on the bench and mete out justice. *Judge Tyson. Your Honor.* He smiled. Spencer had to admit he'd like people to stand up out of respect when he entered a courtroom. It was an action he'd performed countless times when he defended his client. The bench was imposing, the black robe impressive, and being addressed as Your Honor was heady indeed.

Yes. He would do as Damon recommended and stop seeing Jenah. Thankfully, he didn't have to drop her right away. He had sixty days to continue to enjoy the woman who'd offered him the best sex he'd ever had in his life.

He stood up, dropped several large bills on the table, waved to the bartender and walked down the corridor to the elevator. He entered an empty car and punched the button for the third floor. It rose quickly, quietly stopping at the designated floor. The door opened and Spencer came face-to-face with Jenah.

"Where are you going?"

"Where the hell have you been?"

Spencer clamped a hand around his paramour's upper arm, forcibly dragging her down to the suite where he'd told her to wait for him. He unlocked the door and pulled her inside. "It's apparent you didn't hear me when I told you to wait in the room for me."

Jenah Morris tossed back the thick, highlighted, chemically straightened hair that had fallen over one eye. The peekaboo cut had become her signature hairstyle much like 1940s pinup girl Veronica Lake. The style added mystique, but it also concealed the fact that she had different-colored eyes. It wasn't easy for a black girl growing up in Pittsburgh with one brown and one blue eye not to become the object of rude stares and ridicule.

Pushing out her lower lip, she pouted. "I got tired of waiting."

Taking off his suit jacket, Spencer draped it over the back of a chair in the dining area. "Don't I make it worth your while to wait for me?"

A sly smile parted Jenah's full lips as she watched Spencer Tyson undress. She still couldn't believe she'd gotten him to fall in love with her. She was more than aware that he was married when they'd met on election night in the bar of a downtown D.C. hotel. They'd managed to find a spot where they could talk without shouting, and hours later they went upstairs to a suite where they had shared the most mind-blowing sex she'd ever had.

She'd moved to D.C. to join the staff of a Pittsburgh congresswoman, and had contemplated moving back to the Steel City before Spencer changed her mind. They couldn't be seen together publicly, and she understood that, but now she wanted more. Jenah wanted to become Mrs. Spencer Tyson.

Shrugging out of her coat, she let it slide to the floor. Pulling the hem of her blouse from her skirt's waistband, Jenah began what she called her dance of seduction. She swayed back and forth to a nameless tune in her head, removing each article of clothing like a professional burlesque dancer. Whenever she knew she was going to see Spencer she exchanged her panty hose for a bustier and thigh-high hose. The bustier clinched her waist and pushed up her breasts, bringing Spencer's hungry gaze to linger there.

"Do you like what you see?" she crooned, stepping out of her heels.

Spencer smiled, his gaze shifting from her breasts to his groin. "Do you like what *you* see?" His enormous erection strained against boxer briefs.

"Let it out, baby," Jenah whispered.

Reaching under the waistband, Spencer exposed his swollen penis, holding it and watching Jenah's expression change from curiosity to awe as it continued to grow longer and larger.

"Come and lick it, Jenah."

She approached her lover, sank to her knees and flicked her tongue around his sex. It began with a tentative flick, then her mouth opened and she took as much of him as she could without gagging.

Jenah was so aroused that the moisture bathing her core trickled down her inner thigh. She'd gone down on Spencer, but he never went down on her. She realized their lovemaking was lopsided, but she didn't want to say anything that would make him stop seeing her. However, all that would change once they were married.

Spencer bared his throat, growling as Jenah's mouth worked its magic. He wanted to come in her mouth, but only after he went inside her. Reaching down, he eased her large golden breasts from the bustier, smiling when he saw the large bloodred nipples. Jenah Morris was lush, curvy from her lips to her long, sexy legs. She'd become his private dancer, performing on cue. She was only twenty-six, yet she had a sexual repertoire rivaling an experienced courtesan.

Easing his penis out of her mouth, he placed it between her breasts, smiling while she masturbated him, alternating licking each of her breasts. The uninhibited coupling moved to the bedroom, articles of discarded clothing trailing behind them.

Jenah lay on the bed, legs bent at the knees and arms raised above her head. She didn't have to wait long before Spencer loomed over her, his dick grazing her thighs. He placed his hands on her knees, spreading her legs until she felt the muscles pulling in her groin.

"You're hurting me," she gasped when he applied more pressure than necessary.

Lowering his body, Spencer buried his face in the large breasts. "I'm sorry, baby. You know I'd never hurt you."

"Love me, Spence."

Grasping his erection, he eased the rigid member into her vagina. "I love you," he whispered. "I love you when we're together. I love you when we're not together."

He told her what she needed to hear, only because he wasn't ready to give her up. Damon Paxton has issued an ultimatum and he would follow through. He would continue to sleep with Jenah, getting his fill before he settled down to become a father, judge and a faithful husband.

Jenah was the only woman he'd slept with and not used protection. He'd accompanied her to an ob-gyn in Philadelphia to have her tested for STDs and to be fitted with an intrauterine device. And she was the first single woman who'd become his mistress. Spencer preferred sleeping with married women, because all they wanted was sex without declarations of love or happily ever after.

"Fuck me, daddy," Jenah chanted when she felt every inch of his prodigious penis moving in and out of her. Internally she was a big woman, and Spencer was the first man who'd been large enough to bring her to climax.

If possible, he became longer and harder, and she bucked wildly while trying to get closer when he thrust into her with the power and speed of a piston. Grabbing her breasts, she squeezed them as orgasms tore her asunder. She screamed over and over as they kept coming. Spencer's triumphant growl overlapped hers; he ejaculated, a hot rush of semen filling her core.

They lay joined, waiting for their respiration to return to a normal rhythm. It was another half a hour before they stirred to begin the dance of desire again.

Chapter Twelve

"Mari."

"Sí, m'ijo," Marisol answered without glancing up. She'd spent most of the morning sorting receipts and writing checks.

Bryce walked into the office, sinking down to the chair beside her desk. Although they worked out of home offices they rarely got to see each other until the evening. Most times Marisol was out of the house before ten to meet with clients and vendors, while he got up later, lingering to make breakfast. He wasn't much of a cook, but he could prepare a more than passable breakfast. If there weren't leftovers from the night before, Bryce usually skipped lunch and waited for his wife to return. Most times Marisol opted to cook rather than eat in one of the many wonderful Georgetown restaurants.

Their marriage had been one of adjustment: culture and lifestyles. He'd been born into money, while Marisol had grown up below or at the poverty line. He knew which college he would attend and he'd learned everything about politics while sitting on his grandfather's knee, and when his grandfather retired and his father went into semiretirement Bryce took the reins, shepherding the company in another direction because the complexion of politics and the country had changed yet again.

He stared at the profusion of ebony curls falling around Marisol's face in sensual disarray. "I have a new client for you."

Marisol's head popped up and she smiled at Bryce. "Who is she?"

His sandy-brown eyebrows shot up. "It's not a she."

Resting her elbow on the desk, she cradled her chin on the heel of her hand. Without makeup Marisol looked twenty-two rather than thirty-two.

"Then who is he?"

"Congressman Wesley Sheridan."

"Where is he from?"

"St. Louis."

She blew out a breath. "Missouri or Kansas?"

"Missouri. He just bought a house and would like you to decorate it."

"Thanks for the referral, *m'ijo.*"

"That's all you're going to say?"

"I said thank-you. What else do you want me to say?"

"Don't you want to know about Wes?"

Marisol gestured to the computer monitor. "I'll look him up online." It was something she did before agreeing to take on a client. She wanted to know what to expect before meeting them.

"That may be too late."

She angled her head. "What aren't you telling me, Bryce?"

"We're meeting today for lunch."

She looked at her shorts and tank top. "I hadn't planned to go out this morning."

Reaching over, Bryce ran his fingers through her mussed hair. "What if I order in?"

Smiling, Marisol rose slightly and kissed him. "Thanks, *m'ijo*."

He returned her smile. "Anything for you, baby. I'll call and tell him we're going to meet here."

Marisol wanted Bryce to leave so she could massage her temples. She hadn't wanted to tell him that she had a headache—again. It was the third one this week, and this time it'd lasted for two consecutive days. She went to bed with a headache and woke with one. The headaches had begun when she'd first enrolled in college and after a battery of tests specialists determined they were result of tension. Even after she took a tranquilizer the headaches continued, so she'd stopped taking them.

"What time is your meeting?"

Bryce glanced at his watch. "Twelve-thirty."

She nodded. It was ten-fifty. "As soon as I finish up here I'll set the dining-room table."

"Don't forget to change into something less revealing. I don't need Wes leering at you with his tongue hanging out of his mouth."

Marisol clenched her teeth, intensifying the pain in her head. "I believe I'm mature enough to know what is and what isn't appropriate for a business meeting."

"It's just a reminder, Mari."

She waved him away before she said something she wouldn't be able to retract. "Go, Bryce, so I can finish writing checks."

"Why do you have an attitude?"

"I don't have an attitude."

"Well, you sound like you do."

Covering her face with her hands, Marisol took deep breaths in an attempt to relax. "I don't have an attitude, but if you're looking for one then you're out of luck, because I have a monstrous headache."

"Why didn't you tell me about the headache?"

"There's no reason to tell you."

"Yes, there is, Marisol. Have you forgotten that I'm your husband?"

She rolled her eyes. "As if you'd let me forget."

"What's that supposed to mean?"

"You always make it sound as if I'm your possession. Like this house and everything in it. I'm not some inanimate object on display. Do you realize whenever we go out together you always monitor what I'm wearing?"

"I just want to make certain you look nice."

Standing, Marisol came around the desk. A sweep of lashes touched her cheekbones when she stared at the design on the area rug. "In case you've forgotten, I do have degrees in fashion *and* design. I think that qualifies me to know what I *should* wear or what looks best on me."

Bryce cradled her chin, raising her face. "I...I haven't forgotten, baby. It's just that the first time my mother met you she said you looked like a homeless ragamuffin. She—"

"Your mother!" Marisol gasped, cutting him off. "You scrutinize what I wear because of something your mother said how many years ago!" The outfit she'd worn was gypsy-inspired, and she'd had no idea beforehand that Bryce was taking her to meet his parents.

Bryce tightened his hold on her face. "Baby, baby. You don't understand. I didn't mean for it to come out like that."

"*¡Yo no puedo creer esto! El todavía escucha a mami.*"

"Speak English!"

"Learn Spanish," she spat out.

"You said something about my mother, didn't you?"

Marisol jerked his hands away from her face. "You bet your ass I did. I said I can't believe you're still listening to your mother. You're a thirty-six-year-old man, not an insecure six-year-old looking for mommy's approval."

"I don't want you talking about my mother."

"But it's okay for her to talk about me."

Bryce closed his eyes. "Can we discuss this some other time?"

"No," Marisol said. "I don't want to talk about it at all. I want you to leave me alone so I can finish with my banking."

"I don't know why you refuse to use my accountant. He handles all my expenses."

She held her hair off her face with both hands. Marisol loved Bryce, but he had the annoying habit of trying to convince her that what worked for him should work for her. "Why do we argue about the same thing over and over?"

"We don't argue, Mari. We have discussions."

"Okay, we have discussions. I've told you before I want to keep my design company completely separate from your consulting business. I don't care how much money you make or lose, and you don't need to know about mine. That's why we have different accountants and file separate corporate tax returns."

Bryce threw up his hands. "That's asinine. We're married. We're supposed to be a couple, but it's as if we live together but are living separate lives. Now you know why I don't want to bring a child into *this shit!*"

Hot tears pricked the back of Marisol's eyelids. "You're right." Maybe it was a blessing in disguise that she and Bryce weren't parents. Walking over to the door, she grasped the knob. "Please get out of my office." She waited for Bryce to leave, slamming the door so violently behind him the prints on the wall shook.

Pressing her back to the door, Marisol exhaled. How had she been so clueless? She'd talked about Bethany Paxton being a trophy wife when she'd also become an ornament. Over the years Bryce had bought her enough jewelry that she could open her own store. Then there was the walk-in closet with mink, sable, fox and chinchilla coats, jackets, vests, scarves and earmuffs. You would have thought she lived in Alaska where the winters were long and bitterly cold instead of the D.C. region.

Realization washed over Marisol like an icy wave. She had no one to blame but herself. Bryce was the ringmaster and she had become the main attraction. He would introduce her as "my wife" before mentioning her name.

Deanna was right. She was Bryce's *muñeca*. A doll he'd put on display to impress his mother and those in his family who still thought she never should've become a part of their family.

Marisol returned to her desk, picked up the telephone receiver and dialed a familiar number. Her call was answered after the third ring. "Hey, Dee."

"Hey, yourself. What's up?"

"What does your calendar look like for tomorrow?"

"I just have to proof some invitations. Other than that I'm free. Why?"

"I'd like to borrow your shoulder."

"I'm available now if you want to come over."

Marisol grimaced. "I have to interview a new client in a couple of hours."

"Come over after you're finished."

"What about Spencer?"

"He won't be home until late."

Marisol nodded even though Deanna couldn't see her. She

didn't want an audience when she unburdened herself. "Then I'll see you later."

She knew some people viewed her as hard, brusque, but Marisol saw herself as brutally honest. With her there was no pretense, and although she called a spade a spade she was usually open to accept corrective criticism. For the first time since she'd gone into business for herself the excitement of meeting a new client had lost its appeal.

Chapter Thirteen

Marisol didn't know what to expect, but it certainly wasn't the tall, elegant man with silver hair, olive skin and piercing laser-blue eyes. She'd done a quick search of Wesley Sheridan online, reading that he'd been appointed by the governor to fill a congressional seat when a popular representative from a St. Louis suburb resigned after a bribery scandal. It was noted that he was one of eight representatives in the current session who were bachelors. Wesley, with Bryce McDonald as his political strategist, had run and won the seat when his predecessor's term ended.

Bryce, resting a hand on Wesley's shoulder, made the introductions. "Wes, I'd like you to meet my wife."

The slight lifting of Wesley's black eyebrows was barely perceptible when he stared at the petite woman who'd come highly recommended for her designing skills. "Does *the wife* have a name?"

"Marisol," she said, pronouncing it with the Spanish inflection. Smiling, she extended her hand. Bryce had done it again. He'd referred to her as "my wife."

Wesley took the proffered hand, his gaze sweeping over the delicate features of the wife of the man who'd spearheaded his election bid with a stunning runaway victory.

He returned her bright smile with an admiring one. *"¿Habla Marisol español?"*

Marisol's smile grew wider. *"Sí."*

"Tomo eso como un signo que nos llevaremos bastante bien," Wesley said in fluent Spanish.

"So do I," she replied in English, watching the frown forming between Bryce's eyes.

The fact that Wesley spoke Spanish was a good sign, because it wasn't often that she had the opportunity to practice the language. She didn't speak it as well as her grandmother, because like her mother, they tended to intersperse English when they couldn't come up with the Spanish equivalent quickly enough.

"Bryce will show you where you can wash up before we sit down to eat," Marisol continued in a controlled voice although her heart was racing uncontrollably. There was something about Wesley that sparked a modicum of anticipation, because she felt an immediate connection with the gorgeous man.

She walked into the formal dining room and inspected the table with place settings for three. Decorating the town house was what Marisol called her work-in-progress stage. She'd designed the offices on the first floor to reflect her and Bryce's personality. His was furnished with heavy, masculine mahogany tables, desk and built-in bookcases, while hers was in shades of oyster-white and soft blues: white furniture with blue-and-white upholstered chairs, area rugs and framed prints of Audubon flowers and birds.

A gourmet kitchen, formal living and dining rooms, library and media room occupied the second floor. The master bedroom with en suite baths and dressing rooms, three guest bedroom suites and a solarium took up the third floor. If Marisol wasn't in the kitchen cooking or working out of her home office, she could always be found in the solarium reading or watching the flat screen she'd had installed several months ago.

Every time she entered the dining room, Marisol felt as if time had stood still. The Federal-era-decorated space was graced with a wonderful bay window and working fireplace. She'd included a variety of blues often found in a traditional Federal-era setting, ranging from ethereal sky-blue to a rich royal blue. The table with seating for eight and a buffet table were exquisite Federal-style reproductions.

Bryce had ordered dishes from a Georgetown restaurant specializing in authentic Northern Italian cuisine. Marisol had transferred the entrées from take-out containers to covered serving dishes. She had offset the pasta dishes with freshly made *insalata caprese*: alternate slices of tomato and mozzarella, drizzled with olive oil, then sprinkled with salt and fresh pepper and garnished with basil leaves.

Marisol loved cooking, preferring home-cooked meals to those prepared in restaurants because she suspected some of the ingredients they used were the source of her headaches. Her business meetings were usually conducted in a restaurant over breakfast, lunch or dinner. It was a very, very rare occasion—like today—that she would invite a client into her home. Technically, Wesley Sheridan wasn't her client, but Bryce's. He wouldn't become hers until after their initial consultation and when he agreed to and signed her contract.

She'd opened a bottle of red wine, allowing it to breathe, while a bottle of white sat in a crystal faceted bowl filled with ice when Bryce and Wesley walked into the dining room. Both men were in shirtsleeves. Wesley had removed his suit jacket and tie.

Bryce pulled out a chair for Marisol, seating her, while he sat at the head of the table and left Wesley to sit opposite Marisol. "You told me you liked Italian, so that's what we're having for lunch."

Wesley unfolded the cloth napkin, placing it over his lap. "Italian and Caribbean are my favorites." He smiled, his gaze lingering on Marisol. "That's probably why I usually vacation either in Italy or the Caribbean."

Bryce handed Wesley a napkin-covered basket filled with warm semolina bread. "You have to come back one night when my wife makes her roast pork and rice with pigeon peas."

Wesley took a slice of bread. "If you were to ask me what does Christmas smell like in the Caribbean I would have to say *pernil y arroz con gandules.*"

Marisol speared several slices of tomato and mozzarella, placing them on a salad plate. "Where did you learn to speak Spanish?"

Wesley paused, staring at his plate before his eyes moved up and he gave Marisol a long, penetrating look. "My father was in the import/export business, and by my tenth birthday I'd lived in Peru, Mexico and in a few islands in the Caribbean. My mother hired a tutor who lived and traveled with the family."

"It must have been exciting experiencing a new country and culture every few years," she said.

"You would think so, but I always felt like either a gypsy or a military brat, picking up and moving from place to place, while none of them ever felt like home."

Marisol listened, enjoying a Milan-inspired veal scaloppini

with a glass of white wine as the conversation segued to bipartisan politics. Although she kept abreast of political machinations that were the heart and soul of D.C., she had made it a practice not to discuss religion or politics. Lunch ended with coffee and almond cake that literally melted on the tongue. Bryce cleared the table while Marisol led Wesley down to her office.

They sat in cushioned club chairs pulled up to an antique mahogany card table showing Empire influence, circa 1820. Marisol had bought the table at an auction as a gift to herself for her big three-oh. She knew she'd paid more than she'd planned to spend, but rationalized it was an investment.

Wesley crossed his left leg over the right knee and angled his head. Although he'd spent lunch talking with Bryce, it was his wife who'd garnered his rapt attention. A black wool dress ending at her knees emphasized the slimness of her petite frame but did not disguise her obvious curves. Sheer black stockings and a pair of pumps in the same color called attention to her shapely legs and tiny feet. He'd asked several colleagues if they could recommend an interior decorator, and much to his surprise the name of the wife of his former campaign strategist kept popping up.

"Your home is beautiful." Marisol smiled, lowering her eyes in a demure gesture Wesley found incredibly endearing.

"Thank you, Wesley."

"Please call Wes. My father is also a Wesley."

Marisol crossed her legs at the ankles. "Why do men name their sons after them?"

Laser-blue eyes met a pair in dark brown. "I don't know. Maybe it's ego boosting that their name live on after they're dead and gone, but personally I'd never name my son after me."

"Do you have a son?"

As soon as the question was out Marisol realized she'd made a social faux pas. She made it a point never to cross the line between business and personal. People paid her big bucks to make their homes and offices look pretty; she didn't need to discuss anything beyond rugs, lighting, paint colors and furnishings. However, there was something about Wesley that was different. She'd just met him, yet felt as if she'd known him for a while.

"I'm not married."

"Not being married isn't a requisite to fathering a child," she said softly.

"For me it is."

"Good for you."

"¿Por qué diría usted eso, Marisol?" Wesley asked.

"I said it because there are too many children growing up without fathers in their homes," she said, replying in the same language.

"Did you grow up without your father?"

With downcast eyes, Marisol stared at her hands folded in her lap. "Yes." She looked up, meeting his eyes. "I never met my father. The only thing I know is that he was a married man who seduced my seventeen-year-old mother, and when he discovered she was carrying his baby he packed up his family and moved away. I know I have at least one brother and sister, but nothing else beyond that."

"Do you know their names?"

"No. And I don't want to. They don't need an illegitimate sister showing up on their doorstep disrupting their lives."

"I'm willing to bet they aren't half as successful as you are."

"I'd willingly trade in all of my so-called success to find the man who'd fathered me."

"Have you asked your mother?"

Marisol gave him a look parents usually reserved for their children. "Whenever I asked she said he was dead."

Wesley leaned forward. "Dead as in expired?"

"No. Dead in that he was dead to her. When I asked my grandmother about him, she said she didn't know my mother was seeing anyone. It had been one big secret until I came along. My grandparents sent my mom to Puerto Rico to have me, and when we returned we lived with my great-grandmother for a while until Mami moved into public housing."

When Wesley smiled, attractive slashes appeared in his lean face. "So you're a Boricua?"

"Down to the marrow in my bones," Marisol confirmed proudly. "Enough talk about me. Where is your house?"

"It's near Guánica."

"Guánica as in Puerto Rico?" Wesley nodded. She successfully concealed her surprise at his disclosure. "So you're on the Caribbean Sea side of the island."

"Are you familiar with the area?"

Marisol nodded. "I have relatives in Palomas and Guayanilla."

Leaning back in the deep plush chair and crossing his arms over his chest, Wesley studied Bryce's wife. He'd thought of her as an exquisite exotic doll. Everything about her was perfect, and he wondered if Bryce knew what he'd married.

"Maybe you can get to see them when we go down together."

"Hold up, Wes," Marisol warned, switching back to English. "Aren't you being a little premature? I still haven't decided whether I'm going to take you on as a client."

A muscle twitched in Wesley's cheek when he clenched his teeth. The shockingly light blue eyes with the dark centers paled like chipped ice. "When I came here I was under the impression I *was* a client."

"Who gave you that impression?" she asked, switching back to Spanish.

"Your husband."

Marisol affected a wry smile. "Unfortunately, my husband doesn't know how I run my business. I usually have a consultation with the prospective client."

"Which we're having," Wesley interjected.

"Yes. And during that consultation I outline how I work and what I want from said client."

"I'm willing to pay you whatever you want."

"How big is your house?"

"It's a condo. And it's about thirty-three-hundred square feet."

"How many floors?"

"It's a duplex. Six rooms over five."

"Are any of the rooms furnished?"

Wesley smiled. "I have a bed in the master bedroom, a patio set in the kitchen and there are a couple of lounge chairs on the balcony. Other than that it's bare bones."

Marisol sat up straight. "I'll have to see it."

"Spring recess for the House is April 18 through the end of the month. So we'll have a two-week window in which to go down."

She got up, Wesley rising with her, and walked to her desk to retrieve her iPhone. She scrolled through her calendar. She had two appointments, both scheduled for the first week in April. Then there was Deanna and Spencer's dinner party on the sixteenth. "I'm free during your recess."

Reaching for the phone attached to his belt, Wesley entered a reminder to make travel arrangements for two to Puerto

Rico. "I'll call and let you know once I've firmed up our travel plans."

Marisol picked up a business card, walking over and handing it to Wesley. "Call my office number first. If I don't pick up, then try my cell."

He took the card and slipped it into his shirt pocket. "Thank you, Marisol."

She held out her hand. "You're welcome, Wes."

Wesley Sheridan was there, then he was gone, walking out the office and closing the door behind his departing figure. Marisol sat in the chair she'd just vacated, thinking about what had just transpired. Bryce had upstaged her when he told Wesley that she would accept him as a client without her knowledge. It wasn't that she didn't appreciate the referral, but what she didn't need was a husband who did double duty as her agent.

Marisol decided not to say anything to Bryce because she didn't want another argument, or as he put it, a *discussion*.

Chapter Fourteen

Deanna waved to Marisol as she got out of her car and walked up the path to the front door. When she'd called and asked for a shoulder, Deanna could not fathom what Marisol wanted to talk about. She knew it couldn't be marital, because she and Bryce were so much in love. There were times when she envied her interior-designer friend because she didn't have a part-time husband.

Extending her arms, she hugged Marisol. *"Hola, chica."*

Marisol returned the embrace, going on tiptoe to press her cheek to Deanna's. "You sound good. I'm going to make a Boricua out of you before you know it."

"It's all good," Deanna said, laughing. "Come inside. I can't deal with this weather. One day warm, the next day cold."

Marisol slipped out of her coat, hanging it on a wall hook in the Tudor's expansive entryway. "It's nice and toasty in here."

"I keep the heat cranked up because I'm always cold."

"Are you taking an iron supplement?" Marisol asked as she followed Deanna into the kitchen.

"Yeah, but I'm still borderline anemic. Do you want something to eat or drink? And what's up with the 911 call?"

Marisol sat on a high-back stool at the cooking island in the stainless-steel kitchen. "I'll take a cup of herbal tea."

"I just bought decaffeinated peach-flavored green tea. Would you like to try it?"

"Sure."

Resting her elbows on the granite countertop, Marisol watched her friend as she moved confidently around the remodeled, updated kitchen. She'd met Deanna when she and Bryce attended a two-thousand-dollar-a-plate fundraising event in a downtown D.C. hotel. Marisol had been so impressed with the food and decor that she'd asked the event planner for her business card. Their subsequent meeting was to plan a birthday party for Bryce.

They'd become friends—not BFFs who called or texted each other every day, but friends who met on average twice a month as businesswomen who discussed their clients and the challenges they'd faced to grow their businesses. As an only child, Marisol had always wanted a sister, and Deanna Tyson had become that sister.

"What do you think of me?" she asked as Deanna placed napkins and spoons on the countertop.

Deanna stared at Marisol. "What are you talking about?"

"How do you see me? Pretend we're meeting for the first time. What would be your first impression?"

Sitting across from her guest, Deanna gave her a long stare. "If I were really bitchy, then I would hate you."

Marisol's jaw dropped. "You're kidding?"

"No, I'm not. You're every normal man's fantasy. You are petite, and no matter how much you eat you never gain a pound. You have wonderful hair, perfect teeth and skin. I've known you for more than three years and I've never known you to have a zit. Now, tell me what's there not to hate."

"I suffer from chronic headaches."

"I've been saying for a while that you should see my acupuncturist. Those tiny needles work miracles whenever my back goes out from being on my feet for days at a time."

Marisol nodded. "I'll try him only because I've been overdosing on drugstore headache medications."

"We've temporarily solved your headache dilemma. What's really bothering you, chica? Wait," Deanna said when the light went off on the electric kettle. "Don't say anything until I bring you your tea."

Three minutes later Marisol told Deanna everything in between sips of fragrant green tea. She held up a hand. "I know, Dee. I'm my husband's *muñeca*. And I can't believe I've allowed him to inspect what I wear like I'm his kid. I was so busy jumping all over Bethany about being a hood ornament for Damon when I'm no different. The only difference between me and Bethany is that she has children and no career."

Reaching across the space separating them, Deanna grasped Marisol's hand, staring at the diamonds in her wedding rings. "It's not going to be easy to undo what you've allowed to go on for six years."

"Try seven. It began before I married Bryce. I was in my Bohemian phase and all of my outfits were a bit funky. I had wild hair and favored flowing fabrics with shocking colors. It was the last time I actually felt completely free, and the last time I didn't complain about having a headache." Marisol reversed their hands, squeezing Deanna's fingers. "A neurosurgeon told me my headaches were brought on by tension. He was wrong, Dee. It's more like frustration. I'm frustrated that I can't get pregnant, and subliminally resent Bryce inspecting me before we go out together."

Deanna's expression stilled, growing serious. "How long have you been trying to get pregnant?"

"Two years."

"Have you had your estrogen checked?" Deanna asked.

"Yes. It's normal."

"It doesn't have to be you, Marisol. Maybe it's Bryce."

Slumping in the stool, Marisol narrowed her eyes. "What aren't you saying, Dee?"

"Have you considered that you may not have a problem? That it could be your husband with a low sperm count?"

A wry smile twisted Marisol's lips. "I don't think so. He told me he got a girl pregnant when they were in college, but she decided to have an abortion."

Deanna sipped her tea, staring at Marisol over the rim. "Maybe you just need to relax. Elections are over, and Bryce probably has a lull before campaigning starts up again. Why don't the two of you go away for a week or two? Lie in the sun and make mad crazy love to each other. I'm willing to bet you'll come back with a bun in the oven."

Marisol crossed her arms over her chest at the same time she affected a sad smile. "Life can be a bitch. I was a virgin until I was twenty-five only because I didn't want to end up like my mother—pregnant, poor and single. Bryce and I dated six months before I slept with him for the first time, but only after he'd put a ring on my finger. Once he realized I'd been a virgin he swore I would be his forever. Now that I think back, he made it sound as if my virginity was some kind of prize, a trophy he could put in a display case for his personal pleasure."

"You're not going to leave him." Deanna's query was a statement.

"No. I love him, Dee. And if Bryce isn't going to change, then it's up to me to change. But I don't intend for it to be so drastic that we'll end up in divorce court."

Deanna shook her head. "I've seen you and Bryce together enough to know that he loves you, and if he's as possessive as you say, then you'll be together for a very long time."

Marisol's expression did not reveal her inner feelings. She didn't want to correct Deanna about Bryce's possessiveness because he wasn't. He was controlling. "Enough bitchin' and moaning," she said instead. "Have you ever met Wesley Sheridan?"

"Yeah. A couple of times. Why?" Deanna asked.

"He bought a house in Puerto Rico and he wants me to decorate it."

"That's strange, because he just bought the co-op he was renting in Adams Morgan before he won his seat in a runoff election." Deanna pushed out her lips. "I wonder if the silver fox is getting finally getting married."

"Is he seeing anyone?" Marisol had found herself intrigued by the young politician who spoke Spanish as if it was his first language.

"I don't know. D.C. is a strange city. Either everyone knows everyone's business, or they can be as tight-lipped as a secret service agent guarding the president. I was born and raised here, my dad was a secret service agent, my mother a schoolteacher and one year I worked as a senate page. I've seen members of Congress come and go, and some who were there when I was a kid are still around, so there aren't too many politicians I'm not familiar with. Now, take Wes Sheridan. Aside from him being nice on the eyes, he's not what I consider the prototypical politician. He doesn't have the connections some of the others have, so he's his own man. He's never been seen with a woman, so there are rumors about his sexual orientation. Maybe he's gay or maybe he isn't. And if he is, then that could be the reason why he'd want a clandestine hideaway."

"A duplex hideaway that has eleven rooms?"

Deanna whistled softly. "That's a lot of space for one person."

"It depends on how it's configured. I'll take pictures to show you the layout."

"When are you going?"

"Wesley mentioned flying down during the recess."

"Make certain you don't leave before…" Deanna's words trailed off when Spencer walked into the kitchen. She glanced at the clock on the microwave. It was four forty-five. "I thought you were working late."

Spencer undid the top button on his shirt, then loosened his tie. "I must be coming down with something, so I decided to come home early." He smiled at Marisol, but it was more of a grimace. "Hi, Marisol."

"Hey, Spencer."

Deanna closed the distance between her and her husband, placing her hand on his forehead. His face was flushed, eyes glassy. "You feel a little warm. Why don't you go upstairs and get into bed and I'll make you a hot toddy."

"All I need is a few hours of sleep and I'll be all right."

"That's what's wrong with you, Spencer. You don't get enough sleep," Deanna said accusingly.

He frowned. "Please don't start in with the nagging, Dee."

"Since when is concern nagging?" she countered.

"I'm going to bed."

Deanna waited until she and Marisol were alone again. "Spencer is worse than a kid whenever he gets sick."

Marisol slid off the stool. "That's because men are nothing more than big kids. Thanks for the tea and for letting me dump on you. Call me later with the name and number of your acupuncturist." She hugged Deanna. "Go take care of Spencer. I'll let myself out."

It wasn't until the return drive to Georgetown that Marisol realized she was pain-free. Gripping the steering wheel with one hand, she massaged her temple in a circular motion with the other. She smiled. The headache was gone. She'd decided to take Deanna's advice and see her acupuncturist only because she'd exhausted all other options.

Opening the front door, she found Bryce pacing the length of the hallway leading from the entry to the half bath and utility kitchen they used during work hours. She and Bryce had decided beforehand that the entire first floor would be solely business-related.

She waved to him as she started up the staircase, but he gestured for her to stop before he placed a hand over the mouthpiece of the cordless receiver. "Don't go up yet, Mari."

Slipping off her coat, Marisol dropped it and her handbag on one of a trio of armchairs in what doubled as a sitting area. Bryce nodded several times to whomever was on the other end of the line, and then pressed a button, ending the call. He approached her, brushing a light kiss over her mouth.

"Do you have anything planned this coming weekend?"

"Nothing. Why?"

"My sisters are getting together and throwing a surprise forty-fifth anniversary party for my parents before Dad takes Mom on their around-the-world cruise."

Marisol wished she'd had a prior engagement so she wouldn't have to accompany Bryce. "Where is it?" Her tone was flat, void of emotion.

"It's going to be at Georgina's."

"Is she cooking?"

Bryce gave Marisol a pointed look. "That's not funny."

"I'm sorry." After more than ten years of marriage his spoiled and overindulged older sister couldn't boil an egg.

He smiled when seeing her lips twitch. "No, you're not. But to answer your question, she's having it catered." Bryce reached for her hand, leading her into his office. He sat on a leather love seat, bringing her down to sit on his lap. "How did it go with Wes?"

Resting her head on Bryce's shoulder, Marisol closed her eyes. "Well. He spoke Spanish, which gave me a chance to practice mine."

"His ability to speak fluent Spanish helped him get elected."

"He's very bright."

"Are you going to take him on as a client?"

She nodded. "Yes. It's been several years since I've been to Puerto Rico—"

"Puerto Rico?"

Marisol felt Bryce go still, as if he'd been paralyzed by a powerful tranquilizer. She sat up straight, meeting his stunned gaze. "Didn't he tell you that the house is in Puerto Rico?"

"No, he didn't. When he said he bought a house I'd assumed it was somewhere around here."

"Sorry, *m'ijo*, but this time it's not within driving distance."

"I don't like it."

"What don't you like?"

"That you are going away with a man."

Pushing against his shoulder, Marisol forced Bryce to release her. "What's wrong with you? The man is a client, not my lover."

Bryce blushed. "I didn't say he was your lover, Mari."

"Then what is it you're saying? I need to hear it."

"I guess you can say I'm jealous."

"Jealous of what, *m'ijo?*"

"Wes is an attractive man and—"

"And so are you, Bryce," she said softly, cutting him off. "Wesley Sheridan isn't my first male client and hopefully he won't be my last. None of them have ever crossed the line between business and personal because that's something I won't tolerate. You're a D.C. insider, and I want to know if you've ever heard any gossip about me and another man."

"No, babe."

She kissed him. "Then I don't want to hear about me and Wesley Sheridan. I'll go with him to Puerto Rico to see his house, then I'll help him select what he needs to make it a home."

Bryce's gaze softened as he stared at the tiny round face with the luminous dark eyes. He pantomimed zipping his lips. "The topic is moot."

"Good." Marisol kissed him again, then stood up and left her husband's office. She didn't know what had sparked Bryce's sudden jealousy, but she did not intend to dwell on it. She knew she had to prepare herself to come face-to-face with her in-laws in a week, and she also had to select an appropriate gift for a forty-fifth wedding anniversary.

Chapter Fifteen

Bethany sat in the small, cramped office occupied by her former mentor. *Oh, how the mighty have fallen,* she thought, staring at Nathan Nelson as he shifted through stacks of papers and unopened letters.

He'd been her mentor at the television station, but that didn't exclude him from being a bully *and* a tyrant. When she was first assigned to the D.C. affiliate he had taken her under his wing and protection, but what Bethany hadn't known was that he'd also wanted to get into her panties. She'd resisted sleeping with her bosses to get a promotion, and it was no different with Nate. What she'd come to respect about the man was that he took rejection well. To him, no meant no, and after he'd dealt with that he'd slipped fluidly back into the professional journalist who had been responsible for the network earning a string of awards during his tenure. Earlier in his career he'd won a coveted Pulitzer for uncovering the CIA's involvement in the overthrow of a Central American president, replacing him with a U.S.-backed puppet. Now in his late sixties, he sat in an office in a less-than-desirable D.C. neighborhood that was smaller than her kitchen, dwarfed by stacks of old magazines and newspapers. His eyes were rheumy, breath smelling of alcohol, and his rumpled shirt and pants looked as if they hadn't seen an iron since leaving the factory. His mussed gray hair was oily, which meant it needed washing, and the stubble on his chin was sparse and scraggly.

Bethany, sitting on the edge of the cracked leather chair, met dull gray eyes. "What happened to you, Nate?"

His chin wobbled slightly. "My world fell apart after my wife left me and I hit rock bottom. She had a barracuda for a lawyer who just about cleaned me out, and when the head of the network gave me my pink slip because I couldn't get up and come to work on time I dropped out of life for a while."

She waved her hand. "What do you call this?"

Nate looked at the young woman who appeared as if she'd just stepped off the set for a Ralph Lauren photo shoot. Ten years ago she'd been a fresh-faced ingenue looking to make a career in television reporting, and now she was the wife of one of the most influential men in Washington, D.C. He'd always known she was ambitious, but thought that ambition was directed at her career, not landing a much older and very wealthy husband.

He affected a lopsided smile. "It's my office."

Bethany wrinkled her nose. "It's not much better than a hovel. In fact, it's a pigsty."

"It's my motherfucking hovel," he snapped.

Bethany stood up as if jerked up by a taut wire. "Talk to me like that again I'm going to walk out of here."

Nate waved at her like he was swatting fly. "Sit down and don't take yourself so seriously. You've heard and said worse than *motherfucker* and you know it, princess."

Bethany sat down again. Nate was right. "I try to monitor my language now because I have kids."

Nate sucked his teeth, and then opened the top drawer in the desk to retrieve a toothpick. "How old are they now?" he mumbled, picking his teeth as Bethany averted her gaze.

"Abby is eight and Connor turned five in January."

"Who do they look like?"

She smiled. "They look me, but have Damon's eyes."

Nate returned her smile, validating he hadn't seen a dentist in a very long time. "You know they used to call you the blonde Liz Taylor because of your violet eyes. Just watching you onscreen used to make me hard. Sorry about that," he said when spots of color dotted Bethany's pale cheeks. "You told me you wanted a job."

"I need a job, something to do in my spare time."

"How much spare time do you have?"

"A lot," she admitted.

Nate ran a hand over his face. "I just put out my last edition of a paper I was doing for several local churches in the area, and I've been mulling over the idea of putting together a tabloid geared to who's who and who's doing who in D.C. Fortunately, I still have a few contacts in the capital district that are willing to dish on their enemies. If I decide to go through with this, then I'm going to need someone on the inside. You, Bethany, would be that inside reporter."

Her eyes opened wider. "You want me to spy on people?"

"It wouldn't be spying. It would be more like listening in and reporting back what you hear. Not at any time would we print names, because that would make us to liable to lawsuits."

Bethany shook her head. "Did I just hear the pronoun *us?*"

"They would sue me and the paper."

"That's better."

"You're married to a Washington insider, so it should be easy for you to get dirt on some of the women who have shunned you. Yes, Bethany. Don't look so shocked. I told you I still have my contacts. I know you attend fundraisers with Damon, but not the more private functions because the wives of his business associates still look down on you as the woman who destroyed Damon and Jean's marriage."

"Their marriage was over even before I'd entered the picture. Dear sweet Jean Paxton was a whore. She slept with any man who came through her front *and* back doors, and that included the pool boy and deliverymen. The only one she wouldn't sleep with was Damon."

"Do you know this for a fact?"

Bethany nodded. "Yes."

"Can you prove it?"

She nodded again. "Damon waited for Jean to take their daughter with her when she went to visit her mother, then he had the house wired with hidden cameras. Once he'd recorded hours showing Jean in bed with different men, he showed it to his attorney. When Jean was shown the footage she had no reaction. They had a quickie divorce, Damon gave her the house and a sizable settlement and three months later I married Damon."

"Do you know the names of the men she slept with?"

"Some of them. But I'm not going to tell you. What I do know is the names of her friends who were also cheating on their husbands."

"Are they still married?"

"Yes."

Lacing his fingers together, Nate leaned forward. "How would you like to get even with the bitches?"

"I don't know, Nate. I don't believe in an eye for an eye."

"What do you believe in, princess?"

Bethany lowered her gaze. "Karma."

"What if we speed up karma?"

She crossed her legs and angled her head. "What exactly do you want?"

"I want to sell newspapers. And nothing sells like tabloid gossip. Go online and people are blogging and tweeting. Turn on the TV and all you see are reality shows with out-of-control parents, children and elected officials. I'm sixty-eight years old and I'm barely making ends meet after paying rent on my apartment and this place. If it wasn't for my pension and social security, I'd have to move my bed here and cook on a hot plate. I haven't seen my grandkids in five years because my daughter says she doesn't want her children to know their grandpa is a drunken bum. Yeah, I drink, but it helps me forget what I had and lost."

Opening her handbag, Bethany took out her checkbook. "How much do you need?"

"I don't need your money as much as I need dignity. And selling newspapers will do that for me. Come on, princess. Help an old man out."

Bethany stared at the broken man who'd made it possible for her to rise quickly as a television journalist at the D.C. affiliate. She had been slated to become a weekend anchor if she hadn't given it up to become Mrs. Damon Paxton. "Okay, Nate. Tell me what you want."

He gave her a wide grin. "I want you to accompany Damon to as many parties and fundraisers as time allows. I'm certain your husband will be pleased to show off his beautiful wife. Keep your eyes and ears open for anything you think will sell copies. I'll create a column and an anonymous byline for you. I'll also tie it into the internet with a blog." Nathan paused. "Why are you looking at me like that?"

"It's ludicrous."

"No, it isn't, princess. The column will be titled 'Fact or Fiction, Real or Rumor?' You can be as creative as you want with the column that will become the catalyst for the *Daily Dish*."

"What's the *Daily Dish?*"

"It's your blog."

"I don't blog, Nate."

"You'll learn. I also plan to set up a Facebook page for the paper, and between blogs and tweets we'll be back in business. Everything will be done online, so you won't have to come to this upscale neighborhood and my posh office," he drawled facetiously.

Bethany thought about Nathan's proposal. There was no doubt she would help him out financially, but what was in it for her? "What's in this for me?" She'd spoken her thoughts aloud.

Leaning back in the creaking antique executive chair, Nate laced his hands over his protruding belly. "I can get you a part-time position with the station editing copy. What do you say?"

She was hard-pressed not to show her excitement. "I thought you were persona non grata."

Nate winked at Bethany. "I still have a little juice with some folks in HR."

Bethany appreciated Nathan putting in a good word for her, but she was still ambivalent about gathering information and dishing on people who'd unfairly judged her. She wasn't proud that she'd slept with a married man, but she hadn't experienced any guilt, either. However, Damon's reluctance to out his wife had made Jean a martyr and Bethany a pariah. When she'd spoken to Damon about it his response was that he didn't want Paige to know about her mother's sexual escapades.

"Do you mind if I think about it?" What she didn't tell her former mentor was that Damon didn't want her to work until Abigail and Connor were older.

"I do mind, but I suppose I don't have much of a choice."

"Let me sleep on it, Nate. I'll call and let you know tomorrow. Now, if I don't write the column will I still get the job at the station?" Bethany had to know whether Nate was stringing her along just to get her to write for him.

"Of course, princess. Have you ever known me to go back on my word or break a promise?"

She shook her head. "No." Bethany picked up her handbag, shaking it to make certain she hadn't picked up an insect. "Clean up this office and clean up yourself, Nate, because underneath the trash and dirt is your dignity."

"Damn, princess. You really know how to hurt a guy."

"I'm serious, Nate." Reaching into her bag, she took out her wallet and dropped a handful of bills on the paper-littered desk. "I'll be back in a couple of days. If I walk in here and this place looks the same, then you'll have my answer."

Nathan waved his hand. "I can't clean this up in a couple of days."

Bethany pointed to the large bills. "I gave you enough to hire someone. All of this paper is a breeding ground for rodents and insects. There's also enough money for you to get a haircut and a professional shave. Please don't make me regret working with you again. And another thing."

"What's that, princess?"

"Cut down on the booze and make an appointment to see a dentist."

He saluted her. "Aye, aye, ma'am."

"I'm serious, Nate."

"Okay," he said, sobering. "When are you coming back?"

"Friday morning. That will give you four days to get your act together."

"We're going to be a helluva act, princess."

Bethany smiled. "We'll see about that."

She replayed all that had happened on the return drive to Falls Church. Nathan Nelson wanted revenge and he wanted his fight to become her fight. Bethany knew if she'd been warmly accepted as Damon Paxton's wife her free time would've been filled with charity events and social luncheons. She was thirty-five, and like fifteen-year-old Paige she didn't have one close friend.

Thinking of Paige reminded Bethany that the girl would turn sixteen before the end of the school year. She'd never had a sweet sixteen because her parents couldn't afford it, but that was not the case with Paige.

Bethany wasn't certain if her stepdaughter would accept the idea of having a sweet sixteen with all of her classmates present to help commemorate the all-important milestone birthday, but she would present it to Damon first and get his feedback before asking Deanna to plan the celebration.

Chapter Sixteen

Bethany lay facedown on the massage table, reveling in the magical touch of the masseur kneading the knots in her shoulder blades. She'd kept her promise to herself to work out with her trainer three times a week, limit her intake of wine, increase the servings of fruits and vegetable and protein intake and cut back on red meat. The result was she'd lost eight pounds in three weeks. She'd managed to drink six to eight glasses of water a day, which had eliminated the puffiness under her eyes, while a Botox treatment had erased the tiny frown lines between her eyes.

It was the last week in March, and the evidence of spring was apparent with blooming flowers, budding trees and much warmer daytime temperatures. Spring was a time of renewal, and Bethany Collins Paxton felt renewed. She knew she'd surprised Nathan when she told him she would do the column and blog, and had shocked Damon when she announced she would accompany him to a party hosted by the CEO and several board members of a major pharmaceutical company.

Whenever Damon received an invitation to an event he'd always asked whether she wanted to go with him, and her reply had always been no. This time she'd said yes, because if she was going to glean information for her column and blog, then as a good reporter she had to be there.

The soft background music, dim lighting, scented candles and the walls covered with gauzy fabric added to the surreal setting as Bethany willed her mind blank and she fell asleep under the relaxing ministrations of the incredibly talented masseur.

"Wake up, Mrs. Paxton. You're going to have to turn over."

Eyelids fluttering, Bethany moaned in protest. Holding the sheet to her breasts, she turned over and immediately closed her eyes again. The reason she frequented the spa was because it was a one-stop beauty establishment. The services included facials, massages, hair and makeup, manicure and pedicures. After the massage she would shower and have her hair styled, and the makeup technician would make up her face. In order to save time returning home, she'd brought the dress, shoes and accessories she'd planned to wear with her. She'd also called a car service to pick her up and drive her directly to the hotel.

Damon had lost track of the number of times he'd looked at his watch as he waited for his wife to walk through the doors to the Four Seasons. His expression brightened when he saw her. She was stunning in a gown that was an exact match for her magnificent eyes. A front slit showed off her long legs with each step. Closing the distance between them, he pressed a kiss on her moonlit hair pinned off her face. There was something about her pale, delicate beauty that called to mind a young Grace Kelly. The magnificent tanzanite-and-diamond drop earrings were a gift he'd given her following the birth of their son.

"You look amazing," he whispered in her ear.

Lowering her eyes, Bethany affected a demure smile. "Thank you, sweetheart. You look handsome, as usual. I hope I don't have to shank a few of these bitches tonight for coming on to my man," she whispered.

Pulling back, Damon stared at his wife as if she were a stranger. He'd never known her to exhibit a modicum of jealousy. "Why would you say that?"

"I know I rarely go out with you, so I don't know if you're being hit on."

"I wouldn't know it if I was being hit on." He ran a finger along her jawline. "I promised you the day we married that I'd never cheat on you, and I haven't."

Bethany met his eyes. "And I believe you, Damon."

Taking her hand, he tucked it into the bend of his elbow over the tuxedo jacket. "Let's go in now." It was the cocktail hour, a time when Damon was able to reconnect with those he knew and a few he'd planned to get to know.

Bethany held back. "I need to check my wrap."

"Don't worry about that. I'll get someone to take it for you." He gestured to a familiar bellhop. "Please put this in coat check, and then bring me the ticket." Damon handed the man Bethany's black silk, hand-beaded shawl and surreptitiously slipped him a large bill.

"No problem, Mr. Paxton."

Bethany pressed her bare shoulder against Damon's silk-and-wool jacket. "That was easy."

"I've always told you it's not what you know in this town, but who you know. I make it my business to know the right people regardless of what they do for a living. It's not who owns the hotel, but those who run it that are important. What if a bellhop delivers your luggage with important documents to the wrong room, or the concierge neglects to inform you that something you're expecting is at his station? One mistake could make or break a deal."

"Why is it always about the *deal?*" Bethany asked softly.

"That's the only four-letter word that's music to my ears. When I'm able to get some elected official to agree to vote for something my client wants, and we shake hands and say 'it's a deal,' I quickly forget about the asses I had to kiss to make it a reality."

"I don't envy you, Damon."

Reaching for a flute off the tray of a passing waiter, Damon handed it to Bethany, then took one for himself. "I don't envy me, either." He touched his glass to his wife's. "Here's to many more nights out together."

Nodding, she took a sip of the bubbly wine. "I've neglected you for long enough. The people in this town should know that we're still a couple."

Damon smiled. He hadn't married Bethany because of her beauty and intelligence, but because he'd actually fallen in love with her. Although he was old enough to be her father, he'd never thought of her as a daughter. She'd been twenty-four when he saw her in person for the first time, and he'd found himself slightly off balance when she'd approached his table and handed him her business card with a request she would like to interview him for a news feature she was working on for her station. He waited a few days, then called her. They had dinner in an out-of-the way restaurant in northern Virginia, talking about everything but what she wanted in her interview. They met several more times, and the night Damon made a reservation to eat at an inn several miles from Leesburg it had changed them and their relationship. Bethany had offered him the best sex he'd ever had in his life. Once he slept with her he'd forgotten any other woman existed—and that included his estranged wife.

Jean had cheated on him before they were married, but he had forgiven her when she claimed it was the first and only time. When she'd come to him months later with the news that she was pregnant, Damon did the right thing and married her. He was approaching forty and he was ready to settle down with a wife and children.

The year Paige celebrated her third birthday Jean moved out of their bedroom. She claimed she didn't like sex and sleeping with him made her physically sick. It wasn't until a year later that he'd found telltale signs that she was sleeping with another man. The condoms her lover had discarded in the trash had come in neon colors, something he hadn't and would never use. Damon hadn't wanted to believe his wife had made love to another man in their home.

He'd sought out other women to take care of his physical needs, and once he met Bethany he knew he had to end his sham of a marriage. On the advice of his lawyer he had the cameras installed, and when Jean and her attorney viewed the footage all agreed divorce was imminent. Damon knew he probably would've still been married to Jean and sleeping with other women if he hadn't met Bethany Collins.

Bethany was a good wife and mother, and he knew she was having a rough time with Paige, but he prayed the two would eventually declare a truce where they could tolerate being in the same room at the same time.

Bethany tapped his shoulder. "There's Deanna and Marisol, the two women who helped me get it together at the Red Cross dinner."

Damon pressed a kiss to her pale hair. "Go talk to them, baby. I'll come and get you when it's time to go into the ballroom to eat."

He watched the gentle sway of her hips in the body-hugging gown. If he'd felt an iota of guilt sleeping with other women while married, it had vanished like a wisp of smoke once he met Bethany. Damon paid a private investigator to delve into the former beauty queen's background. She had no criminal record—not even a traffic ticket. During the eighteen months she'd worked as a recurring character on a top-rated daytime soap Bethany had dated a few Hollywood actors. The tabloids never reported her involvement with alcohol or drugs, so she was touted as the good girl who loved bad boys.

She finally got her big break when she landed a job with an Indianapolis news station. A year later she transferred to Washington, D.C., as a political correspondent. Ratings soared whenever she was on camera with her beautifully modulated voice and hypnotic eyes. When Damon saw her in the restaurant he'd known immediately who she was.

He went still when he felt a hand on his shoulder. Turning, Damon stared into the light brown eyes belonging to Spencer Tyson. The attorney's face was thinner than it had been during their last encounter.

Damon offered his hand. "How's it going, Tyson?"

Spencer shook Damon's hand. "It's all good."

Resting a hand on Spencer's back, Damon steered him over to a corner in the crowded room. "Did you take care of that business we discussed? That situation at the Victoria," he said in a voice barely above a whisper.

Spencer stared at the amber liquid in his highball glass. "Not yet. Don't forget you gave me sixty days."

"And you intend to take every one of them, don't you?"

"Look, Paxton—"

"No, *you* look!" Damon hissed between clenched teeth. "You're not equipped to play in the big leagues, because it's apparent some hungry, power-seeking cunt means more to you than a judgeship. She can't be *that* good, or is it you can't see the bench because her double Ds are blocking your view?" Damon leaned closer. "You don't have to stop fucking her because I've just withdrawn my offer. You're on your own… *son.*"

Turning on his heels, he walked away, leaving Spencer staring at his departing back. He didn't want to believe a man as ambitious as Spencer Tyson would forfeit a chance to sit on the bench for a piece of ass.

Bethany exchanged air kisses with Marisol, then Deanna. "Y'all look so nice tonight."

"Careful, Miss Sweet Tater Queen, but your country is showing," Deanna teased.

Bethany glanced around to see if anyone had overheard her. "Girls, y'all don't know hard it is for me not to sound like a 'Bama. I paid a speech coach a ton of money to help me lose my accent, but every once in a while it comes back."

Marisol, resplendent in red, rolled her eyes upward. "Don't worry about it. *Está entre amigas,* so you can be yourself, chica. I said you were among friends," she explained when Bethany gave her a blank stare.

Bethany flashed a two-hundred-watt smile. It was the first time since she'd become Mrs. Damon Paxton that a woman had called her *friend.* "I'm honored to be your friend, chica."

Marisol shook her head. "Mari or Marisol will do, thank you."

"I have a part-time job," Bethany said quickly.

Deanna and Marisol shared a knowing look. "Good for you. What are you doing?"

"I'm writing copy for the television station where I used to work. It's not very challenging, but at least I'm out of the house a couple of days a week." Bethany didn't tell Marisol and Deanna that she had also agreed to work for Nathan Nelson. That she had come with Damon with the anticipation of overhearing something she could use to debut her column and blog with the impact of a shot heard around the world.

"How are you getting along with your stepdaughter?" Deanna asked, continuing with her questioning.

Bethany drained her flute, then placed it on the tray of a passing waiter. "We keep our distance. She comes in from school and hides out in her room until it's time for dinner. Damon, unless it's absolutely impossible, always makes it home in time for dinner. Of course she's on her best behavior because she doesn't want to hear her father complaining about coming home to a household in turmoil."

"Good for him," Marisol said. "At least he's a hands–on father."

"It's because his parents divorced when he was young, and he got to see his father during holidays and every other summer. Since his dad has been diagnosed with the early stages of Alzheimer's, they've grown very close."

"Now that you're working I suppose you won't have time to meet for lunch," Marisol said to Bethany.

"I make my own hours," Bethany said, "and I've only committed to two days a week."

"Business is slow for me right now," Marisol admitted, "so I'd like to invite you and Deanna over for lunch one day next week."

Deanna accepted a napkin and speared a tiny Moroccan-style meatball with a toothpick. "Count me in if you're cooking. If not, then I'm not coming."

Bethany's gaze shifted from Deanna to Marisol. "What's on the menu?"

"*Tostones, camarones ajillo, polla asado.*"

"This country girl needs you to translate for her."

Marisol laughed. "Fried green bananas, shrimp in a garlic sauce and roast chicken. And, if either of you aren't dieting, then I'll make either white or yellow rice."

Deanna gave Marisol a direct stare. "When have you ever known me to diet?"

"Yo no sé."

"Neither do I," Deanna countered.

Bethany waved her hands. "Hold up, girlfriends. Y'all are going to have to slow down with the Spanish. I took French in college."

"Does this mean I can talk about you in Spanish and you won't understand a word?" Marisol teased.

"Not if I don't cuss you out in French first," Bethany countered, grinning like a Cheshire cat. Her smile faded and her eyes grew cold when she spied a tall redhead with bottle-green eyes. Years ago the spiteful woman had embarked on a campaign to slander her at every opportunity.

Tiffany Jones's eyes were as large as saucers when she recognized her. "Bethany Collins."

"Shame on you, Tiff," she chided. "I know it's been a while, but have you forgotten that I'm now Bethany Paxton?" Bethany gave her a saccharine smile that did not quite reach her eyes. "Tiffany, do you know Deanna Tyson and Marisol McDonald?"

Pulling back her shoulders, Tiffany nodded. "Of course. I spoke to them earlier."

"That's good. I truly detest making introductions," Bethany drawled facetiously. "By the way, how is your grandson?"

Natural color drained from the redhead's face, leaving it a sallow yellow shade. "He's well. Thank you for asking."

Bethany tapped her forehead with a forefinger. "If I remember correctly, he should be about Connor's age. I always take my children and a few of their friends to see the cherry blossoms, then to the botanic gardens, so if you're not doing anything tomorrow I'd like to invite you and your grandson along. Afterward we'll go to a restaurant for lunch, then come back to my house where Damon makes ice cream concoctions like parfaits, hot fudge and brownie sundaes and vanilla egg creams."

Marisol cleared her throat. "If Damon can make a real good black-and-white sundae, then I'm willing to tag along as a chaperone."

Bethany winked at the interior designer. "I'd love to have you, Mari."

Deanna held up a hand. "Count me out. I have an engagement party tomorrow."

Bethany raised her pale eyebrows, staring directly at Tiffany. "What about you, Tiff? Can I count you in? After all, you've never been to our home in Falls Church."

"I'll have to ask my daughter whether I can bring Bobby."

Bethany attempted to frown, but the muscles between her eyes were frozen because of her recent Botox treatment. "I was under the impression you had sole custody of your grandson because of your daughter's substance abuse."

"I do, but I still ask her."

"Stop playing, Tiffy!" Marisol snapped. "If you don't want to come, then just come out and say it."

"I...I didn't say I didn't want to come."

At that moment Bethany could have hugged and kissed Marisol. She was more than aware of the campaign of salacious gossip Tiffany Jones had spread on behalf of her former BFF Jean Paxton. "Is that a yes?"

Tiffany's mouth tightened noticeably. "Yes."

Bethany's eyes sparkled like precious jewels. "I always contract for a driver to take us around. We'll pick you and Bobby up around nine-thirty. The driver will wait five minutes, then we're onto the next pickup."

Tiffany offered a relaxed smile for the first time. "We'll be ready at nine-thirty."

Bethany opened and closed her hand. "See you tomorrow," she said in singsong.

Deanna shook her head, smiling when Tiffany left. "You are no good, Beth-Ann."

Marisol rested a hand on her hip. "And why did you put that *puta* on the spot?"

Bethany rolled her eyes. "Because that *bitch* made my life a living hell, that's why. I could never do to her what she'd done to me. She called me everything but a child of God, and if Damon wasn't who he is we would've been run out of Washington on the proverbial rail."

"What did Damon say or do?" Deanna asked.

Bethany shook her head. "Nothing. He said what goes around comes around. Those things have a way of working themselves out where only those involved get to see it."

"I don't like confrontation," Deanna admitted, "but I don't think I'd be able to stand by and let some heifer slander me like Tiffany did you."

"I hear you, *amiga*." Marisol pushed out her lips. "I'd ring her doorbell, and when she answered I'd give her an old-fashioned East Harlem beatdown with a ball bat."

Bethany laughed. "Back in Parkers Corners we used a riding crop. It takes a long time, if ever, for the welts to go away. But I'm not going to beat up on Tiffy Jones. She got her payback when her sweet little Juliette, which sugar wouldn't melt in her mouth, fell in love with a MS-13 gang member, got pregnant *and* hooked on drugs."

Deanna adjusted the neckline of her Grecian-inspired black silk chiffon gown. "Mrs. Jones is in some serious denial, because she tells everyone that Juliette is clean and attending college on the West Coast when the poor child has been shuttled from one rehab treatment center to another because she can't stay clean. The other patients call her Lindsay Lohan because of her red hair."

"How do you know this?" Bethany asked Deanna.

"You forget I plan a lot of events in D.C., and my clients love to gossip about one another. Even the so-called best friends."

Marisol nodded. "I hear you, chica. If I don't tell you my personal business, then no one in this town knows it."

"You know my personal business," Bethany chimed in.

Marisol wrapped an arm around Bethany's waist. "What you say to Deanna and me will never be repeated."

For the first time since reuniting with Nathan Nelson, Bethany felt conflicted, seriously so because she'd promised him a gossip column. And that wasn't possible unless she divulged some of what she heard and/or had been told. What she had to figure out was a way to write the column without revealing her source. She knew Nathan would never reveal the name of his reporter, but that still didn't mean she shouldn't take the necessary steps to protect her identity.

"It's the same with me," Bethany lied smoothly.

Chapter Seventeen

Marisol opened the door, frowning at the two women standing on the other side. "I told you not to bring anything."

Deanna lifted a gaily colored shopping bag. "I brought my celebrated margarita."

"And I brought a pint of Damon's homemade bing cherry ice cream and blackberry sorbet for dessert," Bethany said, the slow Alabama drawl creeping back in her voice.

Marisol stepped back. "If that's the case, then please come in."

Bethany's jaw dropped when she stared up at the hanging fixture in the town house's entry. "Oh, my word. This place is beautiful. I should've hired you to decorate my house."

"Your house is very nice," Marisol told Bethany.

"My house looks like a museum. Your house looks like a home."

Deanna handed Marisol the shopping bag, took off her jacket and hung it on the wall hook. "Marisol decorated my house a couple of years ago. You can always have her do yours, Bethany."

"I'm seriously thinking about it."

"Remember, we don't discuss business during our luncheons," Marisol reminded Bethany. "Now, come upstairs. Instead of eating in the dining room, I thought the solarium would be more relaxing. It's on the third floor," she said to Bethany. "And unlike Deanna, I don't have an elevator."

"And I can count on one hand how many times I've taken it," Deanna said, following her hostess up the curving staircase with elaborately carved newel posts. "The only time it comes in handy is when we have guests and entertain upstairs."

"Damon wanted to buy a house inside the Beltway, but at that time I wanted to get as far away from D.C. without moving out of Virginia. Even though Falls Church is only a little over two square miles and six miles from D.C., it still feels like a different world."

"I'll give you a tour after we finish eating," Marisol promised Bethany. "One more flight and we're there." She glanced over her shoulder at Bethany. "The only time we dress up is when we eat out. Otherwise it's jeans, sweats and running shoes."

Bethany glanced down at her pumps. "I'll remember that the next time. And the next time we'll meet at my house."

"Cook or catered?" Deanna asked.

"Girl, please," Bethany drawled again. "I learned to cook as soon as I was old enough to reach the stove. Paula Deen has nothing on me when it comes to Southern cooking."

Deanna smiled. "Collards, corn bread, potato salad and biscuits?"

"Country ham, peach cobbler, fried chicken, smothered pork chops, chicken-fried steak with white gravy—"

"Enough!" Deanna shouted. "You're making me more hungry than I already am."

"That does it," Marisol announced. "The next time we meet it'll be at Bethany's."

Deanna walked into the room that always reminded her of a hothouse. It was filled with potted palms, trees and exotic flowers. Marisol had set a table in a corner from which wafted the most delicious smells. She'd made it a practice not to eat breakfast before she and Marisol got together for lunch.

"Sweet Hannah," Bethany gasped. "Why do I feel as if I'm in Hawaii with all of these orchids?"

"Try Puerto Rico," Marisol corrected. "They're the same variety that grows outside my cousin's house. And because I couldn't bring plants into the country I had to order them from an exporter. I had a hard time getting them to grow until I installed a special heating and cooling system where I could regulate the humidity. Now they're taking over the room. I have to keep cutting them back and giving away the cuttings. Would you like a few?"

Bethany shook her head. "I'm good at growing vegetables, but not flowers."

Marisol pointed to a door on the right. "There's a bathroom over there if you want to wash up. As soon as I put the ice cream in the freezer we can eat. Deanna, will you please pour the cocktails?"

As promised, Marisol had fried thinly sliced green bananas, passing the plate around before she did a bowl filled with mojito—a garlic dipping sauce to top off the tostones. She'd also prepared shrimp in a garlic sauce for her guests, a savory white rice and roast chicken with a garlic rub and a green citrus salad.

"There are toothbrushes and mouthwash in the bathroom

you'll probably want to use before you leave, because with the garlic I know your breaths will be kicking."

Bethany sat, spreading a napkin over the chocolate-brown suede skirt she'd paired with a brown turtleneck and a hot-pink suede bolero jacket and brown suede and leather boots. She was overdressed, but it was only the second time she'd met for the girlfriends' luncheon. "Where's your handsome husband, Mari?"

Marisol passed Bethany the plate of shrimp. "I know you're not talking about someone's handsome husband. Damon Paxton is as fine as they come."

"Here, here," intoned Deanna. "Damon is as smooth as creamy peanut butter—the type you eat out the jar with a spoon, because anything extra would spoil the taste."

Covering her face with her napkin, Bethany blushed and laughed. "Y'all just ought to stop."

"Es verdad," Marisol said in agreement. "Bryce is handsome in a preppy sort of way and Spencer is cute, because his freckles make him look boyish, but Damon *es todo el hombre.* That's why those other women were so angry when he married you."

"One thing I don't plan to do that his first wife did, and that is cheat on him."

Deanna chewed and swallowed a forkful of salad with a delicious dressing. "So, they both were cheaters."

Bethany kept her eyes downcast on her plate. "I know two wrongs don't make it right, but Jean was the first to cheat on Damon. I don't know if it was before or after she moved out of their bedroom."

Marisol picked up the crystal goblet with the chilled pale green liquid. She took a swallow. "I really don't like that cheating business. My dad was a married man who cheated on his wife with my mother and I was the result of that liaison.

I'm not being judgmental, Bethany," she said when seeing her pained expression, "it's just that I pray it won't happen with me and Bryce."

"Have you ever suspected him of cheating on you?" Bethany asked.

A beat passed before Marisol said, "I don't think about that. Maybe I'm in denial, but if he is, then I don't want to know."

"I'm with you," Deanna said in agreement. "If Spencer is cheating I don't want to know about it, but if it's true then I'll cut his balls off."

Bethany choked. She covered her mouth, coughing until she recovered. "No. You didn't say you'd cut his balls off."

"Yes, I did, Beth-Ann."

"Have you ever cheated on Spencer?" Bethany asked.

There came another pause as the three women stared at one another. "Once," Deanna confessed.

"*¿Bromea, no está usted?* You're joking, aren't you?" Marisol quickly translated.

Deanna shook her head. "I wish I was. Spencer and I were married about a year and we had a horrible fight where we both said things that should've never been said. I was still working at a hotel as an assistant banquet manager, so rather than go home that night I checked into another hotel across town where I'd once interned. I was in the bar drowning my sorrows with Long Island iced teas when a man sat down next to me and we began talking. One thing led to another and I ended up in his suite and in his bed. Somehow I made it back to my room and fell asleep. When I woke the next day I couldn't remember his face or whether the sex was good or bad."

With wide eyes, Marisol whispered, "What did Spencer say when you went home?"

"He asked me if I'd had fun staying out all night and I told him I did and thanked him for letting me see another side of his personality. Spencer isn't as benign as he looks. South Side Red can be formidable when crossed." It'd only been a month ago when he'd confronted Damon Paxton about flirting with her.

Marisol blinked. "Is that what people call him?"

"You mean South Side as in Chicago?" Bethany asked.

Deanna nodded. "Spencer spent the first ten years of his life there. When some gang members attempted to recruit him, his parents decided it was time to leave. You can take the thug out the ghetto, but it's hard to get the ghetto out the thug."

Marisol shook her head. "He really had me fooled. He's always so polite."

"I'm not saying he isn't polite," Deanna said in defense of her husband. "But just don't back him into a corner."

"I guess you guys made up, because you're still married," Bethany said.

"It took about a week. We sort of tiptoed around each other, being overly polite. I'd go to bed before him, so when he got in I'd pretend to be asleep. Then I decided either I was going to try to save my marriage by offering the olive branch or end it. One morning I asked Spencer if he wanted a divorce, because I was more than willing to give him one, but he told me there wasn't going to be a divorce as long as there was breath in his body. That night we had the best makeup sex I've ever had. I wish it was like that now, because we have to find time to make love to each other."

Bethany took a swallow of her drink. "Sex is good with Damon, but for a man in his fifties he's no longer an Energizer Bunny."

Deanna set down her fork. "At least you're getting some.

I'm seriously thinking about buying a vibrator to take care my needs."

Bethany waved her hand. "That's for single women."

"Wrong, Beth-Ann," Deanna countered. "It's for married women who aren't getting enough. I'm thirty-three and sexually primed. If I were a brief or law book I'd probably see more action with Spencer than I do now. He's gone when I get up and he doesn't come home until I'm asleep. Most times he sleeps in one of the guest bedrooms because I don't want him coming home and waking me up in the middle of the night."

"Why does he come home so late?" Bethany asked innocently.

Marisol gave Bethany an incredulous stare. "Are you aware that Spencer Tyson is a hotshot D.C. attorney who puts in at least seventy to eighty hours a week representing some of the most well-heeled clients in the district?"

"And could it be that not only is he working but also may be out there tomcattin' on his wife? Did I say something wrong?" Bethany asked when Deanna and Marisol glared at her.

"How can you be so clueless?" Marisol whispered. "You just said that Spencer is cheating on Deanna."

"I didn't say he was. I said maybe he was."

"Don't go there unless you have proof," Marisol continued, her voice lowering as her temper spiraled.

"What if I had proof?" Bethany countered. "Would you want to know, Deanna?"

"Do you have proof that Spencer is cheating on me?" Deanna asked.

Bethany's eyes darkened until they were mysterious purple pools. "No. I just don't want some other woman to do to you what I did to Jean despite her messed-up relationship with Damon." She picked up her goblet, taking a long swallow. "This margarita is fabulous, Dee. What's in it besides tequila?"

"I always add Patron for an extra punch."

"Right about now it's punching back."

Marisol dabbed the corners of her mouth. "Don't worry, Beth. I will not let you leave my home under the influence. You can always hang out here until you feel better."

Bethany appeared suddenly alert. "Thanks for the offer, but I know when to stop." And she did. The few times she'd overindulged she'd said things she hadn't meant to say. There was no way she was going to admit to Marisol or Deanna that the network hadn't hired her to write copy, because she'd decided not to go backward. Writing copy was akin to been-there, done-that. She wasn't an intern, but a professional journalist. Bethany also didn't want the word to get out that she'd gone back to work because she and Damon needed an extra paycheck. After all, laws had changed with regard to lobbyists, and their influence on Capitol Hill had been curtailed dramatically.

What she did was accept Nate's offer to write the column. Her chance of gathering information directly from Tiffany Jones had been thwarted when Tiffany and her grandson hadn't accompanied them to see the cherry blossoms and the botanic gardens. Now it was necessary for her to pump her new friends for information she could use for the column.

"You didn't answer my question, Marisol."

"About what?"

"About Bryce? Where is he?"

"He's in New Jersey."

"He does a lot of traveling, doesn't he?"

Marisol's eyes narrowed in suspicion. "What are you doing, Bethany?"

"I don't know what you're talking about."

"Don't you?" Marisol snapped angrily. "You *are* interviewing me."

"No, I'm not. If I'd wanted to interview you I'd have asked you beforehand. And I usually use a tape recorder as a backup. I suppose once a reporter always a reporter. I always ask a lot of questions until I get to know someone." Bethany threw her hands up. "No more questions."

The three women exchanged glances until Deanna broke the uncomfortable silence. "Marisol, you're going to have to teach me how you make your rice."

Bethany knew only quick thinking had helped her dodge a bullet. It was apparent she'd underestimated her two new friends. They were as bright as they were talented. She'd asked too many questions too soon. It wouldn't happen again.

Chapter Eighteen

Deanna smiled at the valet as he opened the driver's-side door. "Thank you. I shouldn't be longer than an hour."

She'd gotten a telephone call earlier that morning to meet a prospective client. The man said he'd been referred to her by a couple who'd used her services for their daughter's wedding—one of less than a half dozen she'd coordinated since establishing Tyson Planners and Events, Inc. The fall and winter months were the busiest for private parties and the spring for fundraisers. Even if she'd had a staff of assistants, Deanna still wouldn't have been able to coordinate every event because of conflicts in scheduling. There were very few days and nights in D.C. when there wasn't something going on in a pub, hotel, ballroom or private home. It was a very socially oriented city.

She walked through the automatic revolving door and into the lobby of the hotel where she'd interned during summers while pursuing a degree in hotel and hospitality management.

Making her way over to the hospitality desk, she gave the

young woman on duty her name and asked her to ring Mr. Richard Douglas's room. The woman pointed to a well-dressed, middle-aged man sitting in the lobby designed to resemble an oasis with a flowing fountain surrounded by exotic plants, ferns, palms and flowers.

"Mr. Douglas is sitting over there."

"Thank you."

Deanna closed the distance between her and the man with salt-and-pepper hair. He rose at her approach. "Mr. Douglas?" Raven-black eyes in a deeply tanned face stared at her. There was something in his bearing that communicated he wasn't an American. He was a man of color, and she wondered from where.

Firm lips parted as he flashed a toothpaste-ad smile. He inclined his head. "Mrs. Tyson."

"Yes." She offered her hand and he took it, holding her fingers a bit longer than necessary.

Richard Douglas cupped her elbow. "Would you mind if we conduct our business in my suite?"

Deanna's professional facade did not falter. The man had a slight accent, but she wasn't able to identify it. "Yes, I would mind. We can either talk here in the lobby or in the bar."

Richard took a step, bringing him mere inches from the event planner. "You didn't mind coming to my suite seven years ago."

This time Deanna's expression changed, becoming one of shock and horror. He was the *one*. Richard Douglas was the man she'd slept with what now seemed a lifetime ago. She stood straighter. What were the odds of her reuniting with him after she'd revealed their liaison only two days before to Marisol and Bethany? It was as if talking about it had conjured him up.

"What took you so long to contact me?" Her voice was

shaded in neutral tones. "It's been a long time since that horrific night."

His black eyes flickered. "Horrific for who? It certainly wasn't for me. You were the best piece of ass I've ever had." Deanna turned to walk away, but his hand caught her upper arm, tightening when she tried pulling away. "Please, Mrs. Tyson. Don't make a scene. Let's go over to the tables near the windows so we can talk like civil adults."

Deanna knew when she'd been trapped, but she didn't intend to stay that way. If the man intended to blackmail her, then he was in for a very rude awakening. If necessary, she would tell Spencer about the night she'd stayed over in the hotel rather than live with the fear of being publicly outed.

Richard waved to a waitress carrying a tray with drinks from the bar. "I'll have bourbon neat and please bring the young lady a Long Island iced tea. See, I remember your drink of choice," he said mockingly when Deanna glared at him.

Crossing one leg over the other, Deanna leaned back against the softness of the armchair. She'd debated whether to wear a skirt, but had changed into a pantsuit, saving herself the humiliation of having the lecher staring at her legs. "Big whoop," she sneered. "You'll have to drink it because I'm driving."

Unbuttoning his suit jacket, Richard looped one trouser-covered leg over the opposite knee, staring at the faint pinstripe in the dark blue wool fabric. "If you're unable to drive, then I'll drive you back home and have my driver follow us."

"You're mad if you think I'm going to let you anywhere near my home."

He ran a hand over his straight cropped hair. "Are you concerned that your neighbors will see a strange man driving your car?"

It was becoming more and more difficult for Deanna not to lose her temper. She never would've met with Richard Douglas if he hadn't been referred to her by a very reliable client who'd used her services for what had become that rare wedding where several former cabinet members, a former vice president and heads of state were attendees. What she couldn't fathom was Richard Douglas's connection to them.

"I'm not as concerned about my neighbors as about the man who believes he can blackmail me into sleeping with him."

"Sleeping with me *again*. I watched your face when the desk clerk pointed to me, and there was no indication that you'd recognized me. Why's that?"

"Because I didn't recognize you."

"Is there anything about that night you remember?"

"Yes. I had a fight with my husband and I came here and drank myself into oblivion. I don't remember you, so the fact that you tell me we slept together means nothing."

He leaned closer. "Do you deny having sex that night?"

Deanna knew she could lie and say yes, but knew the lie would come back to haunt her. She'd learned if you told one lie, then you'd have to tell another and another until you wouldn't be able to tell the lie from the truth.

"All I remember about that night is talking to a man, going back to his suite, getting into bed with him, but nothing beyond that until I woke up in my room. You tell me you were that man, but how do I know you're telling the truth? Someone could have told you about the incident and you decided to contact me while impersonating him to run a scam on me."

"Is that what you want to believe, Mrs. Tyson?"

"What else is there?"

"Let me refresh your memory. You told me your room

number, but not your name. You said you'd had a fight with your husband, so you were spending the night at the hotel. We talked about a lot things, but even though you were slightly inebriated you were also very guarded. That told me a lot about you. You are a very strong-willed woman." He stared at her mouth. "After we made love, I cleaned you up and took you back to your room. If I hadn't had an appointment with a business associate we would've spent the entire night together."

"I'm glad *you* enjoyed yourself," Deanna spat out.

He continued to stare at her. "I can't believe you're more stunning now than you were then."

"What exactly is it you want from me, Mr. Douglas?"

"I want a repeat of that night."

Deanna leaned forward, her heart beating painfully against her ribs. "Why now, Mr. Douglas? Why have you waited seven years to contact me about something that reminds me of junior high school bullshit? It's like a boy threatening a girl that if she doesn't sleep with him, he'll tell everyone that he saw her have oral sex with his best friend."

Richard smiled. "I just discovered who you are. There was a photo of you and your husband in the *Washington Post*'s weekend section when the two of you attended a fundraiser last month. I must say you're quite the handsome couple."

"Thanks for the compliment, but I'm not sleeping with you."

"Even if I get word to your husband that his wife hasn't been the paragon of virtue?"

"I don't care what you tell him."

"You will care, Mrs. Tyson, if you find yourself unable to book a kiddie party in this town."

Deanna wanted to slap—no, punch—the arrogant man in the face, but knew it would cause a scene. And there was always the possibility he would have her arrested for assault. She stood up. "Do what you feel you have to do. Have a nice day, Mr. Douglas."

Richard rose to his feet, watching the sensual sway of Deanna Tyson's hips in the tailored gray pantsuit. He'd thought her lovely when she'd sat down next to him in the bar what now seemed aeons ago. He'd sensed her pain and vulnerability immediately, and set out to take advantage of her. He'd plied her with drinks, she crying on his shoulder about the fight she'd had with her husband. Aware that she was intoxicated, he'd coaxed her back to his suite where he'd undressed her, then made love to her. Even in her drunken haze she'd responded to him, pleading with him to love her as much as she'd loved him.

He never would've met Deanna Tyson that night if he hadn't come to the hotel, checking in as a guest in order to ascertain whether it would be a suitable investment for a group of men who had more money than they'd known what to do with. The fact that it was drug money made little difference to Richard Douglas. The fees he'd earned negotiating money-laundering deals had made him a very wealthy man. It had only taken one day for him to inspect the premises and one night to make love to a woman whose memory he hadn't been able to rid himself of.

He hadn't been in D.C. in seven years, and seeing Deanna's photograph in the newspaper had been so unexpected that he'd thought he had imagined it. Richard had discovered she now owned and operated her own business, but knew he couldn't approach her outright. So, he did the next best thing. He'd asked someone to refer him. Even though he'd gotten Deanna to meet him, what he hadn't anticipated was her refusing his offer even with the threat of blackmail.

Unfortunately, he had misjudged her. Now he was forced to use another approach.

Deanna drove with one hand on the steering wheel, the other clamped over her mouth to keep from screaming. She was less than a mile from her home when she pulled over to the curb and shifted into Park. Reaching for her cell with shaking hands, she managed to punch in Marisol's number on the first attempt.

It wasn't until she heard her friend's voice that the tears she'd kept in check overflowed. "Where are you, Marisol?"

"¿Qué pasa?"

"Please speak English! I don't have time to translate whatever it is you're saying." Deanna sniffled loudly before reaching for several tissues in her handbag on the passenger-side seat.

"What's the matter? Talk to me, Deanna!"

"I…I have to see you. I need to talk to you." The words were falling over one another.

"I'm on my way home. I'll be there in five minutes. If you get there before me, then wait."

Chapter Nineteen

By the time Marisol had pulled Deanna into her office and closed and locked the door, Deanna was able to recall everything that had happened in the hotel lobby with vivid clarity. Marisol handed her a glass and a bottle of chilled water. "If you want something stronger I'll get it for you."

She shook her head. "Drinking is what got me into trouble."

Flopping down beside Deanna, Marisol held her free hand. "Tell me everything, chica."

Deanna did, leaving nothing out. She closed her eyes when she heard the slow exhalation of her friend's breath. "I know, you know and Bethany knows the truth. He'd admitted he didn't even know my name until he saw the picture caption. If he'd had a tape of our tryst, then it wouldn't have taken him seven years to find me."

"Are you saying that he's bluffing, Dee?"

Deanna opened her eyes, meeting Marisol's stare. "The only thing I'm admitting is that he freaked me out, because even if I'd been hypnotized I don't believe I would've been able to recall his name or face."

"Aren't you afraid he's going to tell Spencer?"

"I have two options, Mari. Either I tell Spencer the truth or I lie. But I doubt if he will believe the lie because that night is stamped on his brain like a permanent tattoo."

"Does he ever bring it up?" Marisol asked.

"It's been years since he's mentioned it."

"What do you think will happen if you tell Spencer the truth about that night?"

Deanna lifted her shoulders. "Either he'll forgive me, or we'll split up."

"I don't like this, Dee. The sick bastard has your cell phone number, probably your home address, and there's no doubt he knows where Spencer works. What if he decides to contact you again?"

"I'm not going to meet him again."

"The man sounds deranged, Deanna. He's probably obsessed with you, and that means he's going to be trouble. I…" Her words stopped when she stood up. "Let me talk to someone first."

"No, Marisol. I don't want anyone else to know about this."

Marisol rested her hands at her waist over a pair of slim cut jeans. "This person I trust with my life. What I tell him will stay between the three of us." She gave Deanna a long stare. "Do you trust me?"

A silence ensued while Deanna met her best friend's eyes. "Yes."

"Good. Then, let me help you."

A beat passed, and then she said, "Make the call."

Deanna couldn't understand any of Marisol's conversation because she'd spoken rapid Spanish to the person on the other end of the line. She took a deep swallow of the cool water, puzzled at the turn her life had taken. Her marriage was on solid footing, her business was growing and solvent and the following year she and Spencer would try for a baby. By the time they celebrated their tenth anniversary she hoped to be a mother.

But a mysterious man, someone who'd come to her in a surreal nightmare, had reemerged to threaten all she held dear; she loved her husband and the marriage they'd worked so hard to preserve. What Richard Douglas didn't know was that she had no intention of giving in to his demands or fleeing as if she were a frightened rabbit. Although her father had retired from the U.S. Secret Service he still knew enough insiders on the White House detail who would be willing to protect her from her would-be blackmailer.

Deanna forced herself not to dwell on what had happened earlier but on Marisol's promise to help her. If it had been left to her she would've called Spencer at his office, demanding he come home because of an emergency. As well as she'd believed she knew her husband, Deanna could not predict his reaction to being told that she had cheated on him.

Either he would kiss her while professing to love her despite her breaking their wedding vows, or he would lose all semblance of control and show her the dark side of his personality. She prayed it would be the former.

"He wants to talk to you."

Marisol's voice broke into her thoughts. She handed her the cordless receiver. Deanna took the phone. "Hello."

"Deanna."

"Yes."

"May I call you Deanna?" asked a deep male voice speaking flawless English.

"Please."

"Deanna, I want you to listen very closely to what I'm going to tell you. Marisol told me about this pestilence that's attempting to blackmail you. I want you to tell me everything you know about this man."

"There's not much to tell."

"How did he introduce himself? How tall is he? What does he look like? How old do you think he is?"

Deanna hesitated, trying to remember if he'd towered over her once he stood up. "He told me his name is Richard Douglas and he's at least six-one or two. He has cropped salt-and-pepper hair, but his face is unlined. I estimate he's between forty and fifty."

"What type of hair texture does he have?"

"Even though it's straight, it's also coarse."

"What about his features?"

Deanna chewed her lip. "They weren't European. He's a man of color, but I couldn't determine from where because of his accent."

"Can you identify the accent?"

She shook her head, then realized the man on the other end of the line couldn't see her. "No. One thing I know is it isn't Spanish."

"Did it sound Caribbean?"

"It wasn't any Caribbean accent I've ever heard." She paused. "Now that I think back I believe it could've been German or Russian." A soft chuckle came through the earpiece.

"He doesn't look European, but his accent may be European."

"Look…"

"You can call me John."

"Okay, John. When Richard Douglas asked to meet with me I was under the impression he wanted to contract my services to host an event. At least that's what he told me. I had no idea I would be blindsided by a cretin who wanted me to sleep with him or he would tell my husband about an incident that happened years ago. If he hadn't taken me off guard I would've told him that my husband knew all about my indiscretion. That would've shut him down completely and I wouldn't be here talking to you."

"It didn't happen, Deanna, so we're going to have to deal with the fallout. What color are his eyes?"

"They are dark, probably black. He was well-dressed. In other words, his suit did not come off a department store rack."

"What about jewelry, Deanna? Was he wearing a ring or rings, watch or earring?"

A beat passed. "He wasn't wearing an earring, and I don't remember any rings. He may have been wearing a watch, but I couldn't see it because his shirt had French cuffs. Wait a minute."

"What is it?" John asked.

"He wore cuff links. They weren't yellow gold, so they had to be either silver, white gold or platinum." Deanna smiled despite her dilemma. "And before you ask, they weren't monogrammed. They were oval with a diamond chip in the center."

"That information is very helpful. Is there anything else you remember about him?"

"I don't think so."

"Was his shirt cuff monogrammed?"

Deanna exhaled a breath. "If it was, then I don't remember. I don't know if this will help, but he wore wingtips and I recognized the designer because my husband has several pair in his closet." She gave John the name of the shoe designer.

"You just narrowed my search from searching from

millions to probably less than ten thousand. There aren't too many men willing to pay more than two thousand dollars for a pair of handmade shoes. I'm certain I will find this Richard Douglas—if that is his actual name."

"He'd checked in to the Brandon-Phillips under that name."

"He may not have checked in."

"What do you mean?" Deanna asked.

"Marisol told me that you asked the desk clerk to ring his room, but he was already sitting in the lobby."

"What aren't you telling me, John?"

"He didn't have to check in to the Brandon-Phillips, but uses the lobby and/or bar to conduct business. A lot of businessmen do it, and that includes the late Howard Hughes. But there's something about Mr. Douglas that puzzles me."

"What is it?"

"It was obvious he'd gotten a room at the hotel years ago, because he'd taken you there to rape you. Yes, Deanna, the man raped you. If you were under the influence, then he took advantage of you. The fact that you didn't remember his face or the act bears this out. So if he comes after you again, then we can arrange for the police to arrest him for rape."

"Do you think he's going to contact me again?" Deanna asked. "When I answered his call, his number but not his name showed up on the display." Reaching for her cell, she repeated the numbers to John.

"Odds are that he will call you again. And when he does I'm going to take him down. Marisol will program my number into your cell. You won't see numbers but stars. When he contacts you again, tell him to call you back in half an hour, because you're busy with a client. When he calls back, tell him you are willing to meet to discuss his indecent proposal. I want you to suggest a meeting at DuPont Circle, but I doubt if he'd want to be that exposed. He'll probably want to go back to the Brandon-Phillips."

"I'm not going to sleep with him."

"You don't have to. Think of him as a blind date. Try and sit in the lobby rather than in the bar and I'll take it from there."

Deanna felt her stomach muscles contract. "What are you going to do?"

"Deanna, I wouldn't presume to tell you how to plan a banquet, so please don't ask me how I catch bad guys. Don't say anything to your husband. Go about your business as if this never happened. The less suspicion you raise, the better. Meanwhile, I'm going to talk to the guy who referred him to you to see what I come up with."

"If word gets out that my clients are being interrogated then I might as well close down Tyson Planners and Events, Inc. completely."

John laughed again. "Don't worry, Deanna. I have my methods that will never compromise your company. Now, could you please give Marisol the phone?"

Deanna slumped back in the aubergine-and-lime-green silk striped settee; for the second time within an hour a man she hadn't known had impacted her life. The man who'd identified himself as John seemed confident that he could get Richard Douglas to withdraw his threat.

Marisol took the phone, again speaking in Spanish. She ended the call, replacing the receiver in its cradle. Sitting on the corner of her desk, she met Deanna's unflinching stare. "It's going to be all right."

"Are you that certain, Marisol?"

A small smile tilted the corners of her mouth. "I'm very certain. Juan—John to you—will take care of everything."

Deanna chewed the inside of her cheek, a habit she'd worked for years to rid herself of. "What does he do?"

"I don't know, Dee. I asked him once and the look he gave me was enough to say, *If I tell you, then I'll have to kill you,* so I never asked again. I know Juan from the old neighborhood, and there's nothing I wouldn't do for him and he for me. Bryce gets a little jealous whenever he comes around, but I'm not going to stop being friends with him because my husband catches an attitude because I have male friends."

Deanna pushed a profusion of twists behind her left ear. "I keep telling myself that if I hadn't said anything to you and Bethany about that night we wouldn't be having this conversation."

"I know you're not talking about letting sleeping dogs lie?" Marisol asked.

"That's exactly what I'm saying. We've shared secrets before and never have the chickens come home to roost."

Marisol crossed one high-heeled booted foot over the other at the ankle. "What are you trying to say, Dee? That you don't trust Bethany?"

"I'm not saying that. It's just that I feel we shouldn't say too much around her."

"You know I wasn't feeling her when we first met, but after hanging out with her this past weekend I've changed my opinion of her. She's really a good mother. When we went back to her house and I got to see her and Damon together there's no question that they're really in love with each other."

"Maybe I'm being overly superstitious, but I'm going to monitor what I say around her." Deanna pushed to her feet. "After you give me John's phone number I'm going home to take a couple of aspirins and then I'm going to bed. Tomorrow I have to drive to Reston to check out a converted barn for Senator Walters's daughter's sweet-sixteen party. She wants a Western theme along with the ubiquitous saloon, dance hall girls, bales of hay and a mechanical bull."

Marisol laughed softly. "Hee-haw!"

Deanna smiled for the first time since she'd gotten up earlier that morning to see Spencer off. "A Western theme is child's play compared to a beach party or a cruise ship. I'd planned one where the parents invited their daughter's classmates and close friends for a spring break sweet sixteen. They sailed down to Hilton Head, checked in to a hotel and partied for the week. They were exhausted, sunburned and so quiet during the return trip that you could hear a rat piss on cotton."

"That must have set them back a pretty penny."

"Try two twenty-five."

"Are you telling me they paid two hundred twenty-five thousand for a party for a sixteen-year-old?"

"I am," Deanna confirmed.

"*¡Coño!* That's tuition for four years of college plus a car."

"It was what I call wretched excess. The kids ate lobster and caviar every night, while their parents drank champagne like water." She sobered. "I can't thank you enough for lending your shoulder, chica."

Marisol waved her hand. "How many times have I cried on your shoulder? Too many to count," she said, answering her own question. "Give me your cell and I'll program Juan's number. After he takes care of your parasite, he'll ask for your phone and will delete the number."

Deanna wanted to tell Marisol she would agree to anything short of murder to right the wrong, to undo the single act that could possibly destroy her marriage. She loved her husband unconditionally, and prayed she would be able to get out of this dilemma unscathed and with Spencer still unaware that she'd been unfaithful.

Chapter Twenty

Deanna was going through her checklist of attendees when she realized she wasn't alone. Glancing up, she saw Spencer's broad shoulders spanning the doorway to the office. It was six-fifteen, and she was shocked that he'd come home so early.

She smiled at him. He'd removed his jacket and tie and rolled back the cuffs to his shirt. "Hi."

Spencer returned her smile. The sound of Aretha Franklin's distinctive voice flowed from hidden speakers. "I like your music choice."

"'Natural Woman' is my anthem." Deanna had bought several CDs featuring classic songs and instrumentals spanning six decades. "Did you eat?"

She wondered if her voice sounded strained to Spencer, because it didn't sound natural to her. It was as if she had morphed into the 1950s Donna Reed stay-at-home mom, asking her loving husband how his day was when her insides were churning into knots. If only he'd known that earlier that afternoon she'd met with a man for whom she'd opened her legs, and if her life had depended upon it couldn't remembered his face or his name.

He nodded. "I had my assistant order something for lunch but when I didn't get a chance to eat it I had it for an early dinner."

Standing and coming from behind the workstation, Deanna walked over to Spencer, touching her mouth to his. "How is Kate getting along with her husband?"

"They're doing much better after going to marriage counseling."

Deanna gave him a too-bright smile. "That's good. I've always thought of them as such a cute couple."

Spencer frowned. "Cute or not, the man should've never put his hands on her no matter how angry she makes him."

Not wanting to talk about angry husbands, Deanna patted Spencer's chest. "You know you're going to have to eat more than one meal a day to regain the weight you lost."

Wrapping an arm around Deanna's waist, Spencer pulled her close. "You worry too much."

She smiled. "I can't worry about my baby?"

"Sure you can, but not more than I worry about you."

Deanna kissed him again. "Playa."

"I wish. How was your day?"

"It was good. I hung out with Marisol for a while. Bethany Paxton couldn't make it," she lied. Deanna didn't know why she'd mentioned Bethany's name, but Spencer knew she had invited her and Damon to their dinner party.

Spencer's impassive expression did not change. The name Paxton made him want to punch walls. He still could recall in vivid clarity his conversation with Damon Paxton. He'd held out the carrot, then pulled it back when he wouldn't do his bidding. Spencer didn't want anything to do with Damon

Paxton; but not only had Deanna befriended the man's wife, she'd also invited them to their upcoming dinner party.

Now that Damon had reneged on his promise there was no reason why he should stop seeing Jenah. Just when he thought he was bored with her, the extremely talented woman came up with something completely new in her sexual repertoire to make him change his mind. Sleeping with Jenah validated all the reasons why men slept with prostitutes.

However, Spencer didn't think of her as a prostitute because he didn't actually pay her for sex. This didn't mean he hadn't given her money to buy something nice for herself every once in a while, and he did put her up in the suite at the Victoria, permitting her to charge whatever she wanted to eat or drink to his bill—a bill he always paid in cash. There was no way he was going to pay the expenses for his extramarital affair with a credit card and inadvertently leave the receipt lying around for Deanna to find. When he'd married Deanna he'd promised her it would be for life.

"I didn't know you and Bethany were tight."

"I'm not tight with her like I am with Marisol. She's more of a friend. What's the matter, Spencer? Is there something about her you don't like?"

Reddish-brown eyebrows shot up. "Nah. I don't know her, so there's no reason for me not to like her."

"How about her husband? Didn't the two of you have drinks?"

Spencer nodded. "We had a few drinks, talked politics and that was that. It's not as if he invited me to his home for dinner."

"Well, they're coming here in two weeks."

"How many have responded?"

Closing her eyes, Deanna leaned into Spencer. "So far

eighteen of twenty-four are coming. My brother and sister are still questionable. They're still trying to get sitters."

"What about your parents? Can't they watch the kids?"

"Mom and Daddy are going away to golf camp that week, so they're not available. Are you smirking?" Deanna asked when Spencer turned his head. "You are," she accused when she saw a flash of white teeth. "You know you're not right when it comes to my family."

Tightening his hold on Deanna's waist, Spencer picked her off her feet. "You know I like your family. It's just your sister's badass kids that get to me. Why do they have to scream so much?"

"They're kids, Spencer. That's what they do."

"Not our kids. We're going to have kids, Dee. Lots of them."

"The only way we're going to have lots of kids is if we have a couple of sets of twins," she countered.

Spencer set Deanna on her feet. "Twins run in my family. My dad, aunt and a few cousins are twins."

He stared into the wide-set light brown eyes staring back at him. Deanna was the total woman: pretty, intelligent, creative, ambitious and loyal. She had been a faithful wife, while he'd slept with four women during his eight-year marriage. He thought of women as cars; he traded them in every two years. However, he doubted whether Jenah would last a year. She'd begun nagging him again about leaving his wife and marrying her. Why would he marry a woman he'd slept with while married? If she was willing to have an affair with a married man, then there was no way she would remain faithful to him.

"I know it's early, but can I interest you into going to bed with me?"

Deanna moved closer, anchoring her arms under Spencer's shoulders. "I don't know, lover. I may need some convincing."

Gathering her hem of her sweatshirt, Spencer searched for a firm breast, gently squeezing it until the nipple hardened against the lace cup of her bra. "How's that?" he rasped in her ear.

A dreamy smile softened Deanna's features. "It's nice."

"Just nice?"

"Mmm-hmm."

"Maybe you need more convincing," he said, grinning from ear to ear.

Deanna caught her husband's lip between her teeth, suckling it. "I think I do." This was the husband she'd missed: the teasing, prolonged foreplay. Lately, their lovemaking was intense, frenetic. Spencer pushed into her, pumped like a crazy man, then as soon as he came he'd roll off and fall asleep.

One of the reasons she'd married Spencer Tyson was because she'd fallen in love with him *and* the sex had been incredible. He was as exciting to look at completely nude as he was when he made love to not only her body but also her mind. He was able to make her forget every man she'd known or slept with.

Deanna had confessed to something she'd never told anyone—and that included her mother. She didn't know why she'd told Marisol and Bethany about cheating on Spencer, but decided she'd carried the guilt long enough and had had to unburden herself.

The guilt had returned, but this time it had a name and face. John had cautioned her to carry on with her life as if she'd never met Richard Douglas, but Deanna wondered how long she could keep up the pretense that her life was as rosy as a 1950s family sitcom. That every problem or crisis would be solved within the thirty-minute time slot.

"Maybe I do need a tad bit more convincing." She needed Spencer to make love to her, if only to forget what had happened earlier that afternoon.

Going to his knees, Spencer untied the drawstring to her sweatpants, pushing them down her hips and legs. Pressing his face against the triangle of silk, he inhaled her essence. "You smell sweet, baby."

Women he'd slept with refused to understand why he wouldn't put his face between their legs, but what they didn't know was that most intimate act was reserved exclusively for his wife. Sliding his hands under the narrow waistband to her bikini panties, he eased them down, smiling. Deanna had talked about having her pubic area waxed, and it was apparent she had followed through. Running his fingertips over the neatly shorn hair, Spencer pressed a kiss there.

"Please, Spencer." His name came out a quivering whisper when the tip of his tongue grazed Deanna's clitoris. He knew exactly what to do to arouse her as a rush of moisture bathed her throbbing core. She was pleading with him to penetrate her, but he was in no hurry to engage in the frantic coupling of their recent lovemaking. She pleaded, afraid that she was going to climax before she felt Spencer inside her.

Deanna forced herself to think of any- and everything else but the throbbing pleasure threatening to take her beyond herself. From the very first time she and Spencer shared a bed, Deanna couldn't remember a time when she didn't want him. Even when they disagreed vehemently about something she'd wanted to lie beside him at night. Whenever he came home late, or didn't come home at all because he and the other attorneys were preparing for trial, when she woke to find herself alone loneliness would weigh on her like a stone.

Spencer was her husband, partner, lover and occasionally her roommate. Legally they were connected, yet there were times when they were physically disconnected and Deanna didn't know what to do to bring them closer together.

Spencer had eased her down to the carpeted floor, his hands cupping her hips as he continued his sensual assault. It was as if he hadn't eaten in days and his intent was to gorge himself because he didn't know when he would be able to eat again.

Deanna closed her eyes, her head thrashing from side to side and praying for the torture to end. "Love me, baby," she pleaded. "Please love me."

Spencer pressed a kiss to his wife's inner thigh before he moved up her body and claimed her mouth, allowing her to taste herself. He inhaled the familiar fragrance stamped on her silken skin like a permanent tattoo. Even if he were blind-folded he would be able to pick out Deanna in a darkened room with a hundred women.

Within minutes their clothes were strewn over the deep pile of the pale blue-gray carpeting, Deanna's sweatshirt and pants providing a barrier between her naked hips and the carpet. The first and only time they'd made love on a carpet, she'd been left with rug burns on her hips and back. Grasping his penis, Spencer stroked it, his gaze fixed on his wife's face as she watched him until he'd achieved a full erection. The sex may have been good with Jenah, but that's all it was—sex. He screwed his mistresses, but made love to his wife. She lifted her head and he rubbed the head of his penis over her mouth, grinning when she licked the tiny drop of secretion on the tip.

Deanna opened her legs wider and she wasn't disappointed when Spencer guided his erection between her thighs and penetrated her, both sighing in unison. It had been much too long since they'd shared a tender moment of lovemaking. Lifting her hips, she met his slow, strong thrusts. Then she lifted her legs, wrapping them around his waist. After that everything ceased to exist. She forgot about her clients, the man who'd attempted to blackmail her into sleeping with him and her empty womb. Nothing mattered except that she had gotten her husband back—if only for a few minutes.

A moan of ecstasy slipped through her parted lips when Deanna felt passion inch its way up and down her body, heating her blood. She was hot, then cold, and hot again. Then she rose to meet Spencer in a moment of uncontrolled and overwhelming passion that left her temporarily mute.

The hardened flesh sliding in and out of her body sent spirals of ecstasy washing over her until she felt as if she were drowning in a pleasure so intense that it scorched both her mind and body. "Oh, baby," she crooned over and over until it became a litany.

Spencer smiled. "Is it good, baby?" he asked, quickening his motions until Deanna's breasts danced liked buoys in rough seas.

"Yes! Yes!"

"It's so good to me, too." Spencer had lied. It was better than good. It was spectacular. Every time he made love to Deanna he was reminded of how much he loved her. "Oh, shit!" he gasped when the muscles in her pelvis gripped him like a vise, holding him fast. They eased for a nanosecond before they gripped his penis again, this time tighter and much longer.

"You like that, don't you?" Deanna crooned in Spencer's ear. A guttural sound was his response. She'd practiced Kegel exercises ceaselessly until her pelvic muscles were strong enough to stop urination, while enhancing sexual responsiveness. She squeezed him again. "Am I hurting you, baby?"

"No...no," Spencer stuttered as his scrotum tightened. "Damn!" he screamed when she squeezed him tight enough to stop him from coming. The pleasurable torture went on until he felt himself slipping away. The next time Deanna released the vise on his penis, Spencer grasped her buttocks, holding her while he pumped his hips, thrusting faster and harder until the dam broke and he ejaculated, semen exploding like the back draft from a jet engine. Her moans filled his ears when the muscles in her vagina contracted again, this time from multiple orgasms.

They lay together, waiting for their hearts to resume a normal rhythm. Spencer still hadn't been able to figure out why he cheated on her with other women, because there wasn't anything Deanna had done to send him into another woman's bed. He had tried analyzing why he was an unfaithful husband when he'd never been an unfaithful boyfriend or fiancé. It had taken weeks, months of reflection and the only thing he'd been able to come up with was the time he and Deanna had had that explosive argument and she'd stayed out all night. She'd punished him, and he'd punished her—over and over again. He'd planned to see Jenah, but then changed his mind when the annoying woman said they had to talk—about a future together.

She'd begun talking about marriage days before Christmas, and he'd told her over and over there could never be a future for them, but it was as if Jenah was deaf. As much as he hadn't wanted to admit it, Damon Paxton was right. The woman was a liability. And because he hadn't given her up when Damon suggested, she had cost him a judgeship. Pulling out and rolling off Deanna, he lay on his back, staring up at the ceiling.

"You've been in Washington long enough to know it's never about the husband or the wife, but the couple." Of all the things the lobbyist had said that afternoon, he'd remembered that statement. It was apparent he hadn't been thinking clearly,

because all he'd thought about was ending the meeting with Paxton because Jenah was upstairs waiting for him. She was waiting to have sex with him when he should have been home making love to his wife.

"Are you all right, Spencer?"

Deanna's contralto had broken into his thoughts. "I don't know, baby."

"Why not?"

"I'm scared to look and see if I still have a dick."

Rising on an elbow, Deanna glanced at his groin. "It's still there."

Spencer smiled. "What were you trying to do? Eviscerate me?"

Deanna pulled the flaccid sex away from his thigh and pressed a kiss along its length. "Never. I love making love with you too much to tamper with the family jewels."

"Speaking of family. What do you say we try and increase ours? Don't look at me like that, Dee. I'm serious. Stop, baby," he said when she fell on him, placing kisses over his face.

Tonight signaled a change, because Spencer had decided he was going to become a faithful husband and hopefully a better father than he'd been a husband.

Chapter Twenty-One

Deanna scooted forward when Spencer stepped into the Jacuzzi and sat down behind her. A smile tilted the corners of her mouth. She couldn't remember the last time they'd shared a bath, or even a shower.

The light from a full moon silvered the bathroom through the skylight, and with dozens of flickering candles and the haunting strains of one of her favorite sound tracks coming from the in-wall iPod ports wired to ceiling speakers in every room in the house, Deanna felt as if she and Spencer were on their honeymoon. They'd gone to the Italian Riviera for two weeks and had lived a hedonistic lifestyle. Most times they were out of their clothes more than in. They'd slept nude, swum nude and worn a minimum of clothing while dining.

"Are you comfortable, baby?"

She moaned and closed her eyes. "Very." Deanna wanted to tell Spencer she wasn't as comfortable as she was happy—happy that she'd gotten her husband back. When she'd taken time to reexamine what had gone wrong with her marriage, she hadn't been able to come up with one plausible reason why she and Spencer were growing further and further apart. If it wasn't for fundraisers or dinner parties that required an escort, they wouldn't be a couple.

"I've missed you so much." Her thoughts had just slipped out.

Wrapping his arms around Deanna's waist, Spencer pushed his groin to her hips. "I've missed you, too. But that's going to change."

"How?" she asked.

"We're going to spend a lot more time together. I want you to let me know when you have a free week so we can go away."

A warning bell went off in Deanna's head, and she wanted to ask Spencer *what's up?* but didn't want to appear suspicious or ungrateful. She'd spent so much time complaining that she didn't get to see enough of him, and now when he was offering a romantic getaway she was going to question why.

"Where are we going?" she asked instead.

Spencer pressed his mouth to the nape of her damp neck. "Anyplace where it's warm. This winter is the first one since I left Chicago that really got to me."

Deanna smiled. "Now you know D.C. winters can't compare to Chicago's. It's just that we've had more snow this winter than we've had in years."

"That's why I want to get away. How does St. Croix sound to you?"

Her smile became a full grin. "It sounds wonderful." She also wanted to tell Spencer that winter was over, but again she decided not to mention it.

"It's the perfect place for us to make a baby," he whispered in her ear.

Deanna gasped when she felt the hardened flesh pushing

against her buttocks. Turning to face Spencer, she straddled him while at the same time grasping his erection and guiding it between her thighs. Throwing back her head, she moaned as he lifted his hips and pushed inside her.

In a moment of madness Deanna forgot about Richard Douglas and his threats. The only thing that mattered was the blood-engorged flesh sliding in and out of her vagina. There were three reasons why she'd married Spencer Tyson: intelligence, ambition and sex. And at times it was the sex that seemed to supersede his other assets. He was the first man to make her come by just staring at his hard-on. If there was a contest for men who were hung like a horse there was no doubt her husband would be a winner.

The warm bubbles swept around their writhing bodies as Deanna tried to get even closer. Spencer shifted and she looped her legs around his waist. Holding tightly to his strong neck, she leaned back, screaming when she felt him touch her womb. She screamed over and over as the orgasms continued to come until she gave one last shudder and collapsed against Spencer's chest.

Spencer reversed their positions, his hips moving faster and faster until he felt the familiar tingling at the base of his spine. Grasping Deanna's breasts, he squeezed them tightly while surrendering to an ecstasy that left him mewling like a wounded animal. It didn't matter how many women he'd slept with; none could come close to what his wife offered him. He hadn't been the first man in her bed, but since making her his wife he knew he was the only man who'd been in her bed.

Bethany tapped lightly on her daughter's bedroom door before pushing it open and walking in. Abigail sat at her desk, the wires from her iPod in her ears, while she sang loudly.

Leaning against the door frame, Bethany smiled and shook her head. It was obvious her daughter had multitasking down to a science. Abigail could listen to music, talk and do homework all at the same time.

Bethany had to admit that she and Damon had produced two very attractive children with above-average intelligence. They had also inherited their father's driving ambition. For them it couldn't be just good, but exceptional. When Abigail had an assignment to identify the differing parts of a flower, she'd embarked on a project to have Bethany purchase fresh flowers at a florist, then painstakingly separated the flower with tweezers and displayed them under glass.

Her teacher and principal had recommended she be skipped to the next grade, but Bethany wouldn't approve it. Although her daughter was academically ahead of her peers, it wasn't the same socially. There were times when the eight-year-old acted more like five or six when she couldn't get her way. Her temper tantrums had subsided to once or twice a month, but they were back with more regularity now that Paige had come to live with them.

Bethany approached Abigail, running a hand over her ash-blond hair. Large dark blue eyes looked at her before Abigail gave her a sweet smile and pulled the buds from her ears.

"How's the homework, Abby?" Bethany asked.

"It's good."

She peered at the page where Abigail had completed several math computations. Bethany had decided to compromise with the direction of her daughter's education. The child would take advanced classes, but would remain with children her own age in her homeroom.

She kissed the sweet-smelling moonlit strands. "How are things in school?"

Abigail turned off her iPod. She pursed her lips. "It's okay."

Bethany's pale eyebrows lifted a fraction. "Just okay, sweetheart?"

"I'm not fighting with Melissa anymore."

Reaching for Abigail's hands, Bethany eased her from the chair and led her over to the daybed in an alcove. When she'd had her daughter's room decorated she'd purchased the daybed for Abigail because it was where she lounged in the space that had become her play corner. The space was a quintessential girl's room, with white furniture and pink accents. The duvet on the double bed matched the tiny rose-sprigged design on the daybed cushions and pillows and the wallpaper in the play area.

"I didn't know you were fighting with Melissa." Bethany's voice was soft, calming.

Abigail pulled her legs up in a yoga position. Blond wavy hair concealed her face when she leaned forward. "We weren't really fighting, Mom. Melissa got mad when she thought I said that her mother was a slut. But I didn't say it, Mom. It was Hannah who'd heard her mother call Melissa's mother a slut because she found her in bed with Jason Babinski's father."

Cradling Abigail's head to her chest, Bethany kissed her hair again. She knew the women because their children were in some of the same classes, but she hadn't accepted their invitations to join them for coffee. Maybe it was time she became more responsive to their offers.

"I'm glad you finally worked it out, baby. And, you know what I've told you about repeating gossip."

Abigail nodded. "What goes around comes around."

She had warned her children about repeating what they'd overheard others say, while Damon was adamant about them not using profanity. Bethany knew she was being hypocritical, because she was about to do exactly what she'd cautioned her son and daughter not to do: repeat gossip. Waiting until Connor, Abigail and Paige had left for school and Damon for his office, she had gone to the home office, closed the door and retrieved the flash drive she'd concealed on a bookshelf behind a stack of romance novels.

Salacious gossip she'd overheard she'd typed for the column "Fact or Fiction, Real or Rumor?" She would blog the *Daily Dish* on a netbook that Nathan had given her. Bethany had repaid Tiffany Jones in spades when Damon had inadvertently mentioned that her daughter had left rehab to take up with an L.A.-based Mexican-American mechanic. Bethany's scathing, acerbic wit came through when she wrote: *It is apparent a D.C. doyenne's strung-out daughter checked out of her posh L.A. rehab spa because she prefers chorizo instead of breakfast links with her eggs.*

Now she had Libby Archer and Jason Babinski Sr. to add to the list of cheaters. Bethany thought about what Deanna had told her about her about cheating on Spencer, but that was old news. What she wanted was something new, fresh. She had made certain to save everything on the flash drive instead of her home computer, because Bethany didn't want anything traced back to her. And she knew Nate would never reveal his source. He'd reassured her no names would ever appear in the column or blog—only innuendos, insinuations and ambiguities.

"I'm not going to stay long. I just came in to see how you were doing."

"I'm almost finished with my homework," Abigail said.

"Don't stay up too late."

Abigail kissed her mother's cheek. "I won't."

Bethany walked out of Abigail's bedroom and across the hall to Connor's. She peered in. The glow from several nightlights revealed he was in bed. She and Damon never had to tell Connor to go to bed. Because he required more sleep than most kids his age in order to be alert, her son made certain to get at least ten hours of sleep on school nights.

She continued down the hallway, stopping at Paige's bedroom. Bethany was surprised to find the door open. Paige would come home from school and remain cloistered in her bedroom until it was time for dinner. She was usually talkative during the meal, but once the table was cleared she retreated to her room and closed the door until the following morning.

Bethany met Paige's startled gaze as she sat on her bed. "Hi." Her greeting was shaded in neutral tones.

"What do you want?" Paige spat out.

"Please watch your tone," Bethany warned.

"Yeah, yeah, I know. This is your house."

"This is also your home, Paige, so that means everyone respects one another."

Walking in, Bethany sat on a chair near the door. What had surprised her when Paige had come to live with them was that her bedroom was always incredibly neat. Mrs. Rodgers had remarked that all she had to do was change Paige's bed, clean her en suite bath, dust and vacuum. She never had to pick up clothes or shelve books, which made the housekeeper's job an easy one.

Paige rolled her eyes. "What–eva."

Bethany decided to overlook her stepdaughter's surly attitude. "I want to know if you want a sweet-sixteen party."

Paige's lip curled. "Yeah, right."

"Is that a yes or no, Paige?"

"That's means you must be on the pipe. Who the hell would I invite to my party?"

Again, Bethany ignored the insolence. "How about the kids in your class?"

"I don't want anything to do with a bunch of losers."

"Why are they losers?" Bethany asked.

Falling back on the pile of pillows behind her shoulders, Paige stared up at the ceiling. "All they do is get high and have sex."

Years of performing in front of a camera came into play when Bethany's expression did not change with the teenager's admission. She didn't want to acknowledge that children who'd come from good homes were getting high on drugs. But she was relieved that despite Paige's anger and hostility she hadn't gone along with the others. The last thing she needed was to deal with a drug-addicted, promiscuous adolescent.

"Are there any kids in your school who you'd want to invite?"

Paige lifted her shoulders under an oversize black T. "There are a few, but they're not in my class."

"How many would you like to invite?"

There came a beat of silence before Paige said, "I'll let you know."

"When, Paige?"

"When I think about it."

"Don't think too long, because I need to talk to an event planner about what you'd want."

"Do you mean what *you* want?" Paige snapped nastily.

"This is not about me," Bethany countered. "I'm not the one turning sixteen."

"What if I don't want a sweet-sixteen party? All I want is a nose job, and Daddy said I could have one."

Bethany pushed off the chair, coming to stand. "If you don't want a party, then you won't have one. Good night."

Turning on her heel, she walked out of Paige's bedroom and closed the door behind her. Not having to become involved in planning a party for Paige eliminated what Bethany knew would become a misgiving for making the suggestion. She'd wanted a party to celebrate her sixteenth birthday, but not when her parents couldn't put food on the table. Her mother had surprised her with her favorite dessert—lemon-filled coconut layer cake and a pearl necklace. It hadn't mattered that the pearls were imitation and the coating would soon peel off, but for Bethany that had become a birthday to remember.

Five years later she'd received another memorable gift for her twenty-first birthday—a strand of twelve millimeter golden South Sea pearls from Mikimoto. The actor she'd been dating at the time was a closet gay who'd been touted as one of Hollywood's sexiest men. She'd kept his secret, and when he'd asked what she wanted for her birthday, Bethany had told him a strand of pearls. They continued to date until her contract with the soap wasn't renewed.

After she'd left L.A., Bethany decided to reinvent herself when she concentrated on her new profession as a news journalist. It was a decision she never regretted. She'd married a D.C. power broker, had her dream house and two beautiful children. Her life was as perfect as it could get. The exception was Paige.

She'd promised herself to try and get along with the recalcitrant girl by extending the olive branch, but she still wasn't getting through to her. Perhaps, she mused, it was time she stopped trying.

Chapter Twenty-Two

Marisol cradled a tall glass filled with freshly squeezed lemonade. She'd held on to the glass to give herself something to do with her hands.

Was she bored?

Yes.

Did she want to go home?

Yes!

She wanted to be anywhere except in Bryce's sister's Annapolis family room eating tasteless food. How, she mused, could Georgina contract with a caterer whose dishes were so bland they could've passed for her own?

"What are you thinking about, *m'ija?*" Bryce whispered in her ear as he flopped down beside her.

"How I wished I would've remembered to put a bottle of *sofrito* in my purse to sprinkle on my food," Marisol whispered back.

"Stop it, sweetheart. The food's not that bad."

Shifting slightly, she stared at Bryce, drowning in his baby-blue eyes. "How can you say that after eating my food?"

Leaning closer, he kissed her cheek. "No one can match you in the kitchen or in the bedroom."

Marisol wanted to tell him that for all that went on in the bedroom she still wasn't pregnant. Deanna and Bethany had cautioned her to relax, and she wanted to tell them that if she was any more relaxed she would be comatose.

She took a sip of lemonade, then let out an audible sigh. Marisol knew if she didn't stop obsessing about becoming pregnant she was going to go crazy. After all, she wouldn't be the first woman who wouldn't be able conceive. It also wouldn't be the end of the world—at least not her world.

"Please take this," she said to Bryce, handing him her glass when his two-year-old niece extended her arms for Marisol to pick her up. "Come, baby girl, and give Titi some love." The little girl with a mop of dirty-blond hair and large soft brown eyes planted a wet, noisy kiss on her cheek. "Thank you, Jessica." Turning her head slightly, she kissed the toddler. Jessica put two fingers in her mouth, closed her eyes and went to sleep.

Marisol lost track of time as she, too, closed her eyes, shutting out the activity going on around her as she held the sleeping child. She felt Bryce when he got up, heard the shrieks of children as they chased one another in and out of the room. If it hadn't been raining they would've played outdoors on the expansive property with outdoor basketball and tennis courts and inground pool.

She'd managed to spend the day with Bryce's family without fanfare. His sisters had greeted her with polite smiles and impersonal embraces. Their children were more effusive, calling her Titi or Aunt Mari, while her mother-in-law was speechless for a long moment when she'd given her a pair of sapphire-and-diamond earrings and sapphire-and-gold cuff links for her father-in-law. The card had read from her and Bryce, but his parents knew she'd been the one to select the jewelry.

"Are you practicing?"

Marisol smiled, but didn't open her eyes when Cynthia McDonald sat beside her. "You could say that," she told Bryce's mother.

"Bryce told me the two of you are planning to start a family."

Marisol's eyelids fluttered wildly before she was able to look at Cynthia. The elegant woman had celebrated her seventieth birthday days before Christmas, but her plastic surgeon had managed to turn back time, because a recent face-lift and dermabrasion had erased minute lines and wrinkles that left her face smooth, flawless. She'd suspected her mother-in-law had also had her nose done, because it appeared smaller, more delicate.

Why, she wondered, did Bryce tell his mother that when they'd been trying for years to have a baby? Marisol nodded. "Yes, it's true."

Cynthia McDonald's blue-green gaze did not waver. "I know you and I haven't always gotten along, only because I didn't think you would make a good wife for my son."

A sardonic smile twisted Marisol's mouth. "You've changed your mind?"

"Yes."

"What made you change your mind, Cynthia?"

The older woman patted her short coiffed silver hair. "I've noticed a change in Bryce. He is a lot more focused since he's married you. He used to have a nervous energy that I'd found off-putting. It was as if he had to prove to his father that he had I think he called it the 'chops' to continue the family business."

"Bryce is a brilliant political strategist," Marisol said in defense of her husband.

"I know that and you know that. But it has taken Bryce a long time to come to that realization, and I have you to thank for that. Being married to you has given him stability."

"So, now you approve of me?"

Cynthia blushed as she lowered her gaze. "It's not that I disapproved of you, Marisol. It's just that I thought he could've done better, not realizing you were that better. Some of the women Bryce used to take up with came from good families, but they had the morals of alley cats. Even after they were married they'd continued to sleep around. Have you seen the film *White Mischief?*"

Marisol searched her memory. "No, I don't believe I have. Why?"

"It's about a group of bored, elite British colonial expatriates living a hedonistic existence in a region of Kenyon known as Happy Valley. They were notorious for drug use, drinking and adultery and were very promiscuous. Bryce and his friends had created their own Happy Valley in Annapolis, Maryland, whenever they got together."

"Are you saying he was into drugs and orgies?" The query was a whisper.

"Don't look so shocked, Marisol. I'm certain you've smoked dope."

"That's where you're wrong. I've never taken drugs."

Another flush suffused Cynthia's face and neck. "I'm sorry for being presumptuous. Will you please forgive me?" Marisol nodded. "Well, I can't say the same for my son. I don't know why I'm telling you this, but you should know there had been a nonstop trail of women coming and going until Roger told him he had to get his own apartment. He moved out, but continued to hang out with his friends. Then it stopped. I have to assume that's when he met you."

Marisol wanted to tell Cynthia that she'd never witnessed Bryce taking drugs. And she wondered if he was having unprotected sex with other women because two years into their marriage he'd developed a latex sensitivity.

"I told Bryce I would divorce him in a heartbeat if he ever cheated on me."

Cynthia patted Marisol's thigh. "I hope that never happens. And I can't wait until you and Bryce give me a grandchild."

"Don't you have enough grandchildren?"

"When you get to my age you'll realize you can never have enough grandchildren. There's just more to love and spoil."

Marisol gave Cynthia a sincere smile, knowing it was going to happen. Whether naturally, through artificial insemination or adoption, she knew she was going to become a mother.

"I'm going to check my voice mail before I come up," Marisol said to Bryce as he headed for the staircase.

Lowering his head, Bryce kissed her cheek. "I'll check mine after I take a shower."

Marisol entered her office and sat down behind her desk. She punched in the pass code to retrieve her messages. There was one from Wesley Sheridan, asking her to call him to set up a meeting to discuss their travel plans. She dialed his number, counting off the rings until there was a break in the connection.

"Wes Sheridan."

She smiled. "This is Marisol. I'm returning your call."

"*¿Cómo está usted?*"

"*Bueno.*"

"Do you have anything planned for tomorrow?" Wesley asked in English.

"Tomorrow is Sunday."

"I know that."

Marisol stared at the Waterford paperweight on her desk. The red heart had been a Valentine's gift from Bryce. "I don't work Sundays."

"It's not work. I want to invite you and Bryce over for an informal get-together. I'm using it to thank key people on my campaign committee."

"Why didn't you call Bryce?"

"I did. But when he didn't pick up I decided to call you."

"Let me check with Bryce to see if he's available."

"Even if he isn't, I'd still like you to come."

There weren't too many occasions when Marisol attended a social gathering without Bryce. She wanted to decline Wesley's invitation, because Sundays were for sleeping in late and lazing around the house. She didn't cook or go out to eat. If they didn't eat leftovers, then Bryce ordered in. Sundays had become her day of rest.

"After I talk to Bryce I'll call you back." She hung up, walked out the office and climbed the staircase to the second floor. Marisol found Bryce standing under the oversize showerhead in a free-standing shower, shampooing his hair. She stared at the spray of water sluicing over Bryce's slim, toned physique. He didn't work out, but playing tennis several times a week kept him in peak condition.

He smiled, beckoning her. "Come join me."

"No thanks. I plan to take a bath later." She was looking forward to a leisurely soak in the tub.

Sitting on a chair in the master bath, Marisol admired her decorating handiwork. She'd decorated the bath in the Regency period with Wedgwood green. Pull-up chairs, two armchairs, a French fainting couch, neoclassical art, book-case and fireplace were more reminiscent of a library than a bathroom.

"Wesley wants to know if you have anything planned for tomorrow."

Bryce turned his face up to the flowing water. "I told Tate Drysdale that I would drive up to meet him in Richmond. Why?"

"He's inviting us to an informal gathering at his place."

"Tate and I have postponed our meeting twice, and we really need to talk if he's thinking about running for re-election. I'll probably stay overnight, so I want you to go without me."

Marisol knew it was impossible for Bryce to meet her later, because the congressman lived a hundred miles away from D.C. She knew if Wesley wasn't Bryce's client she would've declined, but he was also her client.

"What time are you leaving?"

Turning off the water, Bryce reached for a towel from a stack on a teakwood bench. "I'm going to try to be on the road before sunrise."

"Do you want breakfast?"

Blotting the water from his hair, he tossed the towel into a basket, and then reached for a bath sheet to dry his body. "No. I'll stop and eat once I'm outside Richmond."

Marisol stared at the marble floor. "I'll call Wesley and let him know that I'll be coming alone."

Bryce wrapped the towel around his waist. "Why do you make it sound as if you're going to an execution?"

"You know I like to chill out on Sundays."

Dropping an arm over Marisol's shoulders, he pulled her close to his damp body. "Sweetheart. It's only one Sunday." He kissed her nose. "And remember that Wesley's *our* client."

"And you'll remind me in case I forget, won't you?"

Bryce cupped her bottom. "You can bet your cute ass I will."

Marisol reached out and grabbed his butt over the towel. "You keep feeling me up and I'm going to make you cry." He dropped his hand. "Coward," she taunted. The first time she'd performed fellatio Bryce had literally lost control, and he had made her promise to never do it again.

"Hell, yeah," Bryce confirmed, walking into the bedroom, while Marisol retreated to her office to call and confirm her attendance at Wesley Sheridan's informal gathering.

Chapter Twenty-Three

The buzzer rang, disengaging the lock, and Marisol pushed open the outer door to the town house. She'd taken a cab from Georgetown because it was impossible to park in Adams Morgan on weekends. She could see why Wesley had elected to live in a neighborhood that locals called the city's Latin Quarter. It came alive at sundown, with residents in their twenties and thirties crowding sidewalks and filling the many restaurants, funky bars and nightclubs.

The neighborhood was one of her favorites, because not only was it ethnically diverse but it also had wonderful ethnic restaurants. The few times she'd come with Bryce they'd stayed up until the break of dawn relaxing in coffeehouses and listening to live music. Coming to Adams Morgan reminded Marisol of the Parisian Left Bank.

When she entered the spacious vestibule she heard voices raised in laughter coming from an apartment at the end of the hallway. The door was ajar; within seconds it opened wider and she came face-to-face with Wesley Sheridan. If it hadn't been for his premature silver hair she wouldn't have recognized him. He was dressed entirely in black: pullover sweater, slacks, slip-ons and wire-rimmed blue-tinted glasses.

Marisol smiled at her host, handing him a decorative shopping bag. *"Hola otra vez."*

Wesley took the bag, then, angling his head, kissed her cheek. "Hello to you, too. Thank you for coming, but you didn't have to bring anything."

"Bryce told me you have a fondness for Spanish wine."

Wesley smiled, flashing gleaming white teeth in his deeply tanned face. "He's right. Although I'm sorry he couldn't make it, I'm glad you decided to come because I'd like you to tell me what you think of my apartment."

He stood aside and Marisol walked into an entryway, her practiced gaze taking in everything in one sweeping glance. "I'm surprised you say apartment and not your home. Which one is it, Wes?" she asked, untying her cashmere shawl and draping it over her arm. Turning on her heels, she stared up at him. The tinted lenses wouldn't permit her to see his eyes clearly.

"I suppose it's my home." He took her wrap, placing it on a chair beside a rustic wooden table. Resting his hand on the small of her back, Wesley steered her into the living room.

Marisol came to a complete stop when she saw Bethany and Damon Paxton. Her gaze swept over the small group in an attempt to see who else she recognized. The others were strangers. Smiling with Bethany's approach, she exchanged an air kiss with her. The blonde was the epitome of casual chic in a sleeveless red sheath dress that was a striking contrast to her pale skin and hair.

"Don't you look nice," Bethany crooned. "Isn't she beautiful, Wesley?"

Marisol saw Wesley stare at her off-the-shoulder black

jersey wool dress hugging her body like a second skin. End-ing at her knees, it appeared even shorter with her four-inch heels.

"I'm glad Bryce isn't here to hear me say that I think his wife is stunning." Wesley rested his hand on Marisol's back. *"¿Le puedo conseguir que algo tomar?"*

She stiffened with his touch, then relaxed once he removed his hand. "I'll have club soda with a twist of lime."

Wesley angled his head. "Are you certain you don't want anything stronger?" he asked, switching fluidly back to English.

Marisol smiled. "Quite certain."

"After I get your drink I'll introduce you to everyone."

"Come and talk to me," Bethany said when Wesley walked to the portable bar. "How do you know Wesley?"

"Nice outfit," Marisol said complimenting her.

"Thanks. But you didn't answer my question. What's your connection to Wesley Sheridan?"

"He happens to be my client."

"You decorated this place?"

"No. He wants me to decorate his vacation home."

"By the way, where's Bryce?"

"He couldn't make it because he had a prior engagement," Marisol explained. "Why are *you* here?"

"I came with Damon. Now that I'm working I find myself wanting to get out more."

"Are you still working at the station?"

"Yes and no."

"Which is it, Bethany?"

"I used to go into the station a couple of days a week, but now I just email everything in," Bethany lied.

Marisol smiled. "Sweet. I'd love to be able to work in my jammies, but no such luck."

"You're the one with the glam career."

"It's not as glamorous as you think."

"You make homes beautiful."

"Only after I go through weeks and months of frustration and aggravation when people change their minds umpteen times because they don't know what they really want."

Bethany moved closer to Marisol. "You know it's my turn to host a luncheon. And when you come I'll give you a complete tour of my house this time, and want you to be completely honest when you tell me its tacky."

When Marisol had gone back to Bethany's house after their trip to the botanic gardens she'd come into the house by a side door that led directly into a designer kitchen. "If the rest of the house is anything like your kitchen, then you'll get a passing grade."

"It's the bedrooms I'd like you to look at."

"Who decorated them?"

"I did," Bethany confirmed.

A hint of a smile parted Marisol's lips. "Then I'll be certain to be brutally honest."

"What do you think of this room?"

Marisol stared at the soothing blue-gray color on the living room walls. "I like it."

"Why?"

"It works because it has a traditional arrangement, but it's not too formal because Wesley incorporated informal fabrics and accent pieces. The white trim on the mantel and French doors emphasize the architectural detail of the coffered ceiling. I like the off-white chairs, love seat and sofa with accent pillows in blue, gray and white. The collection of vases and the mirror on the mantel appear to be antiques, and the silver candlesticks also look like antiques."

"Hey-y-y, girlfriend," Bethany crooned. "You do know your stuff, don't you?"

"Did you think I was a fraud?"

"No, no, no," Bethany countered quickly. "I'd heard you were good…" Whatever she attempted to say was preempted when Wesley returned with Marisol's drink.

Winking, Wesley gave Bethany a slow smile. "I'm going to kidnap your friend so I can introduce her to the others."

"Don't forget she's married."

Wesley's expression changed, becoming a mask of stone as he gave Bethany a long, penetrating stare before his gaze shifted to Marisol. "That's something I can never forget."

"What do you think you're doing?"

Bethany froze. She hadn't noticed Damon when he'd come up behind her. "What are you talking about?" The calmness in her voice masked the rush of anxiety, making it difficult for her to draw a normal breath.

Damon moved closer, his breath feathering over her ear. "I heard what you just said to Wesley. I happen to know the man well enough to say that he'd never hit on another man's wife. He's honorable and was *very* idealistic, darling."

"Why do you say *was,* Damon?"

"I'm a lobbyist, and that means I sell influence. One of my clients wanted him to vote for something that would've been in their best interest. Initially when I approached Sheridan, he wouldn't give me the time of day. There's an Italian saying— 'one hand washes the other and both hands wash the face.' Sheridan wanted something for his congressional district and my people made it happen for him. And when he ran for his congressional seat, unlike some candidates who have to rely on volunteers, he was able to hire the best political strategist and team in the country. The folks you see here are the key people on that team."

"In other words, he was bought out."

"I'm not saying he was, darling. It's just that he's become the consummate politician. Now, tell me why did you warn him about Bryce McDonald's wife?"

"I see the way he looks at her, Damon."

"She is a beautiful woman, Beth."

It was obvious Damon couldn't see what she'd seen because she'd lost count of the number of times she'd been on the receiving end of a subtle yet lecherous stare. And Wesley had stared at Marisol as if she was something to devour. Marisol had admitted the silver-haired, handsome young congress-man was her client, but an uneasy feeling told Bethany there was something more to their relationship. Call it instinct or intuition, it was something she'd learned not to ignore. Following up on a lead or an anonymous tip was what had put her on the fast track as a journalist.

"That she is, Damon. I can see why Bryce fell for her."

Damon's arm went around Bethany's waist. "Your claws are showing, babe. I've never known you to be jealous of any woman."

"I'm not jealous, Damon."

"If not, then what are you?"

"I'm just curious."

Damon kissed her ear. "You know what happened to the curious cat."

It got killed, Bethany mused. She smiled when she recalled the retort about satisfaction bringing it back. "I'm not going to answer that. Can you be a dear and get me a wine spritzer?"

"Can I leave you alone without you getting into trouble?"

Shifting slightly, she pressed her breasts to Damon's chest. Flashing a sexy moue, Bethany stared up at him through lowered lids. "Why don't you leave me alone and find out?"

He rested a hand on the curve of her hip. "I'm going to call Mrs. Rodgers and let her know we'll be late. Very, very late."

She closed her eyes. "Where are we going?"

"We're going to check into a hotel, order room service and make love until we pass out from exhaustion. Then we're going to take a nap, then get up and do it again and again and again."

Bethany smiled. "That just may take all night, my love."

"Then it will take all night and probably into tomorrow. It's been a while since I've taken a day off."

Bethany opened her eyes while curbing the urge to squeal like an adolescent girl at a concert. It had been a long time since she and Damon had checked into a hotel together. "Where are we going?"

Damon tightened his hold on her hip. "I've discovered a place where certain gentlemen stash their mistresses."

She recalled the times when she'd waited for Damon in hotels and inns when he was still married *and* living with Jean. Bethany would've invited him to her apartment if her ultra-conservative religious landlady hadn't kept watch on who was coming and going.

"Don't forget I, too, was a mistress."

"True, babe. But the difference is I married you."

Bethany nodded, her eyes following Wesley as he introduced Marisol to the members of his staff. His hand barely touching her waist may have appeared impersonal to others, but not Bethany. And when they headed in her direction she noticed a look in the young congressman's eyes that was more than familiar. It was the same look she'd affected when she saw Damon Paxton in that restaurant that now seemed a lifetime ago. Wesley wanted Marisol McDonald.

"I suppose introducing you guys would just be a formality," Wesley said, smiling.

Damon, reaching for Marisol's hand, dropped a kiss on her knuckle. "Yes, it would. It's always nice seeing you, Marisol."

Marisol patted Damon's hand. "This man makes the best vanilla egg cream south of Brooklyn."

"It took me years before I realized there were no eggs in egg creams," Wesley admitted.

Shifting slightly, Marisol gave Wesley a bored look. "What would someone from St. Louis know about eggs creams? It's a New York City thing."

Smiling and winking at her, Wesley said, "And what would someone from the Big Apple know about pork steaks?"

"What the heck are pork steaks?" she asked.

"We'll save this discussion for another time, because it's time we go into the dining room to eat."

The silent, efficient waitstaff escorted everyone into the dining room, seating them with their respective place cards. Pushing serving carts, they filled plates with a sautéed vegetable medley, date-stuffed chicken breast with Madeira sauce, prime rib and sole meunière. Wineglasses were emptied and refilled with red, white and rosé wines that were the perfect complement to the expertly prepared food.

Marisol had sat at the opposite end of the table from Wesley because she was the only one who'd come without an escort. She made a mental note to get the name and telephone number of the caterer to pass along to Georgina. Hopefully her sister-in-law would appreciate the offer rather than take it as a slight.

Peering over the rim of her water goblet, she noticed Wesley staring in her direction. She wanted to see his eyes behind the tinted lenses. Bethany's warning about her being married continued to nag at Marisol. What had she been trying to insinuate? That Wesley was the type to go after married women?

Taking a sip of water, she touched her napkin to the corners of her mouth. First Cynthia McDonald had revealed Bryce's sordid life as a bachelor and now Bethany was hinting at Wesley possibly sleeping with married women. Marisol knew D.C. was a place of secrets, secrets deals and secret liaisons. It was glittering and glamorous, and a place where political machinations were more important than sex. What she didn't want was to be caught up in one or the other.

She had decorated the homes of judges, senators and representatives, and she had also had clients who'd asked her to assist architects when they'd decided to renovate their residences. Her services were in demand, but lately Marisol had become much more discriminating because she didn't want to overtax herself and exacerbate the recurring headaches. Luckily she hadn't had one in more than a week, and for that she was grateful and appreciative.

"May I please have everyone's attention." Wesley had raised his voice to be heard above the soft conversations going on around the table. "Firstly, I would thank you for taking time out to come here this afternoon." He nodded to a woman holding a basket. "Robyn is going to come around and give each of you a little something from me to show my appreciation for your dedication and hard work that helped me to win my congressional seat. Please don't open them until you leave." One black eyebrow rose a fraction. "Marisol, Robyn will give you something for your husband. I know everyone here has heard me say more times than they can count that I wouldn't be here without Bryce McDonald."

"Here, here," came a chorus from the assembly.

"Last and certainly not least," Wesley continued, "I'd like to thank Damon Paxton. Some of you may not know it, but without Damon you would've become volunteers and not paid staff." He raised his water glass and there was another chorus of approval.

The gathering lasted for another hour, when a variety of desserts, ranging from sliced fresh seasonal fruit, tarts and compotes accompanied by coffee, tea and cordials was served. Marisol lingered behind the others when Wesley said he wanted to give her something.

When he took off his glasses she realized why he'd worn them. His eyes were red and swollen. "What happened to you?" she asked.

"Allergies. I'm going to take a couple of Benadryl before I go to bed tonight."

"Why didn't you take them earlier?"

He smiled. "I didn't want anyone to think I was under the influence." He took her hand. "Come with me."

Marisol followed Wesley down a wide hallway to a room he'd set up as a home office. It was quintessentially masculine, with an ornately carved oak desk, matching built-in bookcases, leather chairs, walls covered with framed prints and photographs of athletes. He picked up an envelope off the glass-covered desk, handing it to her.

"In there are tentative plans for our trip to Puerto Rico. If the dates don't fit into your schedule, then please let me know."

Marisol scanned the single page of type. Wesley had arranged for them to spend two weeks on the island. They were scheduled to fly into Ponce on a private jet. A driver would pick them up at the airport and drive them to Guánica. She looked up at him. "I don't think it's going to take me more than a week to set up plans for each room."

"I realize that. But I just thought you'd want to spend some time with your relatives in Palomas and Guayanilla."

Her pulse quickened. "Are you sure you don't mind hanging out with my relatives?"

"Of course I don't mind."

She lowered her eyes. "Thank you, Wesley."

"You're welcome."

Wesley walked her outside where he hailed a taxi, waiting until she was seated, and then he closed the door. Gazing out the back window, she stared at him until he became smaller and smaller, then disappeared from her line of vision.

A week from now she would be on a jet flying to Puerto Rico for business and pleasure. But the man accompanying her wouldn't be her husband, but her client. The last time she'd gone to Puerto Rico to visit relatives Bryce refused to go with her, saying he hadn't wanted to impose on her time with her family. When her aunts and cousins asked her about her husband, Marisol had lied and said he was working.

What she didn't want to think of was that her husband had stayed in D.C. to see another woman. *Damn you, Cynthia!* Why had Bryce's mother waited six years to tell her about Bryce's sexual escapades? As far as Marisol was concerned, what she didn't know couldn't hurt her.

Chapter Twenty-Four

The driver got out and came around to help Bethany out the car, then waited for Damon to emerge. "Please call me, Mr. Paxton, when you're ready to leave."

"I won't need you until tomorrow morning," Damon told his driver. "Enjoy your evening."

The driver smiled. "Thank you. The same to you and Mrs. Paxton."

Damon caught Bethany's hand, tucking it into the crook of his elbow as he led her to the entrance to the Victoria. It had been a long time—in fact, it was before he and Bethany were married since they'd checked into a hotel to do nothing more than make love. He'd had a few reservations about marrying a woman twenty years his junior, but Bethany had surprised him because she appeared genuinely happy as a wife and mother. He hadn't asked much from her, with the exception that she remain a stay-at-home mother until Connor and Abigail were older. He'd witnessed the negative effects on children of two working parents: lack of boundaries, higher incidents of substance abuse and unplanned pregnancies.

The doorman held the door. "Good evening. Welcome to the Victoria."

Bethany gave him a friendly smile. "Thank you. How did you find this place?" she whispered to Damon.

"I told you it's a stash house for mistresses."

"Did you ever bring your mistresses here?"

"No, but I know quite a few men who do."

"It's beautiful."

"It is," Damon agreed.

"I've never been in this neighborhood," Bethany admitted.

"The two square blocks that make up this section of D.C. are a well-kept secret. The town houses belong to some of the wealthiest families in the city. Before this place was converted to a hotel it was the residence of a wealthy banker who'd lost his fortune in the Crash of '29."

"I feel as if I should be wearing one of those high-necked white dresses with the bustles from the Victorian era."

"You would've been an exquisite Victorian lady."

"I doubt it, Damon. Remember, my family was and is still dirt-poor."

He had no comeback to Bethany's reference to her humble beginnings. Damon had thought that she would've become accustomed to her new upscale lifestyle. Now he realized why she hadn't wanted to live in one of the more affluent D.C. or northern Virginia suburbs. He'd wanted to live in George-town, Washington's oldest and wealthiest neighborhood, but Bethany had preferred Falls Church because she wouldn't have to run into those who'd been Jean's close friends and staunch allies.

Damon realized once he'd begun seeing Bethany publicly he'd put her in a tenuous position where she'd become a much maligned pariah as a home wrecker, and there was little he could do to counter the accusation without outing the mother of his daughter.

Resting his hand in the small of Bethany's back, he led her to the concierge. The man was dressed in a dark gray tailored suit, white shirt and charcoal-gray silk tie. "I'd like a suite for the night."

The concierge nodded. "We happen to have a charming suite on the third floor. If you have luggage, I'll arrange for someone to bring it up for you."

Damon and Bethany shared a secret smile. "There's no luggage."

"My name is Philip and I'll be here until midnight. Clarence will relieve me, so if there's anything you need he will be available for you. How would you like to check in, Mister...?"

"It's Paxton. Damon and Bethany Paxton."

Philip took a surreptitious glance at their matching wedding bands, smiling. "Would you like dinner in your suite?"

Again, Damon and Bethany exchanged a glance, she shaking her head. They'd sat down to eat at three at Wesley's. "We'll have something light in the bar, but I doubt whether we'll want a full dinner." Reaching into the breast pocket of his jacket, Damon removed his credit-card case, handing Philip one.

After they were checked in and given room keys, Damon steered Bethany into the bar, seating her at table for two in a corner where a towering palm provided them with a modicum of privacy.

Light from a candle on the table was reflected in Bethany's brilliant violet eyes. "I like this place," she said, glancing around the rosewood-paneled area.

"Would you like us to rent a suite here?"

Settling back in her chair, she stared at something over his shoulder. "What would we use it for?"

"Date night. If the president and the first lady have date night, why shouldn't we?"

"You want to date me?"

Reaching across the table, Damon held on to Bethany's hands. "Yes. Only because we've never really dated. It's true I would meet you in hotels, but those weren't actually dates. The few times I took you to a social gathering because it required a partner didn't count. I want to take you out to dinner, or to a movie, but instead of going home we can come here and you can make as much noise as you want when we make love."

Bethany blushed. "I'm not the only one who makes noise."

"You're the screamer, Beth."

"I only scream when you hit the G-spot."

Damon angled his head and rested his arm over the back of the chair. "But I don't hit it every time, do I?"

"If you're asking me whether I have an orgasm whenever we make love, then the answer is yes."

"But I don't make you scream every time."

Bethany hesitated, her expression tight, lips compressed. "What are you getting at, Damon? Are you asking if you satisfy me?" He nodded. "May I be honest?"

He nodded again. "Please."

"Sex...I mean making love with you is glorious. We don't make love as often as we did before we were married, but that's to be expected."

"Because I'm getting old?"

Bethany reversed their hands, her thumbs making tiny circles over his knuckles. "It has nothing to do with your age, darling. It's different now that we have the kids. We can't run around naked or make love anytime the moods hits us. If you want to rent a suite here I definitely won't be opposed to it."

Damon's gaze was as soft as a caress. He wondered how he had gotten so lucky. It was as if he'd been repaid for making a mess of his first marriage. "Have a drink with me."

Bethany affected a sexy moue. "Are you trying to get me drunk so you can take advantage of me?"

"Yes."

Throwing back her head, she laughed softly. "Then I'll have what you have."

"Are you certain you can handle a martini?"

"Have you forgotten that my introduction to booze was moonshine?"

It was Damon's turn to laugh. "Do you want to drink them here, or go upstairs?"

"I'd rather sit here. The atmosphere is conducive to seduction."

Raising his hand, Damon signaled a waiter and placed an order for extra dry gin martinis with a splash of Dubonnet and a twist. Waiting until the man walked away, he gazed deeply into Bethany's eyes. "I love you so..."

The rest of his declaration died on his tongue when he heard a familiar voice come from a table behind him. He didn't have to turn around and peer through the fronds of the palm to know who it was. Placing a finger over his mouth, he signaled for Bethany not to talk. He'd cautioned Spencer Tyson to stop seeing Jenah Morris, but apparently from what he was saying to her, it had come back to haunt him.

"You can't be pregnant," Spencer spat out between clenched teeth.

"Do you want to see the results of my test?" Jenah asked.

If he was like some of the guys he'd known in his old

neighborhood he would've slapped Jenah off her chair. He'd asked Jenah to meet him at the Victoria not to make love to her but to break it off—for good. He and Deanna had agreed to start trying for a baby, and that meant a total commitment to his wife. He'd cheated on her for the last time.

"I tell you it's over and you come at me with phony 'I'm having your baby,' nonsense. It's the oldest trick in the book and I'm not falling for it."

"It's not a trick, Spencer."

"What happened to your IUD?"

A sly smile parted Jenah's lips as she peered at Spencer through the fringe of hair covering her blue eye. "I had it removed."

"What the hell for?" Spencer was hard-pressed not to scream at Jenah.

"My periods were too heavy and I was losing time from work, so I went to my doctor and had him remove it."

"Why didn't you use something else?"

"I had to decide whether to go back on the Pill but…"

"But what, Jenah?"

"I thought about how nice it would be to have your baby."

Spencer's hands curled into tight fists. "You scheming bitch! You deliberately got pregnant because you thought I would leave my wife, didn't you? Well, let me tell you something. I wouldn't give a fuck if you had a dozen of my kids, I still wouldn't marry you."

Jenah's eyes filled with tears, but somewhere she found the strength not to let them fall. "But you told me you loved me," she said in a strangled voice.

"A man will say anything when he has his dick in a wet pussy." Reaching into the pocket of his suit trousers, he took a money clip and placed a wad of bills on the table. "Get rid of it, bitch, or I'll make you regret you ever drew breath."

Jenah slapped at the money. "Do you think you can buy me off?"

Spencer stood up. "Everybody has a price, Jenah. Even you."

Jenah also came to her feet. "Maybe Deanna needs to know that her husband has been creeping on her."

"You stay away from my wife or you'll find D.C. hazardous to your health."

"Are you threatening me, Spencer Tyson?"

"No, ho."

"If I'm a ho, then you made me one."

Spencer had heard enough. "You were a ho before we met. Someone who isn't wouldn't open her legs to a man within hours of meeting him. Have a good life," he said in parting as he walked out of the Victoria, unaware that the couple sitting behind him had overheard his damning conversation.

Bethany's eyes were as large as silver dollars as she clamped a hand over her mouth. "Oh, my gosh!" she whispered through her fingers. "Do you think I should tell Deanna?"

Damon ran a hand over his face. "Stay out of it, Beth."

"But she's my friend."

"I don't care if she was your sister, I want you to stay out of it. If Spencer doesn't say anything to his wife, then you shouldn't."

"Didn't Tiffany Jones tell Jean about you and me before you did?"

"It didn't matter if she did, because my marriage had been over for years. All that was left was a divorce. Tyson and his wife are still very much together."

Bethany recalled the conversation she'd had with Deanna about cheating. The event planner had said if her husband was cheating, then she didn't want to know about it. But if she'd discovered it was true she would "cut his balls off."

"I won't say anything to her." She'd promised Damon she wouldn't tell her friend about her unfaithful husband, but she didn't promise him that it wouldn't appear in her column. "Who is she?" she asked instead.

"She works for congresswoman Earline Canton."

"From which state?"

"Pennsylvania."

"I feel sorry for her, Damon." He looked at Bethany as if she'd taken leave of her senses.

"Why?"

"Because she fell for the oldest trick in the book. Spencer tells her he loves her, so she deliberately gets pregnant in the hope that he'll leave his wife and marry her."

"She's pathetic, Beth. She's a girl trying to play a woman's game."

Bethany had to agree. She didn't know how old the woman Spencer had called Jenah was, but she couldn't have been that naive. Even in her early twenties Bethany was smart enough to know not to play the pregnant game. It had taken her a while to come to the realization that she was actually Mrs. Damon Paxton, and it had become more of a reality once Abigail was born. She'd succeeded where so many women had failed. The country girl had come to the big city and landed not only a wealthy man but one that was rumored to have as much power as the president. As a lobbyist Damon's power didn't come with two four-year limits or checks and balances. And everything he did wasn't subject to scrutiny *and* transparency.

Chapter Twenty-Five

Deanna took a step back, surveying the room that had been decorated to resemble a Japanese teahouse in the third-floor ballroom. A trio of Japanese lanterns was suspended over a table set for twenty, their light reflecting off the red tablecloth and a gold-embroidered runner.

One corner of the large room had been transformed into a garden with an indoor fountain surrounded by bonsai plants. Low tables were covered with white and red candles that would be lit within minutes of the arrival of her first guests. Tall, narrow windows were covered with white panels that resembled rice paper. Futons were set up around the perimeter of the room for her guests to lounge on before or after dinner. The florist had delivered vases of white flowers she had positioned around the expansive space and in the unlit fireplace.

She'd set up serving tables where the caterer and her staff would set up a buffet for casual dining, and the bartender had arrived and was going through the inventory in the built-in bar. Spencer had offered to stand in as bartender, but Deanna had convinced him to play host while she conferred with the caterer and his staff. Instead of her two favorite caterers she'd contracted with a man who'd earned a reputation for preparing Asian-fusion dishes that had made him a much a sought-after D.C.-area chef.

"It looks nice, Dee."

She turned to find Spencer standing at the entrance to the ballroom. He looked incredibly handsome in a white silk shirt with a banded collar piped in black and black slacks. "Thank you."

He walked into the room and stared down at the water falling over the rocks. "The fountain adds a nice touch."

"Help me light the candles, then I want you to dim the lights until you think we achieve the right nightclub atmosphere."

Working in tandem, Deanna and Spencer lit the subtly scented and unscented candles. Deanna stood at the entrance to the ballroom while Spencer tapped the wall switch, lowering the setting on the recessed lights until she told him to stop. Two small lamps on the bar provided enough illumination for the talented mixologist to concoct his exotic cocktails.

Looping her arm through Spencer's, she stared at his profile. She'd noticed a change in her husband, a tenseness that had begun earlier in the week. He'd gone to meet with a client Sunday afternoon and had returned in a dark mood. When she'd asked him about it, he claimed attorney-client privilege wouldn't permit him to talk about the case. However, when he'd joined her in bed later that night he'd made love to her as if he'd been denied sex for months. She was no longer using birth control and it was as if Spencer wanted to get her pregnant as soon as possible.

Deanna wasn't certain why Spencer had changed his mind about waiting another two years, but refused to ask because she'd been nagging him about having a baby. There were moments when she tried imagining how much her life would change once she became a mother. She knew she would have to curtail traveling and refer her clients to another area event planner. She and Roslyn Abrams weren't rivals but friendly competitors. When Roslyn was unable to take on a client because of her schedule she would refer them to Deanna, and she would do the same when scheduling conflicts wouldn't allow her to contract with a client.

And it wasn't for the first time that Deanna had thought about owning and operating a bed-and-breakfast. When she'd gone to Reston to check out the site for her client's daughter's Western-themed sweet-sixteen party, she'd written down the telephone number of the broker advertising the sale of an abandoned two-story farmhouse. Deanna hadn't mentioned it to Spencer, because she knew he loved living in the Tudor, but it was an idea that she'd begun fantasizing about.

What she didn't want to think about was Richard Douglas calling her again. It'd been more than two weeks since she'd met with him, and with each passing day she prayed that she would never hear from him again. If she was ever presented with an opportunity to relive her life, that night would head the list of do-overs. But she realized there were no do-overs in life—just don't make the same mistake twice.

"What do you think?" she asked Spencer.

"I think you're incredible," he said softly.

"I'm talking about the room."

Deanna heard the words, but there was no passion or excitement in Spencer's voice. "Please come with me." She led him out of the ballroom and into their home office, closing the door behind them. "What's the matter, baby?"

★ ★ ★

Spencer stared at the neatly twisted hair Deanna had tucked into a chignon on the nape of her long neck. The black silk tunic and matching slacks were in keeping with the Asian theme of their dinner party. Smoky shadows gave her clear brown eyes a mysterious look. His gaze lingered on her vermilion-colored mouth.

"Nothing's wrong. Why do you ask?"

"You're distant, Spencer. It's as if you're preoccupied with something else whenever I talk to you."

He forced a smile he didn't feel. What he couldn't tell Deanna was that his so-called perfect life had come crashing down around him when Jenah told him she was carrying his baby. Spencer didn't know whether to believe her, but he suspected she'd told him that because she felt it would force him to leave Deanna in order to save face. After all, he wouldn't be the first man to have an extramarital affair and find himself in baby-mama drama.

When he and Deanna had first begun sleeping together he'd used condoms, but after they were married she'd opted to go on the Pill. And that meant whenever he cheated on her he had to use protection. The exception had been Jenah. And having her fitted for an IUD had been his idea, not hers. He'd messed up big-time because he should've continued to sleep with married women who had as much to lose as he did *and* he should've never slept with Jenah without a condom.

"I can't talk about the particulars, but I have to decide whether to defend a client who wants to bring sexual harassment charges against her boss who just happens to be a member of Congress."

"Why don't you give the case to another lawyer at the firm?"

Spencer closed his eyes. "This is a personal client."

A slight frown appeared between Deanna's eyes. "I thought you didn't handle personal cases because you don't have the time."

"I usually don't, but this one is different."

"Why is *she* different, Spencer?"

His frown matched hers. "I didn't say my client was a woman."

Deanna's mouth formed an O. "The member isn't a woman?"

Spencer nodded. He would perjure himself under oath if it meant saving his marriage. "He's thinking about quitting since she's threatened him, so he doesn't know what to do."

Curving her arms under Spencer's shoulders, Deanna leaned into him. "I'm sorry. I thought you were shutting me out."

"You know I would never deliberately do that. I love you, baby."

She smiled up at him. "I love you, too. I need to go downstairs and check to see if Dennis is ready to start setting up the cocktail hour."

"Do you want me to help with anything?"

"You can put on some background music."

"Consider it done."

Deanna had hired a staff of four experienced servers she'd worked with since starting up Tyson Planners. They'd rotated duties, handling coat check and maître d' with waiters, making certain each could fill in at a moment's notice. Her brother and sister had declined because they were unable to find someone to babysit their children, thereby eliminating a possible confrontation between Spencer and Neva.

Bryce and Marisol arrived at five-thirty and the maître d' escorted them into the elevator and up to the third floor.

Marisol stepped out of the elevator, resplendent in a white kimono with a black obi sash.

"Chica! Everything looks beautiful."

Deanna gave her an air kiss, then pressed her cheek to Bryce's. "Thank you and welcome. The bar is open and there are hot and cold hors d'oeuvres."

The elevator brought a steady stream of invitees into the ballroom as they stared in awe at the space the Tysons had set up for entertaining their guests. The invitations had indicated Asian-inspired dress optional, but everyone had worn something that reflected the theme. Most of the women wore jade jewelry, while the men had opted for loose-fitting shirts with mandarin collars.

Dennis Wen and his catering staff had prepared sushi and hot and cold appetizers from Thailand, Vietnam, Korea, China and Japan. The bartender, who went by the single name of Prince, did brisk business pouring, mixing and shaking drinks with his normal silent precision.

Damon and Bethany arrived minutes after six and Deanna went to greet them. "Welcome."

Bethany was like a child in a toy factory. "Oh, my word! This place is beau-ti-ful." The word came out in three distinct syllables.

Deanna felt a warm glow surge through her. It was the first time she and Spencer had entertained since renovating and redecorating the house. "I'll only take some of the credit because Marisol helped me select the furnishings."

Bethany slipped her arm through Damon's. "Darling, would you mind if I redecorate some of the rooms?"

Damon stared at his wife. "I told you the house is yours to do whatever you want with it."

"That does it," Bethany said. "I'm going to talk to Marisol."

Deanna led Damon to the bar, where Spencer stood with an associate from his firm. "What would you like to drink?"

Damon gave Prince his usual martini order, then nodded to Spencer when he turned to look at him. He extended his hand to the attorney. "Beautiful house."

Spencer shook the proffered hand. "Thanks. And thank you for coming." He turned to his associate. "Calvin, I don't know if you're familiar with Damon Paxton."

Calvin Graham held out his hand, his face flushed with color from his second drink in less than half an hour. "Who hasn't heard of Mr. Paxton? I'm honored to meet you, sir. Calvin Graham." The two men shook hands, exchanging the requisite greetings before Calvin walked away, leaving Damon with their host.

Damon's expression did not give away his revulsion for Spencer Tyson's irresponsible behavior. "Is there a place where we can talk in private?"

"Sure. Bring your drink," Spencer suggested when Prince placed Damon's martini on the bar with a cocktail napkin with the Chinese characters symbolizing good health.

Spencer stopped to tell Deanna he and Damon needed to talk, then led the way out of the ballroom and into the office, closing the door behind them. He indicated a leather chair for the lobbyist to sit, then took a matching one. "What would you like to talk about?"

Damon decided to be direct. "I was at the Victoria Sunday with my wife when you were going at it with Jenah Morris."

Spencer's Adam's apple bobbed up and down as he attempted to process what he'd heard. Slumping in the chair, he closed his eyes. "How much did you hear?"

"Enough to know that the lady has accused you of getting her pregnant."

He opened his eyes. "And just what do you intend to do with this information?"

Damon took a sip of the expertly prepared martini, then set it down on a glass coaster on a side table. "You think I'm telling you this to blackmail you?"

"I don't know," Spencer countered.

A sardonic grin touched Damon's mouth. "Regardless of what you may have heard about me, I'm not into blackmail. I don't want to say that I told you so, but I'm going to say it anyway. You may be a brilliant attorney, but you're a dumb son of a bitch when it comes to women. You have to think with this head." He tapped his temple. "Not the one between your legs."

"I don't need you lecturing me in my own home."

"Someone should've lectured you before you decide to pick up the wrong woman to sleep with *and* without protection. Yeah, I screwed around on my first wife, but I made certain those women had as much to lose as I did. Women like Jenah Morris are a dime a dozen, and you stooped to a new low when you took up with her."

Spencer agreed with Damon, but he wasn't about to let him know that. If they had been anywhere but in his home he would've told the older man exactly what he thought of him. Just because Deanna and Marisol had helped out his wife, that hadn't given Damon carte blanche to ingratiate himself into his life. Spencer believed the lobbyist was still smarting from him threatening to kick his ass for coming on to Deanna.

"I don't believe she's pregnant."

"You would know that for certain if you were fucking her with a rubber."

Spencer crossed his arms over his chest. "What's your stake in all of this, Paxton?"

"My wife likes your wife. In fact, Deanna and Marisol

McDonald are the only women who have befriended her since I married her. I love my wife and there isn't anything I wouldn't do to make certain she's happy. She was quite upset when she overheard your conversation with Ms. Morris. Her first reaction was to call Deanna and let her know you've been cheating on her."

Spencer nodded, and had managed not to visibly react to Bethany's reaction. He couldn't understand why women found the need to dime out men because of their intense dislike for the *other woman*. "Women will stick together."

"Not as well as the old boy's club," Damon countered.

"What are you talking about?" Spencer asked, sitting up straight.

"I'm going to help you out."

"Why?"

"Because I know you were breaking it off with Jenah when she dropped the bomb. I'm also indebted to Deanna and Marisol for rescuing Bethany when she had an emotional meltdown. Bethany had been through enough, and I've sworn an oath to protect her and my children. I'm going to do you a favor this one time, but if you fuck up again, then you're on your own."

Spencer stared at Damon, baffled. He didn't know what game Paxton was playing, but whatever it was he wanted no part of it. People like the power broker never did anything for nothing. And he didn't believe he was willing to help him with this dilemma because Deanna had salvaged what was left of his wife's debauched reputation. All of D.C. had buzzed about the blonde television reporter who'd set her sights on a man twenty years her senior and seduced him away from his wife and young child. If Damon hadn't been who he was, his name would've been left off every party and fundraiser list in the nation's capital. But Damon's sphere of influence made him an important ally. He was the go-to guy when individuals, companies and corporations wanted elected officials to tack on pork for their districts.

"What do you intend to do?" he asked.

"I can get rid of your problem."

Throwing back his head, Spencer laughed loudly. "What are you going to do? Have her end up dead in the woods?"

A deep flush suffused Damon's face. "I don't kill people, Tyson. What I can do is get someone to take care of your problem."

"What do you get out of it, Paxton? My firstborn?"

"I'll take godfather and friendship," Damon said flippantly.

"You're kidding."

"Do I look like I'm kidding, Tyson? I told you before that Bethany considers Deanna her friend, and I'd like to keep it that way. And there's no reason why we can't get together as couples every once in a while. By the way, do you golf?"

Spencer smiled for the first time since Damon walked into his home. "Not enough."

Crossing one leg over the other, Damon also smiled. "I belong to a very nice private country club near Falls Church. It has a wonderful nine-hole course. I'd love to invite you as my guest. And if you like the place, then I'll sponsor you to become a member. But not until we take care of your problem."

It took seconds for Spencer to realize Damon could take care of Jenah in a way that would never be traced back to him. What he did do was draw the line when it came to assault and murder.

"Do it, but I don't want her beat up."

Lowering his leg, Damon leaned forward and shook Spencer's hand. "Consider it done, and you won't have to concern yourself with dealing with the lady. It may take a couple of weeks, but my people will make certain once she leaves D.C. for Pittsburgh she won't come back."

Spencer stood up. "I need a drink."

The two men retreated to the ballroom where the noise level had escalated appreciably with the arrival of more invitees. Spencer stood with Deanna, playing the consummate host as he thanked them for coming. He made certain everyone had something to drink and eat as waiters walked around with trays of sushi, Thai chicken on skewers and dim sum.

The sound of soft jazz flowed through speakers as he circulated among the small crowd, his step lighter than it had been in days. Spencer knew he had no choice but to trust Damon Paxton to take care of Jenah. If she'd pretended to be pregnant, then there was no doubt Damon's people would report back to him. But if she was, then he didn't want to imagine how they would take care of it.

Spencer had told Damon that he didn't want Jenah to come to any physical harm, because he didn't want a police investigation traced back to him. After all, he had indirectly threatened her.

He smiled with Deanna's approach. Reaching for her hand, he placed a kiss on her palm. "It looks as if everyone's having a good time."

"Good food, wonderful drinks and people looking to have fun is the perfect combination for a good time," Deanna whispered in his ear. "I notice you and Damon have gotten rather buddy-buddy."

"He invited me to go golfing with him."

Deanna's arched eyebrows lifted slightly with his disclosure. "Where are you golfing?"

"He belongs to a private country club near Falls Church. He claims if I like it, then he'll sponsor me to become a member."

"Are you sure you're going to have time to play golf?"

"I'll make time. It's been a while since that set of clubs you gave me for my thirty-fifth birthday have been out of the closet."

Deanna rolled her eyes upward. "I'll believe it when I see it. I'm glad you're hitting it off with Damon, because now you'll make time for a little R & R."

Looping an arm around her waist, Spencer pulled her closer. "I don't need Paxton for R & R. That's why I have you, Dee. The only time I'm completely relaxed is when I'm with you."

She giggled softly "You keep coming home early and wearing me out I think I'm going to have make a reservation to go to St. Croix earlier than planned."

Spencer pressed his mouth to her ear. "When are you expecting your period?"

"Not for another three weeks."

"I hope it doesn't come. Now that I've wrapped my head around becoming a daddy I can't wait for you to tell me you're pregnant."

Deanna brushed her mouth over his. "It's going to happen, baby. If not next month, then the month after." She knew it would take a couple of cycles for her body to rid itself completely of the properties in the Pill that prevented conception. Deanna refused to become like Marisol, working herself into a state of anxiety if she didn't get pregnant right away. She'd waited eight years, and she would give herself until the end of the year before considering other options.

The elevator door opened and Dennis Wen exited, pushing a cart with a number of serving trays from which wafted the most delicious smells. "Please turn up the lighting, Spencer. It's time for dinner."

Members of the waitstaff stood behind the serving station,

ready to serve those who'd lined up to select what they wanted from the buffet. Another waiter filled water and wine glasses, while another poured hot sake into tiny cups. A pair of chopsticks was positioned beside the knives and forks at each place setting.

Spencer indicated what he wanted on a plate for Deanna, then set it down in front of her when she sat at one end of the table. He fixed a plate for himself, then sat at the opposite facing her. He smiled at those sitting around the table.

"I know I speak for Deanna when I say that I want to thank you for coming out tonight. After we eat and drink I hope you'll stay long enough to relax before we top off the evening with some music and dancing. Those unable to make it home under their own stead are welcome to spend the night. The only other thing I'm going to say is—enjoy!"

Deanna winked across the length of the table at her husband, and she wasn't disappointed when he returned the wink. A month ago she'd felt as if she had been losing her husband, but something or someone had changed him. And for that she was eternally grateful.

Chapter Twenty-Six

Marisol peered out the oval window of the Lear jet when it began to descend; she felt a lump in her throat when she saw the landscape of Puerto Rico come into view. She hadn't told her relatives she was coming because she'd wanted to surprise them, but that wouldn't happen until after she concluded her business with Wesley.

Glancing across the aisle, she stared at the man who disturbed her more than she wanted. There were times she'd caught him staring at her, and it made her feel uneasy. The startling blue eyes, shocking white cropped hair contrasting against his tanned tawny-brown face had women craning their necks to stare at him when they emerged from the limo at a section of the airport where private jets sat on the tarmac.

Marisol wasn't certain whether they'd recognized him as a congressman from Missouri or stared because he was drop-dead gorgeous. He was dressed for the tropical weather: white linen shirt, matching walking shorts and deck shoes.

Bryce had been unusually withdrawn when she'd gotten up

earlier that morning. He'd showered, shaved and was cloistered in his office when the doorbell rang and she'd opened the door to find a liveried driver on the other side. By the time the man had taken her bags and stored them in the trunk of the limo, she'd knocked on his door, pushed it open and found Bryce lying on the sofa with an arm thrown over his face.

When she'd asked him if he hadn't been feeling well, his response had been that he was going to miss her. She'd kissed him passionately, promising to call him every day, then turned and walked out of the house to the waiting car idling at the curb. Within minutes of the driver pulling up in front of Wesley's town house the front door opened and he emerged carrying a Pullman with a garment bag slung over his shoulder. He'd gotten into the car beside her, smiled and then held her hand during the ride to the airport.

Once they were on board the sleek aircraft, Wesley hadn't sat with her, but across the aisle. They were the only passengers, and the two flight attendants were at their beck and call. An onboard chef served an exquisite breakfast of eggs Benedict, scones with clotted cream, mimosas and Blue Mountain Jamaican coffee. After breakfast, she'd reclined her seat and gone to sleep, unaware that when Wesley reclined his seat it wasn't to go to sleep, but to stare at her.

There was a crackling noise before the pilot's voice came through the speakers. "It's ten-eighteen, and Ponce's temperature is now eighty-two degrees Fahrenheit. It is sunny with no report of rain. We should be on the ground in another twenty minutes. I hope you enjoyed your flight."

Wesley came over to sit beside her. "How are you feeling?"

She smiled even though she felt as if he was close, much too close for her to draw a normal breath. "Good. I managed to catch a few winks."

Wesley buckled his seat belt. "You fell asleep right after breakfast."

"It was probably the mimosa. Champagne always makes me sleepy." Her dark eyes met a pair of clear blue ones. "Flying down here on a private jet will definitely make it difficult for me whenever I have to take a commercial carrier."

"How do you fly?"

"Usually I prefer business class when I'm not able to fly first class."

"Do you pay your own travel expenses?"

Marisol nodded. "I do, but the costs are always factored into my fees."

"How do you determine what furnishings go into a particular room?"

"Who decorated your condo?" she asked, answering his question with one of her own.

"It was the widow of the former owner. She decided to rent it after her husband passed away. She moved to Florida to be close to her daughter and grandchildren. Unfortunately she fell and fractured her hip, and eventually had to be confined to a skilled nursing facility. When her children put the property up for sale I was given the opportunity to purchase it as they say for a song. And that included the furnishings. Fortunately for me, none of her children wanted to relocate to D.C."

"Do you have a house in St. Louis?"

"I live in a wing of my parents' house."

"Are you telling me that you never left home?"

"Muy gracioso," Wesley drawled in Spanish.

"I'm not trying to be funny, Wes. I just thought you would've had your own place where you could entertain your *dates*."

"What is it you really want to know about me?"

"Am I that obvious?" Marisol asked.

Wesley smiled. "Yes, you're very obvious. Ask away."

"Were you ever married?"

He smiled. "No."

"Why not?"

"Why do you think?"

Shifting slightly, Marisol turned to look directly at Wesley. "Perhaps you're not into women."

He gave her a long, penetrating stare. "I can assure you that I'm very much into women. It's just that I haven't met one who would make me consider marrying and having children."

"Are you currently dating someone?"

"Why do you want to know?"

"Curious."

"Curious or jealous?"

Marisol made a sucking sound with her tongue and teeth. "You wish."

"I do wish, Marisol. I wish every day that I could be Bryce McDonald and…"

"What?"

Wesley held up a hand. "Please let me finish, Marisol." She nodded. "As I was saying, if I were your husband I would never introduce you as 'my wife.' You would be you—Marisol Rivera, that is, if you'd elected to keep your maiden name. Or you would be Marisol Sheridan, not 'my wife' as if you were an inanimate object put up on display."

Marisol exhaled an inaudible sigh. "So you see me as a trophy wife?"

"You're as much a trophy wife as many other women in the D.C. political circle."

"No, Wes. You've got it wrong. I'm not your typical capital wife."

He smiled. "That's true. You're much more beautiful, and you deserve a man who not only appreciates your beauty but also your intelligence. You may have believed you married up, but it's the other way around. Bryce was the one who married up."

"Now you're talking smack. Have you forgotten that I'm the one who grew up in public housing?"

"It has nothing to do with where one grows up, or how much money you have in the bank. It's about character and inner strength. People like Bryce grow up with a certain sense of entitlement. They believe they can have any- and everything they want because anything and everyone has a price. When I came to your house for lunch I watched the two of you. Bryce didn't look at you as if he loved you."

"How did he look at me, Wes?"

"It was as if you were a rare artifact he'd bid on and won. Something he could put on and take off the shelf when-ever he wanted. And because he owned it, he did what he wanted with it. Please don't get me wrong. I don't think I would've been elected if it hadn't been for Bryce, but I've learned to separate business from personal. When it comes to personal, Bryce McDonald is not at the top of my list of favorite people."

"If that's the case, then why did you invite him to your Sunday brunch?"

"That was business. It was what I refer to as an appreciation gathering."

Marisol nodded. When Bryce had opened the gift Wesley had given him she was pleasantly surprised to discover that Wesley had given him an engraved solid gold pen. She also recalled her heartfelt conversation with Deanna when she'd finally come to the realization that Bryce *was* controlling her life. If it hadn't been for her career she probably would've become a clone of her mother-in-law. Cynthia had given up a career as an attorney to become her husband's social secretary.

She didn't know how Wesley had analyzed her marriage after seeing her and Bryce together for less than an hour, but Marisol knew he was spot-on with his assessment. To Bryce she was never Marisol, but "my wife." She always had to pass inspection before she and Bryce went out together. The only thing he couldn't control was her outspokenness. Initially, when they had met each other he had been somehow taken aback by her frankness. She had always been one to call a spade a spade. There were times when she'd attempted to censor what had come out of her mouth, but had found it hampered her ability to express herself. She was who she was, and Marisol couldn't and didn't want to change even if it meant not having any friends. And the only one she actually considered a friend was Deanna Tyson. Deanna was always there for her, and there wasn't anything she wouldn't do for Deanna. Her association with Bethany Paxton was still too new to consider her a BFF.

However, she felt a kinship with Bethany because of their humble beginnings. Bethany had struggled and worked hard not to repeat her mother's life, and Marisol had worked doubly hard not to repeat Pilar's when she did not become an unwed teenage mother. What she'd inherited from her mother was her drive to better herself. Pilar wasn't content to become the stereotypical welfare mother, sitting around waiting for a handout, but worked hard to earn enough money to support herself and her daughter.

"I am Bryce's wife and partner, not his possession."

"Believe whatever it is you want to believe," Wesley drawled.

"Do you mind if we change the subject?" Marisol asked.

"I don't want to, but I will if it makes you uncomfortable."

"It does."

Marisol didn't want to admit to Wesley that it had taken only one encounter with her and Bryce for him to see what she'd denied for far too long. What she couldn't and didn't want to accept was that she'd allowed her love for a man to redefine what she'd look like in public. If Wesley was able to see through the smoke screen, then who else saw it, too?

A crackling noise came through speakers throughout the aircraft, then the pilot's voice. "Attendants, please prepare the cabin for our descent."

Wesley and Marisol raised their seat backs as they stared out the window to watch the island come closer and closer as the jet banked sharply to the left, heading for the Ponce airport.

Marisol sat inches from Wesley in the rear of a late-model, air-conditioned sedan as it maneuvered in a southwest direction. The tropical heat had hit her like a blast furnace when they'd disembarked, and she was grateful she'd made the decision to change out of her jeans, T and running shoes and into a rose-pink sundress with spaghetti straps crisscrossing her bared back and matching sandals half an hour into the flight.

"Can we stop in Old San Juan before we return to the mainland? I'd like to do some shopping," she asked Wesley.

Stretching out his legs as far as the seat in front of him would allow, Wesley stared at Marisol's delicate profile. He knew he'd struck a raw nerve when he'd brought up how he'd viewed her relationship with her husband. He also knew he had no right to ingratiate himself into her marriage, but the floodgates had opened and the words had come out unbidden.

Wesley had said what he said not to insult Marisol or pass judgment but to make her aware of what was so obvious to him. And he'd wondered how many others had noticed what was apparent within seconds of Bryce introducing Marisol as "my wife."

She'd asked him why he hadn't married and he'd told her the truth. He hadn't met the woman who would make him seriously consider changing his marital status—until now. *She* was that woman who would make him want her as his wife and the mother of his children. How ironic, he mused. The woman with whom he'd found himself so enthralled was married to a man who'd been instrumental in getting him elected to an office where he had been able to effect change for his constituents—some of whom lived in an outlying district with higher than average unemployment.

Placing his hand over hers, Wesley gently squeezed her fingers. "Of course."

Marisol turned to look at Wesley for the first time since they'd deplaned, smiling. "Thank you."

"If you want we can—" The chiming of Marisol's cell phone interrupted him.

Marisol pulled her hand from Wesley's, opened her tote and retrieved her phone. "Hello."

"Marisol, this is Bethany."

She smiled. "Hey, girlfriend. How are you?"

"I'm real good. I've been calling your office leaving messages on your voice mail. When you didn't call me back I got in touch with Bryce, who told me you were out of the country. I told him I'd misplaced the number to your cell, and he gave it to me. I'm saying all that to ask if you're going to be available next week for lunch at my place."

"I'm not going to be available until the end of the month."

"Where are you? Your voice is fading in and out."

"I'm in Ponce."

"As in Puerto Rico?"

She laughed. "The one and only."

"Are you on vacation?"

"No. I'm here on business."

"Don't forget to get in a little pleasure," Bethany teased. "Damon and I went to San Juan six months after we were married, and I don't think I got more than three hours of sleep between hanging out in the clubs at night and shopping during the day."

"I doubt whether we'll have time to visit a club, but I'll probably do a little shopping before I come back."

"We?"

"Wesley and I."

"Wesley Sheridan?"

"Yeah."

"Call when you get back and I'll set a date when we can get together. I'm going to hang up because your voice is fading again."

"*Adiós,* Bethany." Marisol turned off her phone and dropped it into her tote. "I keep forgetting how beautiful this island is," she said after a comfortable silence.

"I never forget," Wesley said. "It's the perfect mix of old and new, primordial and emerging. Although the interior of the house is ultramodern, the overall architecture is reminiscent of Old San Juan. Once you see it you'll know why I decided to buy vacation property here instead of somewhere else in the Caribbean."

"I wouldn't buy vacation property here because I'd never get a chance to relax. Even if I bought a condo in San Juan, if any of my relatives got wind that I was on the island they would harass me. I'd opt for St. Thomas or the Dominican Republic."

Dropping an arm over her shoulders, Wesley pulled her to lean against him. She went stiff for several seconds, then relaxed. "So you've never come here incognito?"

"No, because it would never work. Although my relatives live on the Caribbean side of the island there is always someone somewhere who would recognize me and *chisme* spreads across the island faster than a wildfire."

Lowering his head, Wesley buried his face in the raven curls, wishing he could either turn back the clock where he could've met Marisol before she'd married Bryce or fast-forwarded the clock to where he'd entered politics in his twenties instead of his thirties.

He wanted to ask Marisol if her relatives would disapprove of her living with a man who wasn't her husband while on the island. Although they would sleep under the same roof, they wouldn't sleep in the same bed.

Chapter Twenty-Seven

"*Despiértese, querida. Estamos aquí.* Wake up, Marisol," Wesley repeated, this time in English.

"I'm not sleeping," she said, not opening her eyes.

He sat up straight. "You've been feigning sleep for the past two hours?"

"I was resting my eyes while enjoying having you as a body pillow."

"Perhaps one day you'll return the favor."

Marisol opened her eyes, easing out of Wesley comforting embrace. She hadn't lied. She'd enjoyed his warmth, the lean hardness of his body and the intoxicating scent of his masculine cologne. The driver stopped at a manned booth in front of a set of towering wrought-iron gates.

"I doubt if I'll be able to support your weight, but I promise to give you the best massage you've ever had."

Attractive lines fanned out around Wesley's eyes when he smiled, his gaze caressing the mouth he wanted to kiss. "I'm going to hold you to that promise."

He pressed a button on a remote device and the wrought-iron gates opened. The driver maneuvered slowly over a metal plate and into the cobblestone courtyard, the gates automatically closing behind them. Wesley's condo was one of four, each built on a one-acre lot. His was farthest from the entrance.

When Marisol stepped out of the car she stared up the two-story sand-colored stucco house with a red-tiled roof, second-story wrought-iron balconies and casement windows. *"Es magnífico."*

Wesley rested his hand on the nape of her neck. "It will be even more magnificent after you decorate it." He punched another button on the remote device and a green light on the door handle buzzed softly. He walked into the entryway, then stood off to the side to watch Marisol's reaction. A hint of a smile parted his lips when her jaw dropped and mouth gaped.

Marisol tilted her chin, staring up at the high-ceiling entry rising upward to the second floor. High, wood-beamed ceilings would allow for hot air to rise above the terra-cotta floor. She walked in, her practiced eye surveying the vastness of the living room. Light from a clerestory window illuminated the open expanse of the dining room.

"May I do a walk-through?"

"Of course. Remember, this is going to be your home for the next two weeks," Wesley reminded her.

"It's going to take a while for me to map out each room as a whole, but I just want to get an idea of the dimensions I'll be working with."

"After you complete your walk-through, I'll show you the exterior," Wesley promised.

Marisol climbed the circular staircase to the second floor as cool air flowed from ceiling vents. The condo had been constructed with a central heating and cooling system, although she doubted whether Wesley would ever have to use the heat.

Three large bedrooms with French doors opening out onto balconies had en suite baths that boasted spectacular ocean views. There was a California-king bed in the master bedroom. There was enough space in the room for a triple dresser, armoire and a dressing area with an armchair. Another open space that could be used for a living/dining area or double as a media center overlooked the courtyard. She noticed the fountain in the middle of the courtyard for the first time. A stainless-steel eat-in kitchen and half-bath rounded out the second floor. Walk-in closets and decorative ceiling fans had been installed in all the bedrooms.

Retracing her steps, Marisol returned to the first floor and discovered two large bedrooms—one that could be used for a home office or library. There were ceiling fans and spacious walk-in closets and en suite baths in these rooms, too. She smiled when she walked into the gourmet kitchen to find a glass-covered rattan patio table with four chairs in the breakfast nook.

Wesley was on his cell, talking to someone in Spanish. Not only was he fluent, but his accent was flawless; it was as if Spanish instead of English was his first language. She nodded when he smiled and winked at her. Deanna had referred to him as a "silver fox," while Marisol thought of him as *rico suave.* All of his mannerisms were practiced, precise. It was as if he'd spent hours in the mirror learning how to sit elegantly, and how to angle his head to make it appear as if he was listening intently to every word that came out of the other person's mouth. Then there were his stares—longing, soulful and lusting. And for all her bravado and outspokenness, Marisol was beginning to feel uncomfortable around Wesley.

For a girl who'd grown up in a tough neighborhood where she had to prove she wasn't going to be bullied or taken advantage of by other girls *and* boys, Marisol Pilar Rivera-McDonald was not afraid of Wesley Sheridan but of her own response to him.

Seeing Wesley on the phone was a reminder that she hadn't called Bryce to let him know she'd arrived safely. She retrieved her tote and hit speed dial for her husband's office phone. It rang twice before he picked up.

"What's up, Mari?"

"What's up?" she repeated.

"I have someone on the other line."

"I just called to let you know I got here."

"Have fun. I'll call you later."

She held the phone to ear before realizing Bryce had abruptly hung up on her. Pressing a button, Marisol replaced the phone in the oversize leather tote. An expression of confusion stole across her features as she attempted to process what had just happened. It was the first time since she and Bryce were engaged that he hadn't ended a call with an endearment.

Shaking her head as if to rid her mind of uneasiness and suspicion, Marisol walked back into the kitchen, nearly colliding with Wesley. His hands went to her upper arms, holding her until she'd regained her balance.

"Sorry, Wes."

"Are you all right?"

"I'm fine."

"You don't look fine."

Her eyes narrowed. "What are you talking about?"

Wesley dropped his hands. "You look as if you're ready to rip someone's head off."

Marisol forced a smile she didn't feel. She knew she couldn't afford to agonize over Bryce because it would increase her stress level and she would end up with a headache. Thankfully, she hadn't had one in nearly three weeks.

She patted Wesley's shoulder. "Don't worry. I plan to leave your head intact."

Wesley did smile. "That's good to know," he said, then sobered. "I just called a *tienda de ultramarinos* and ordered enough groceries to last us for at least a week. The days I don't cook we'll eat out."

"Aren't you fancy," Marisol teased. "You say *tienda de ultramarinos* and I say bodega."

"But isn't a bodega more like a storeroom?"

"No, no, Papi," she teased. "To me a bodega is like a super Walmart. It has everything from pots to magazines and, of course, food." She'd affected an accent while wagging her finger, and Wesley laughed so hard he nearly lost his breath.

"What am I going to do with you, Mami?" he asked, once he'd recovered from his laughing jag.

"I don't know, Papi. I will think of something. I'm ready to see outside."

They left the house through a door off the kitchen, stepping out onto a loggia with an outdoor kitchen. Two cushioned chaises made it the perfect spot to begin or end the day.

Wesley took a step, bringing him inches from Marisol. "I'm going to alternate sleeping here and on an inflatable mattress."

Marisol stared him over her shoulder. "No, Wes. You're not going to sleep on those things," she said, pointing at the chaises.

"It wouldn't be the first time I've slept on them. One night when I'd had one too many mojitos I not only slept out here, but I liked it so much I did it the next night."

"I can't put you out of your bedroom. I'll sleep on the inflatable mattress," Marisol volunteered.

"That won't do. You're a guest in my house so you must sleep in the bedroom."

"No, no, no!"

"*¡Sí, sí, sí!*" Wesley countered. "If you'd looked into the closets in each of the bedrooms you would've seen inflatable mattresses. Although you're the first person to come here to stay, I still didn't want to be caught unprepared in case my parents or my sisters came down with their kids. I didn't buy this place for myself, but for my nieces and nephews. Both my sisters are teachers and they usually vacation together. This is the perfect spot for them to come down during school vacations to hang out on the beach."

"Do you want to childproof the house?"

Wesley shook his head. "No. I'd like you to give it a spa or resort look. I'd want the furniture to be functional, but inviting."

"How many children do they have between them?"

"Four. Taryn has two boys ages six and four, and Jennifer has a set of three-year-old twin girls." He held up his hands. "And before you say anything, I'll tell you."

Marisol affected a sexy moue, bringing Wesley gaze to linger on her mouth. "What makes you think I was going to say anything?"

His forefinger touched her left eyebrow. "This goes up just a fraction before you ask a question."

Marisol's fingers circled his wrist, pulling his hand away from her face. "You see a lot, don't you?"

Wesley took a step until they were inches apart. "I see what I want to see, Marisol. I see an incredibly beautiful, talented woman who is in love with life. You have a special *fuego* I find intoxicating. A fire I—"

"Stop it, Wes."

"Stop what, Marisol? Stop telling you not what you want to hear but what you need to hear? Bryce doesn't deserve you."

"And you do?"

The nostrils of Wesley's thin nose flared slightly. "The only thing I'm going to admit to is that I wouldn't treat you as if you were something I bid on and won at an auction. You're nothing more to him than a priceless piece of art or a jewel he'd happened to inherit. What man who loves a woman enough to marry her introduces her as 'my wife'? You have a name. And it is Marisol, not 'my wife.'"

"Don't you think maybe I should take some of the blame for that?"

"Why, Marisol?"

"Because I've allowed it to go on instead of stopping him."

Wesley shook his head. "No, *querida*. I'm not going to let you get out of it by accepting blame for someone else's inadequacies. Bryce McDonald is what I think of as a golden boy. He was born into wealth, never had to concern himself with what college he wanted to attend because Daddy and Grandpa would make it happen by pulling out their checkbooks. Fortunately for *your husband* he has other assets. Men and women find him attractive, and he has an uncanny perception to identify an opponent's weakness and use it against him."

Marisol stared wordlessly at Wesley, her breath catching in her throat. It was as if her brain had shut down within seconds of him calling her *querida,* or *darling.* The word had slipped like an involuntary reflex.

"Did you invite me to come to Puerto Rico to try and seduce me, Wesley?"

He smiled. "Not intentionally."

Both eyebrows lifted. "Not intentionally? But you do admit that you'd like to seduce me?"

"The only thing I'm going to admit is that I wish I'd met you before Bryce McDonald did. I would never treat you with so little respect."

"That's where you're wrong, Wes. I'd never let Bryce or any man disrespect me."

"That's where you are wrong, Marisol. You are Bryce McDonald's beautiful little *muñeca, una muñeca* he takes out and puts on display for other men to see how lucky he is to have you. Close your mouth, *querida*," he cautioned when her jaw dropped again. "I'm saying all these things not to come between you and your husband but—"

"You could've fooled me," Marisol countered.

"The problem is you're not willing to accept the truth," Wesley retorted.

Marisol wanted to tell Wesley that she knew the truth and he was right. She was Bryce's doll; all he was concerned with whenever they went out together as a couple was how she looked. He so wanted to refute his mother's assessment that she was no more than a homeless ragamuffin that he'd spent a small fortune on haute couture and jewelry for her.

Walking over to the chaise, she flopped down on it. Crossing her sandaled feet at the ankles, Marisol stared at the deep rose-pink color on her toes before shifting her gaze to a copse of palm trees. She wondered how much Wesley had surmised from sitting at her table sharing lunch with her and Bryce, or how much he'd uncovered by talking to her husband. If women talked, baring their souls to one another, then it probably was no different with men.

Although she'd never kept track of Bryce's clients or where he was flying off to, she had to know that he and Wesley had spent an inordinate amount of time together in order for him to strategize the congressman's campaign.

"Bryce told you about me, didn't he?"

Wesley walked over and sat on the chaise next to Marisol's. Reaching across the small space separating them, he took her hand, threading their fingers together. "Yes. He told me how he'd met you, how you wouldn't sleep with him until he put a ring on your finger. He wasn't very happy about that because somehow he felt you'd used your body as a bargaining chip. It was apparent his mother wasn't too happy that he'd wanted to marry a Latina, but he was determined to marry you."

Marisol closed her eyes as a cold chill swept over her body. At that point she felt as if she were in the Arctic Circle instead of in the Caribbean. "What else did he tell you, Wesley?"

When Wesley saw her pained expression he regretted having said anything to Marisol about her relationship with his campaign strategist. "I've already said too much."

Sitting up and swinging her legs over the chaise, Marisol practically launched herself at Wesley, landing on his chest. Her eyes narrowed like a cat. "You opened the door, so you'd better let me in, Wesley, or I'm going to call one of my relatives to come and drive me to Ponce where I'll book a flight back to D.C. Then, I'm going to spill my guts to Bryce about everything you've told me about my husband. What's it going to be, Congressman Sheridan?" Pushing into a sitting position, she averted her face.

"Thou shalt not covet thy neighbor's house, thou shalt not covet they neighbor's wife…"

"Why are you quoting the tenth commandment to me?" Marisol whispered.

"Because I've committed a sin."

"What sin, Wes?"

"I'm coveting another man's wife. After I'd asked Bryce to become my campaign strategist we spent a lot of time together. If he was going to take me on as a candidate, I had to tell him everything about myself so he wouldn't be surprised if my opponent uncovered some long-lost secret that might spark a scandal. I gave him the names of every woman I'd slept with, the few with whom I'd had long-term relationships and if I'd ever been involved with men, prostitutes or had engaged in a threesome."

"Did you?"

Wesley also sat up, leaning close enough to Marisol to smell the subtle floral scent clinging to her hair and skin. "No. I've always been one-on-one with women. Very discerning women."

"So discerning or discriminating that you want to sleep with me?"

"Would you prefer I lie, *querida?*"

"I'm not your love *or* your darling, so please stop calling me that. I'm a woman you hired to decorate your house. I can't be anything more to you than that."

A deafening silence followed Marisol's statement. She found Wesley very attractive, but not so much so she'd break her vow to remain a faithful wife. She had no way of knowing if Bryce was a faithful husband, and she didn't want to know if he hadn't been. Her mother-in-law had revealed that Bryce had slept with a lot of women before he'd married her, so Marisol had hoped he'd had his fill of sleeping with other women.

What she had insisted on before sleeping with Bryce was that he get tested for STDs. He'd become angry, walking away, and Marisol didn't hear from him in more than two weeks. They'd reunited when he returned, agreeing to take the test. She also agreed to be tested at the same time and when the results came back, both were negative.

Marisol had lost track of the number of women in her old neighborhood who had been affected with HIV because their sexual partners hadn't wanted to use protection. Some were still living with the disease while too many others had died. Just like she hadn't wanted to become a single mother, she also hadn't wanted to come down with a terminal disease.

The past two weeks had been one of discovery. Cynthia McDonald had disclosed the sordid events in Bryce's life before she'd married him, and Wesley had just revealed Bryce's resenting her insistence that she not sleep with him without a promise of commitment. He'd proposed, given her a ring and she'd given him her virginity. And from her vantage point Marisol realized Bryce had gotten the better deal.

Chapter Twenty-Eight

"Mrs. Tyson."

"Mr. Douglas. What took you so long to call me back?"

A deep chuckle came through the speaker feature. When Deanna saw the word *private* on her cell's display, she'd decided to use the feature and placed a small handheld tape recorder beside the phone to record the conversation. It if hadn't been Richard Douglas, then she wouldn't have recorded the call.

"Are you saying that you missed me?"

"Does anyone miss a pit viper?"

"Careful, Mrs. Tyson. I don't like insults."

Deanna closed her eyes, counting slowly to ten. She'd tried remembering all she had to do if her blackmailer called her again, and right now her mind was a complete blank. And it wasn't as if she could tell the man to call her back while she talked to Marisol, because her friend was in Puerto Rico with Wesley Sheridan. Then she remembered what Marisol's friend John had told her.

"What do you want, Mr. Douglas?"

"You know what I want."

"Say it. Tell me exactly what you want."

"I want you to give a few hours of your time. It can be in the morning or afternoon. I know it wouldn't be easy explaining to your husband why you'd decided not to come home."

"That's where you're wrong. I have events that take me away from home overnight."

"Do you have me on speaker, Mrs. Tyson?"

Deanna was going to lie, but didn't want to spook the man. She had to get enough evidence on him if she hoped to prove him guilty of raping her. "Yes, I do. I need both hands because I'm putting labels on invitations. They have to go into today's mail. If it bothers you, then I'll turn it off." What he didn't know was that she'd gotten up earlier than usual to address envelopes for a *quinceañera*.

"It's okay. Leave it on. Now, back to business. Are you willing to meet with me?"

"Can we talk about this some other time?"

"When?"

"Call me back in half an hour. I really have to get these invitations ready for the mailman, who's going to come here before eleven."

"I'll call you back at eleven."

Deanna's hands were shaking when she ended the call and turned off the recorder. It had happened as John predicted. But the mysterious man had also promised he would catch Richard Douglas in his own trap.

She wished she'd had more invitations to address, or a client or vendor she could talk to in order to make the thirty minutes seem more like three minutes. So she did the next best thing: she paced the floor while watching the clock on the fireplace mantel. At exactly eleven her cell rang again. This time she knew she didn't have the excuse of needing both hands, and that meant she couldn't activate the speaker.

Deanna answered the phone. "Hello."

"Did you finish addressing your envelopes?"

"Yes."

"Did the postman come by to get them?"

"Not yet."

"Thank you for not lying, because I've been sitting in my car in front of your house and so far I haven't seen a mail truck."

"He'll be around. Now I want you to stop using up my cell phone minutes. And I'm not going to talk about what you want on my phone."

"Where do you want to talk?"

"What if you meet in DuPont Circle?"

"Sorry, Mrs. Tyson. I'd rather meet you at the hotel."

"Which hotel?"

"Why, at our favorite little rendezvous."

"And that is?" she asked, stalling for time.

"The Brandon-Phillips, of course. Let me know when you're free and I'll meet you there."

Deanna simulated turning pages in her planner. "I have several meetings with prospective clients and three events this week. Give me your number and I'll call you back."

"I can't do that, Mrs. Tyson. I'll have to call you. And try to make it before the end of the month, because I'm in the States on a sixty-day visa."

Deanna smiled. The man had just given her information she could pass along to John. "Let me see if I can shuffle my schedule to accommodate you. Call me back Friday morning."

"Before or after your husband leaves for work?"

"It doesn't matter. My husband never answers my cell or gets into my business." She hung up without giving him a chance to say anything else, slipping the phone into the back pocket of her jeans. The familiar ring of the doorbell echoed throughout the house. Walking over to an intercom, she pressed a button. "Yes."

"It's Richie. I'm here to pick up your mail."

"I'll be right down."

Deanna took the elevator to the first floor instead of the staircase. When she opened the door, her gaze went past her postman to a black two-door sedan with tinted windows parked in front of her neighbor's house. It took every ounce of self-control not to blurt out *gotcha!* Most of the houses on her street, including her own, were equipped with security cameras after a numbers of cars had been vandalized. First it was flattened tires, then shattered windshields. It was only after more than a dozen cars were spattered with paint that the residents decided it was time to install cameras. The police managed to catch two of the vandals when they were patrolling the area in unmarked cars.

Reaching for the shopping bags with the invitations, she handed them to Richie. "Thank you."

"Have a good day, Mrs. Tyson."

She smiled at the man who'd had the same route for years. He'd told her he'd bought a little bungalow in the Keys, but was waiting for his wife to retire from her nursing position at a local hospital before filing for retirement.

"You, too."

Waiting for the postal worker to return to his truck, Deanna closed and locked the door. Taking the phone from her pocket, she sat on a chair in the entry and scrolled to her contacts. She tapped the number for John.

"Talk to me, Deanna."

She told him everything, including the car parked several feet from her house and Richard Douglas's claim that he was in the country on a sixty-day visa. John asked her for the name of the security company monitoring the cameras and Deanna gave him the password that would permit him to view the footage from her account.

"I'll call you back tomorrow to let you know when you should have another liaison with your admirer."

"Very funny," she sneered.

"I'm sorry. Keep your phone charged. I'll call you tomorrow."

"Thank you, John."

"There's no need to thank me. I've sworn an oath to protect the good citizens of the United States of America. Later, Deanna."

"Later, John."

Deanna clamped a hand over her mouth to keep from screaming. How had a single lapse in judgment ended up with her getting involved in a scenario that was better played out in a Lifetime movie?

Lowering her hand, she clenched her teeth and let out a muffled sound. This was one time when she needed to talk to Marisol, but she was thousands of miles from D.C. If it hadn't been so early or if she wasn't trying to get pregnant she definitely would've had a good strong drink.

She'd gripped her cell so tightly that it left an imprint on her palm. Easing her grip, she called Bethany. She wasn't Marisol, but she was someone who could help her take her mind off her dilemma.

Bethany locked the door to her office, turned on the netbook, went online and pulled up her blog. There were three comments since yesterday and one new comment today.

Katie—4/18: I'm really mad at you, Insider, for teasing me. Can't you give us a hint as to the initials of the member of Congress whose aide is working after hours with another woman's husband?

Bethany typed: The Insider can't do that. I promised hubby I wouldn't say anything, but blogging is typing, not talking.

Roger—4/18: I can't stand your fake-ass. You've got to be a queen looking for attention because you are always talking about hubby. Bee-yotch you wish you had a husband.

Insider: Roger please let me reassure you that I am a queen, but one with real T & As plus the plumbing. If you can't be nice, then this blog isn't for you.

Heather—4/18: I really like your blog. Can't you give us the initials of the aide?

Insider: Double D. Hint: It could be her name or her bra size):

Winnie—4/19: I love the "Cheaters" column in the *Dish*. Why don't they run a contest and see who can come up with the most names of cheaters in D.C.

Insider: I wouldn't want to touch that with a ten-foot pole. I eschew lawsuits involving libel and slander, but more than that I don't want to end up in the Potomac wearing cement boots when I much prefer Prada, Christian Louboutin and Chanel footwear.

Bethany turned off the netbook and hid it in a canvas tote in the back of the closet where she stored magazines and computer supplies. She unlocked the door, then booted up the family computer and went online to check her email.

She was surprised to find an email from one of her sisters. Mary-Beth's loving husband had run off with the town tramp, leaving her almost destitute. She hated to ask, but she wanted Bethany to send her money because she was two months behind in paying her mortgage.

"How dumb do you think I am, Mary-Beth?" she whispered aloud. Her sister's husband was too lazy to make love to his wife, so she doubted he would take up with another woman. Most times it was Mary who worked overtime because Hank was always losing his job because he couldn't get up in the morning.

Reaching for the telephone receiver, she blocked her number before dialing her sister's. Hank answered the call. "Hey, brother. How y'all doin'?"

"Is that you, Bethany?"

"Sho is," she said, lapsing into dialect. "What you up to?"

"Nothin' much. I'm waiting for old man Winthrop to call me to help him haul some lumber for the new addition to the high school."

"That's so nice," she said facetiously. "Where's Mary-Beth?"

"She over at the drugstore putting in a few hours so we can make ends meet."

"You could make ends meet if you got up off your lazy ass long enough to hold down a job."

"Jest you hold on a minute, Beth. You got no call to talk to me like that."

"I'll talk to you any way I want if it involves blood. And you ain't my blood. My sister emailed me asking for money because she says you're behind in your mortgage."

"We is, but…"

"But nothing, Hank. My sister lied, saying you'd run off because she still can't admit that you're a piece of shit when it comes to taking care of your family. You tell Mary-Beth to call me, because I'm not going to answer another email from her. I really don't give a damn about you, but Mary-Beth is my sister and I'm aunt to your kids. Don't forget to tell her, Hank. Because if I have to come to Alabama it will be to move my sister and my nieces and nephews to Virginia."

"Mary will never leave me."

"Keep believing that, Hank."

"I could never stand your uppity ass."

"That's because you tried getting next to this uppity ass. Once I tell my sister what your crooked dick looks like she will get rid of your lazy ass."

"Dream on, bitch! Mary won't believe you and she ain't never leaving me."

"That may be true, but tell her I'm not sending her one penny as long as she's with you."

Bethany's face was beet-red when she slammed down the receiver. She wasn't as angry with Hank as she was with Mary-Beth. Did her sister think she would just write a check and send it to her without checking to see if Hank had actually left Parker Corners?

Shaking her head as if to banish the conversation with Hank, Bethany leaned back in the office chair and read the other emails. Writing the column and the blog had kept her sane, and Nate's *Daily Dish* had become a much-gossiped-about tabloid. Circulation had increased by a few thousand in about a month. Advertisers were waiting online to buy space in the biweekly. In addition to the "Fact or Fiction, Real or Rumor" column, Nate had added another he called "Cheaters."

"Cheaters" was scathing and inflammatory. Nate had sources in the Senate and in the House that gave him updates on who was doing who and what. And without actually naming names, Nate was able to skew the truth enough to avoid being sued.

Bethany had promised Damon and herself that she wouldn't out her friends, but Jenah Morris deserved to get what she got for her chicanery. It was one thing to sleep with a married man, but to deliberately get pregnant with the hope he would leave his wife was despicable.

Not only was Bethany taking oral contraceptives when she'd slept with Damon, but she'd also insisted he wear a condom. Damon had revealed he hadn't slept with Jean in years, but there was always the possibility that they would reconcile. Bethany may have been young, but she wasn't stupid. She hadn't believed Damon was in love with her until after they'd married.

She wanted to ask Damon about Spencer and Jenah but didn't want rouse his suspicion. How could a married man approaching middle age fall into the world's oldest trap by having unprotected sex? Bethany didn't feel as sorry for Spencer as she did for Deanna, praying her friend would never know of her husband's duplicity. Deanna had admitted to sleeping with another man, but it couldn't be construed as cheating.

Her cell rang, and peering over at the display she saw Tyson Planners on the display. "Hey, Deanna. What's up, girl?"

"Are you busy?"

"Not really. Why?"

"I want to get out the house for lunch, but I don't want to eat alone."

"Why don't you come here? I'll fix something light and we can relax while we eat."

"Are you certain you don't mind cooking?"

"Of course not. You have my address, so come on over."

"Thanks, Beth-Ann."

"Anytime, Dee."

Chapter Twenty-Nine

Deanna maneuvered into the driveway leading to the stately Colonial in a charming cul-de-sac. Before leaving Alexandria she'd plugged her iPod into her car's auxiliary port. She'd opened the driver's-side window and sung at the top of her lungs when one of her favorite songs flowed through the speakers. Some drivers gave her shocked stares, while others shook their heads at her off-key singing.

A smile curved her mouth when she saw Bethany leaning against a massive column waiting for her. Dressed in a pair of black stretch capris, matching ballet-type shoes, white tank top and with her hair held off her face with a black headband, the stay-at-home mother was the epitome of casual chic.

Bethany came to meet her as she got out of the BMW, hugging her tightly. "I didn't expect you to open your own door. But thanks for inviting me."

Bethany pressed her cool cheek to Deanna's. "I always give the housekeeper the day off whenever I have company. And there's no need to thank me. You're welcome to come anytime you want." She looped her arm through Deanna's. "Come, let's go inside. I have a neighbor across the street who is nosy as hell. Every time someone drives up I can see her curtains move. One of these days I'm going to open the door naked as a jaybird. That'll give her something to gossip about."

Deanna laughed as she walked into a great room with a soaring cathedral ceiling. It opened out to a living room with furnishings that looked as if they'd been positioned for a furniture showroom ad. The Paxton home looked too perfect, just like its inhabitants. Whenever Damon and Bethany attended a social event it was as if they were walking the red carpet. Everyone looked to see what they were wearing. Both were tall and slender, and their choice of attire always radiated sophistication and elegance.

"Your house is beautiful," she said truthfully.

Bethany smiled at Deanna over her shoulder. "Thanks. I've asked Marisol if she would give me her professional assessment of my decorating skills. I told her I want her to be brutally honest."

"I hope you've come to know Marisol well enough to know that's the only way she knows to be."

Bethany slowed as she turned down a wide carpeted hallway leading into an enclosed back porch. "When I first met her I swore she couldn't stand my guts. But then I realized that was her way, and I really appreciate her candor." She indicated an armchair covered with fabric sprigged with strawberries pulled up to a cloth-covered table with settings for two. "Please sit down. I called her the other day to find out whether she is available for lunch next week, but she's going to be in Puerto Rico until the end of the month."

"Yes, I know," Deanna confirmed, glancing around the garden room with ornaments from the outdoors. There was a collection of armillary sundials, worn urns on stands, an indoor waterfall and fountain and large tank filled with a collection of colorful fish. A table spanning the width of one wall was filled with painted clay and blue-glazed pots filled with a variety of miniature roses, sunflowers, violets and begonia. French doors provided a vista of a wooded area beyond the house where one could watch the change of seasons.

Bethany, removing covers from plates on a nearby serving cart, placed one in front of Deanna. "Did you know she was going with Congressman Wesley Sheridan?"

"Yes, I did." Deanna stared at the plate of spinach salad. Instead of the requisite crumbled bacon and mushrooms, this one boasted walnuts and crumbled blue cheese in a balsamic vinaigrette. "It looks delicious."

"It's one of my favorite salads," Bethany said as she filled water goblets with chilled water. "Which wine do you want? White or rosé?" She held up two half carafes.

"No wine for me, please," she said when Bethany sat down across from her.

Pale eyebrows lifted. "Are you in the family way?"

"I'll know in another two weeks."

"Have you ever been pregnant before?"

Deanna shook her head as she spread a cloth napkin over her lap. "Never. I'm looking forward to becoming a mother."

"What are you going to do with your business?"

"I occasionally work with another event planner when I have a scheduling conflict, and she does the same with me. The difference is that she has a full staff whereas I usually work alone. I have a printer who handles my invitations, a list of caterers and florists, but I'm hands-on with everything else."

Picking up her fork, Bethany stared directly at the event planner. It was as if she was seeing Deanna Tyson for the first time. Her twists were pulled back, allowing for an un-obstructed view of a face with a flawless brown complexion, her eyes a shimmering clear gold-brown that changed color, reminding her of a smoky topaz or tigereye. "Do you plan to give up your business to become a stay-at-home mom?"

Deanna swallowed a mouthful of salad. "To tell you the truth, I would love to run a bed-and-breakfast. I saw a for-sale sign on an abandoned farmhouse not far from Reston that I've inquired about. I have an appointment to meet with the broker next week to see the interior."

"What about Spencer? Is he willing to move?"

"I haven't said anything to Spencer, because I'm not certain whether I'm going to go through with it, and we've just spent a small fortune renovating and redecorating the house in Alexandria."

"How would you like a business partner?"

Deanna almost choked when she took a sip of water. Touching the napkin to the corners of her mouth, she stared numbly at Bethany. "Are you for real?"

Bethany flashed a toothpaste-ad smile. "I'm as real as they come. Damon has more money than he knows what to do with, so investing in an B and B would be a wonderful business venture."

"I thought Damon wanted you to stay home with your kids."

"He does, but that doesn't mean I can't get involved with an outside project when Abby and Connor are in school."

"Overseeing the operation of a B and B is hardly an outside project, Bethany. It's like running a boutique hotel. There's housekeeping, laundry and meals. Then you have to have a groundskeeper, electrician and plumber on-call. And don't forget the all-important ordering, delivery and preparation of food. Last but certainly not least, you must have a bookkeeper to take care of the books."

Bethany grimaced. "I guess it's not as simple as I thought."

"It's simple once it's up and running," Deanna said, smiling. "Remember I have a degree in business with a concentration in hospitality and hotel management."

"Then running a bed-and-breakfast would be perfect for you, Deanna."

"I know. I could have my own suite where I could look in on the baby anytime I want."

Resting her elbow on the table, Bethany cupped her chin on the heel of her hand. "You'd live at the B and B, while Spencer would live in Alexandria?"

"No, Beth-Ann. Of course I'd hire a manager who would live there permanently. There's no way I'm going to have a child and not have Spencer involved in his or her life. It's only recently that I've managed to get my husband back."

Bethany's eyes grew wider. "What are you talking about? You just got him back?"

"I didn't have a husband who would come home at six o'clock and we'd sit down and have dinner together. There were times when Spencer would leave the house before seven and come home at eleven. Before we were married we planned to wait ten years before starting a family because we wanted to establish our careers. Spencer is now junior partner and my business is doing well."

"So now you're having baby-making sex."

Lowering her eyes, Deanna stared at the half-eaten salad. "I don't know if you experienced the same thing, but it's incredible."

Throwing back her head, Bethany let out a peal of laughter. "Honey, please. There was one time when it got so good that

I was close to passing out. Damon thought he was going to have to give me mouth-to-mouth."

Deanna laughed until her eyes filled with tears. The two women talked about the men they'd dated, those they'd slept with and those they fantasized sleeping with. By the time she'd drunk two cups of lemon tea with delicate shortbread cookies, Deanna had all but forgotten about her conversation with Richard Douglas.

"I hope Marisol manages to get in a little fun," she said to Bethany.

"I know if I went away with a man as gorgeous as Wesley Sheridan I'd make certain to have some fun."

Deanna went still. "I know you're not talking about slipping out on Damon."

Bethany flushed a becoming pink. "It's only a fantasy."

"Just make certain that fantasy doesn't become a reality."

Setting down her cup, Bethany gave Deanna a long stare. "I know you had that horrible experience with that strange man, but have you ever had the urge to sleep with a man who wasn't your husband?"

"Not really. Remember, Spencer wasn't the first man I'd slept with, so I'd managed to scratch that itch."

"Don't get me wrong, Deanna. I do love Damon with all my heart, but there are times when I need him to make love to me more than once a week. And, I always have to initiate it. I'm ashamed to say that I lied to Damon when he asked if the reason we don't make love as often as we used to was because he was getting older. I told him it was because we have kids and we can't play the little games that kept our lovemaking fresh."

"Has he had a physical lately?"

She nodded. "Damon has a comprehensive physical twice a year and everything comes back within the normal range."

"It could be his libido isn't what it used to be. There are over-the-counter supplements you can buy in health-food stores to help him."

Bethany sucked her teeth. "I doubt very much if my husband would appreciate me suggesting that he take something to boost his libido."

"The only alternative is to get a vibrator to take care of your needs."

"Believe me, I've thought about it."

"Remember when you told me they were for single women, Beth-Ann?"

"Please don't remind me. Now I'm going to have to eat my words. But I think there may be a silver lining behind this, because Damon is planning to rent a suite at a residential hotel blocks from Rock Creek Park. He says it's a place where influential men stash their whores and mistresses."

Deanna smiled. "So the two of you are going to use the suite only for sex?"

"That's his plan."

"Would you mind if I give you some advice?"

Leaning closer, Bethany couldn't hide her excitement. "Of course not."

"Go to a lingerie shop and buy a merry widow, thigh-high stockings and bustier. And don't forget a pair of five- or six-inch red stilettos. I've heard that there's something about red shoes that turn men on. Black leather and crotchless panties are also turn-ons."

"That's so hoochie, Deanna."

"Men love hoochie, Bethany. Every man I've known who has cheated on his wife was with a hoochie, ho, shank or whatever it is you want to call her. The other woman usually isn't a nice, but a very naughty girl."

"I was once the other woman."

Reaching across the table, Deanna rested her hand on Bethany's. "Planning parties for D.C.'s elite allows me to overhear a lot of gossip. Most times I'm looked upon as hired help, so the doyennes talk as if I don't exist. I've heard a few of them snicker about Jean Paxton's penchant for sleeping with what they consider 'blue-collar trash.' And that includes deliverymen, workmen, the pool boy and/or landscaper. They were proved right when she did marry one of her landscapers. If Jean was doing everything that walked through her door, then I don't blame Damon for finding affection wherever he could. In fact, he was quite the pussy hound until he met you."

Bethany giggled like a little girl. "I've heard him called everything, but not a pussy hound."

"Well, he did have a reputation for sniffing skirts," Deanna said, smiling broadly. "He was very lucky that he found you."

"Did you know that I'd set out to seduce him?"

"No, I didn't. I thought you met by chance."

"Yeah, right," Bethany drawled. "I'd done intensive research about who he did business with and where he liked to eat, then one night I asked the restaurant's maître d' to sit me at a table close to his because I wanted to ask him if I could interview him for a news segment. It helped that I gave the greedy bastard a Benjamin, but it was worth it. I flirted my behind off and before he left Damon gave me his business card and asked me to call him. The rest, as they say, is history. But I turned the tables on him when I made him wait before giving him my panties. I wasn't looking for a lover, but a husband. It paid off in the end when he told me he was going to divorce his wife."

"You did what you had to do to get what you wanted."

"You're right," Bethany agreed. "Have you ever worn black leather?"

"Girl, please. That's my Halloween trademark. I dress up like a dominatrix and Spencer is my male counterpart whenever we go to private parties that look like everyone's ready for a bacchanalia. I spend half the night staring at Spencer's leather codpiece and the other half fantasizing how I'm going to make love to him. Don't forget when you put on your getup that you have to transform your face. Kohl does amazing things to the eyes."

Bethany shook her head. "I'm older than you, yet you know so much more than I do."

"Remember, I grew up here in D.C., while you were growing up in small-town America."

Bethany's expression stilled, growing serious. "I don't know where I'd be now if you and Marisol hadn't come into the bathroom that night. I owe you both my life."

"Don't start with the self-pity, Beth-Ann. You're a survivor. If you hadn't been you never would've left Parker Corners, Alabama."

Her expression brightened. "You know, you're right." She sobered again. "I'm going to ask a favor from you."

"What is it?"

"I'd like to be godmother for your baby."

Deanna saw the violet eyes filling with tears. Suddenly, she knew Bethany Paxton. She was an insecure woman who still wasn't certain of her rightful place in the D.C. social arena.

"What if you share godmother duties with Marisol?"

Pushing back her chair, Bethany came over and hugged Deanna until she claimed she was choking her. "Thank you."

Chapter Thirty

Marisol lay in bed, tossing and turning restlessly. It was her second night in Puerto Rico, and Bryce hadn't called or returned her calls. She'd called his office phone, leaving a voice mail for him to call her back. Twelve hours later she called his cell, believing he could've left D.C. to visit a candidate, but again he hadn't called. Now she'd taken to placing the cell on the pillow beside her so she would hear it when it rang.

Rolling over on her back, she threw an arm over her forehead. Her imagination was beginning to go into overdrive when she wondered if he'd fallen and couldn't get to the phone, or he'd been involved in an auto accident...

"*¡Párelo,* Mari!" she whispered in the darkened, silent space. Agonizing over something over which she had no control was certain to trigger a headache. She turned again, this time to peer at the travel clock on the floor beside the bed. It was after one in the morning.

Marisol knew sleep had become her enemy, so she left the bed, walked to the casement window, opened it and stepped out onto the balcony. Minute lights under the roof tiles il-luminated the balcony. The distinctive croaking whistle of a *coquí,* the small tree frog found only on the island, shattered the stillness of the night.

She stood with her arms resting on the wrought-iron enclosure enjoying the solitude and the smell of salt water. Within minutes her anxiety lessened as she closed her eyes and breathed in the essence of the island that had been home to her ancestors.

Marisol had understood why some of her relatives had opted to leave a place that resembled an emerald paradise for the mainland because they'd felt there were better eco-nomic opportunities, but each time she came for a visit and left Marisol felt as if she'd left a little piece of herself behind. Perhaps, she mused, she should buy a two-bedroom condo in San Juan she could share with her mother.

Every year Pilar complained that it was going to be her last winter in New York, but then come spring she would change her mind. Maybe having a place of her own—a place where she wouldn't have to pay rent or a mortgage—would motivate Pilar to consider early retirement.

Marisol had argued with her mother because she hadn't left the old neighborhood. Pilar had moved out of public hous-ing and into a one-bedroom apartment in a five-story walk-up two blocks from their old housing project, and although West Harlem was undergoing rapid gentrification it had been slower in El Barrio.

Stepping away from the railing, she lay on the chaise out-side the bedroom. Millions of stars littered the nighttime sky, and a near-full moon, silvering the landscape, appeared close enough to reach out and touch.

"What's the matter? Can't sleep?"

Marisol sat up as if she'd been stuck with a sharp

instrument. Wesley stood outside the adjoining bedroom, arms crossed over his bare chest. He wore a pair of white pajama pants and nothing else. The first night he'd slept in one of the bedrooms on the first floor.

"Why are you up?"

Closing the distance between them, Wesley sat at the foot of the chaise, almost tipping it over until he shifted his weight. "I could ask you the same thing. Cute nightgown," he crooned, running a finger along the ruffled hem of her white cotton gown with a revealing neckline.

Marisol swiped at his hand. "Don't do that."

"Don't do that. Don't call me that. You're just full of don'ts, aren't you?"

She stared at the man who'd added to her anxiety. Spending time with Wesley Sheridan hadn't made it easier for her to see how to right the wrongs when it came to her marriage. It was as if Wesley had had a bird's-eye view of everything that had gone on in her home from the time she woke until she went to bed. Had he been that perceptive, or were she and Bryce that transparent? Except for the fact that she hadn't gotten pregnant after trying for two years, Marisol had always thought her marriage was on good footing. However, a man who was interested in her for more than business had made it apparent all wasn't as well as she'd believed.

"If your intent is to harass me, then I'm going back inside."

Holding on to her ankles, Wesley held them fast. "I'm sorry. Is there something wrong with your bed?"

Marisol tried making out his features, but from where he sat his face was in the shadows. She couldn't help but notice his muscled pectorals and incredibly flat stomach. Wesley Sheridan was an extraordinarily handsome male specimen.

"No. It's very comfortable."

"More comfortable than this chaise?"

"I came out because I couldn't sleep."

"Do you want me to make you a hot tea?" Wesley asked, his thumbs making soothing motions over the arch of her foot.

"No, thank you." Smiling, Marisol closed her eyes when Wesley massaged her instep and ankles. "That feels wonderful. Didn't I promise to give you a massage?"

"You did, but right now it's my turn. Talk to me, Marisol."

"What about?"

"About what's bothering you."

She wanted to lie and say nothing, but realized there were few things she could slip past Wesley. It was as if he was so attuned to her Marisol felt as if he could read her mind. She told him about Bryce not returning her calls, the words tumbling over each other as she tried not breaking down.

Wesley's hands stilled. "Do you think something happened to him?"

"I don't know. I can't call his parents because they're out of the country and I don't get along that well with my sisters-in-law."

"What if I have someone from my office call him tomorrow under the pretext that I need some statistics from him? If he answers his phone, then you'll know he's all right."

"Thank you, Wes. When I do get to talk to Bryce I'm going to give him a piece of my mind for making me worry about him."

"Maybe he's busy."

"Too busy to call his wife?"

"Sometimes we dudes aren't too smart."

"Don't make excuses for him, Wesley."

"Just try not to be too hard on him until you find out why he hasn't returned your calls."

If Bryce wasn't in bed with a fever or lying in a ditch

unconscious, then Marisol would know for certain why he hadn't called. He was jealous, jealous that she'd left the country with a man he saw as his rival and/or competition. Lately, Bryce had shown her a side of his personality she'd found more and more repugnant. He'd become a spoiled child, acting out when he couldn't get his way. She knew he was against her going to Puerto Rico with Wesley because he hadn't bothered to walk her to the car and wait until it pulled away from the curb. He resented her not using his accountant, resented her insistence they not file a joint tax return and he resented her struggle to maintain her independence.

Marisol may have unconsciously permitted him to select the clothes she would wear whenever they were out together, but now that she'd been made aware of it, that, too, would change.

"Why do guys always stick together?"

"And you gals don't?"

"Not like men."

"Did you ever see *The First Wives Club*?"

Marisol chuckled softly. "Talk about revenge is a dish best served cold. I loved it!"

"That's what I'm talking about. Guys stick together and women get together to plot revenge."

The topic segued from the inequality between the sexes to her preliminary decorating ideas. She'd spent most of yesterday photographing each room, then uploading the images into her laptop. Each room would have a design floor plan where Marisol would map out the room as a whole.

"You're going to have to determine which season you want for this house."

Releasing her feet, Wesley moved up the chaise and lay on his side next to Marisol. "I don't understand."

"Homes, like people, have personalities. It can be decorated to imbue all the seasons or one or two. Spring signals the melting of snow, warmer days, longer daylight and the emergence of green shoots and the glossy petals of tulips. The mood is light, the air fresh and rooms uncluttered. It also means flowers—inside and out, on walls and fabrics. Because this house is in a tropical climate I'm going to recommend you decorate it in two seasons: spring and summer. It can be romantic, whimsical and uninhibited.

"And because there are going to be children underfoot, you should have furniture that can be easily moved. Tables shouldn't have sharp edges, and if you're going to do a lot of entertaining, then multiple seating arrangements in separate areas offer plenty of room for your guests to mix and mingle. I'll show you what I'm talking about when I design your master bedroom. After I set up the floor plans, then you're going to have to select the furniture styles."

Wesley smothered a yawn with his hand. "I don't want to be rude, but can we discuss this in the morning?"

"Sure."

He stood up, staring down at her. "Aren't you going in?"

"Not yet. Good night."

Wesley held her gaze for a full minute. "Good night."

Marisol watched Wesley's retreat until he disappeared into the adjoining bedroom, silently admiring a pair of broad shoulders, straight spine and narrow waist. Talking to Wesley had temporarily taken her mind off Bryce. She had to believe he was all right, otherwise someone would've contacted her. She'd called Bryce twice and refused to call him again. The ball was now in his court.

Marisol felt her eyelids droop and she got up and went back into the bedroom, closed the windows to keep out the warm air and climbed into bed. This time when she did close her eyes it was to fall asleep.

★ ★ ★

It was the sound of rain and not sunlight pouring into the bedroom that Marisol woke to. Pulling the sheet over her head, she burrowed deeper into the pile of pillows under her head and shoulders. She didn't want to get up, but knew she had to because the sooner she completed the floor plans the sooner she could return to the States. Once Wesley approved the plan for positioning all of the furnishings he would have to approve the colors he wanted for each room. Her recommendations would include paint colors that were in keeping with the tropical climate: watermelon, pear, cantaloupe.

Sweeping off the sheet, she sat up and swung her legs over the side of the bed, her gaze going to the luggage on the floor in a far corner. Now she'd experienced what it meant to live out of a suitcase. The absence of furniture meant that she couldn't empty her bags and put away her clothes in a dresser or chest of drawers. Marisol had taken care not to leave her bags open because she didn't want to bring a creeping or crawling creature back to the States.

The wood floor was cool under her bare feet as she walked over to her Pullman and removed a change of clothes. Thankfully she'd been able to store her toiletries on a countertop in the en suite bath. Forty minutes later, after she'd showered, dressed and made the bed, Marisol walked down the staircase and made her way into the kitchen.

The intoxicating aroma of brewing coffee and the vision of Wesley sprawled on a chair in the kitchen greeted her. He'd rested his bare feet on another chair while flipping through a magazine. His damp hair stood up in tiny spikes from a recent shower and Marisol thought he looked incredibly virile in a pair of faded ripped jeans and white T.

"*Buenos días.*"

Wesley jumped up like a jack-in-the-box, his chair

clattering loudly as it hit the floor. "Good morning." He picked up the chair, offering it to her. "Come and sit. The coffee should be ready in another minute."

Marisol, wearing a pair of jeans with a long-sleeve cotton white top and sandals, folded her body down to the chair. "Thanks. You're up early." It was minutes after seven.

"I'd planned to go for a swim, but I hadn't expected it to rain."

"It'll probably clear up later." She stared directly at Wesley. "I don't want you to call your staffer to ask him to check on Bryce."

"Are you sure?"

She gave him a hint of a smile. "Very sure."

Standing in the shower, it was as if she'd suddenly gotten an epiphany. Marisol had decided she wasn't going to chase after her husband. If he wanted to call her he would. If not, then he wouldn't. For Bryce, her need to remain independent meant they were living together but they were also living separate lives, and that was why he hadn't wanted to bring a child into their current lifestyle.

Well, she had no intention of giving up her career and sense of self to become someone like his mother, who'd waited on his father hand and foot and was available at his beck and call.

Wesley nodded. "It's your call, Mari. But if you change your mind I'm willing to do it."

"I'm not going to change my mind. Today I'm going to do the cooking."

"That's all right," Wesley said in protest. "I didn't bring you here to cook."

"But I want to. How would you like an authentic Puerto Rican meal with rice, beans, tostones and flan?"

Wesley stared, complete surprise on his face. "You cook like that?"

"Yes."

"*¡Maldito!*"

"Damn is right. What if we compromise? I'll cook today and you can cook tomorrow." Wesley extended his hand and she took it. "Do you have a blender or food processor?"

"I'm certain there is a food processor in one of the storage cabinets. Why?"

"I want to make *sofrito,* but I'm going to need cilantro, cachucha or *ajicitos,* bell pepper and cubanelle peppers."

"I'll give you the number to the market and you can ask them to deliver whatever you need."

"How far is it from here?"

Wesley smiled. "Too far to walk. I have an account with the store. I order what I want, then settle the bill before I leave the island."

"Do you ever rent a car to get around?"

"No. Once I get here I usually don't leave until I'm ready to fly back to the States. The developer is breaking ground on the north side of the property to build an nine-hole golf course, indoor tennis court, several inground pools, a building that can be used for private parties and a health spa."

"All you'll need is an on-site supermarket with the requisite pharmacy and a movie theater and you'll never have to leave."

"What about a shoe store?" Wesley teased.

Marisol waved a hand. "Those can be ordered online."

"Coffee's ready," he said when the brewing light on the coffeemaker switched off. "One *café con leche* coming up."

Wesley stood up and went over to make their coffees while Marisol searched the built-in refrigerator/freezer for ingredients she could use to make breakfast.

Chapter Thirty-One

Deanna was certain everyone could see and hear her knees shaking when she walked into the lobby to the Brandon-Phillips. It had taken four days, but Richard Douglas had contacted her again, and following John's instructions Deanna had suggested they meet at the same hotel. She'd also told her blackmailer that she would meet him in the lobby, share a drink, then go upstairs, where she'd fulfill her promise to sleep with him again.

She'd changed her outfit from all-black to a suit with a pencil skirt in a flattering lime-green. It was spring, a time for renewal, the temperatures were in the high seventies, and once she left the hotel she planned to turn the proverbial corner to take her life back. She hadn't met John, couldn't imagine what he looked like, but Deanna knew she had to trust him when he said he would take care of Richard Douglas. Her gaze met and fused to the man rising slowly to his feet with her approach. He was as fastidiously dressed as before, every strand of hair in place.

Richard indicated the chair across from where he'd sat waiting for Deanna. "Please sit down, Mrs. Tyson."

She complied, crossing one leg over the other and bringing his gaze to linger there when the hem of the skirt rose up her thigh. "Don't you think we should dispense with the Mr. Douglas and Mrs. Tyson?"

Bringing his fingertips together, Richard narrowed his eyes. "You hate me, don't you?"

Deanna shook her head. "No, I don't. What I hate is being forced to do something I don't want to do."

Richard lowered his hands. "Then why are you here?"

She leaned forward. "I want you out of my life—for good."

A sardonic smile parted his lips. "What if I want more than just tonight?"

"That's not going to happen. Either you agree to end it tonight, or I'm going home and tell my husband everything."

"You're willing to risk your marriage?"

"So much so that I'm also willing to risk my life."

"Don't be so melodramatic, Deanna."

"Don't be so pompous, *Richard*."

He laughed under his breath. "Given another set of circumstances we would've made a magnificent couple."

Deanna shook her head. "I doubt that. I don't make it my business to consort with criminals. Not only are you a rapist, but you're also a blackmailer."

Richard's expression did not change with her accusation. "I didn't rape you. You went willingly to my room."

"I didn't give you consent, and that means you raped me."

"I'll admit you were under the influence. In fact, both of us were, but let me assure you that you were willing to open your legs for me. Let me remind you that this isn't about your husband finding out that his wife had slept with a man she'd met at a hotel bar, but about your reputation as the consummate event planner. I told you before that I have enough clout that you'll never work in this town again."

"That no longer matters," Deanna said truthfully. After lunching with Bethany she'd come home giving the idea of owning and operating a B and B a lot of consideration. Once her problem with Richard Douglas was resolved, she planned to broach the subject with Spencer.

Richard waved a hand as if swatting away an annoying insect. "Perhaps a cocktail would put you more at ease." Deanna nodded. He raised his hand to get a waiter's attention. "I'll have my usual and please bring the lady a Long Island iced tea."

Deanna stared out the window rather than at the man whose overblown ego told him he could have anything he wanted. When she'd spoken to John, the mysterious voice on the other end of the phone reassured her that when she walked out of the Brandon-Phillips it would be without her having slept with Richard Douglas.

The waiter returned, bringing her back to her situation. Picking up her glass, she held it aloft. "Here's to wonderful goodbyes."

Richard held up his glass filled with bourbon. "Parting is going to be such sweet sorrow. At least for me." Putting it to his mouth, he took a long swallow, peering at Deanna over the rim as she took furtive sips of her drink. His hand shook slightly when he attempted to replace the glass on the table without spilling his drink.

Deanna stared, shocked when she watched him clawing at the tie around his throat as his eyes rolled back in his head, leaving only the whites. "Are you all right?"

"Get up and walk out," a woman whispered in her ear.

Needing no further prompting, she got up and made her way to the revolving doors. Once out on the street a man wearing the hotel's livery moved close to her side. "Don't look at me! Give me your phone."

Reaching into her handbag, she took out her cell phone and handed it to the man without looking at him. She managed to see a pair of white gloved hands, but nothing else. Four seconds later she had her phone; then she walked over to the valet, asking him to bring her car around.

It was over. She had her life back. Deanna didn't know what had happened to Richard Douglas and she didn't want to know. She suspected he was having a heart attack and didn't want to surmise what had precipitated the attack.

Then she did what she hadn't done in a long time. She offered a prayer of thanks. She was thankful that she'd told Marisol, who knew someone able to intervene on her behalf, about her dilemma. She was thankful she hadn't had to tell her husband that she'd committed adultery.

Deanna hadn't thought of herself as a bad wife, but the liaison with Richard Douglas hadn't made her a good wife, either. But she'd been given a second chance to make it right. She would go home, make love to Spencer, tell him about her wish to operate a B and B and continue trying to increase their family.

Jenah Morris quickened her pace. She hadn't noticed the man when she got off the bus to walk the three blocks to her apartment building, but she felt as if he was following her. She chided herself for not taking a taxi from the club where she'd hung out with her friends because she had wanted to save money, because as a single woman with a child on the way she couldn't afford to splurge.

The money Spencer had given her to have an abortion she'd deposited into her savings account. Maybe if she took on a part-time job she could save enough money to tide her over while she was on maternity leave. Then there was the matter of child care. There weren't many agencies that took in newborns, so that meant she had to look for someone responsible to take care of her baby before she returned to work.

The night Spencer had walked out on her Jenah had briefly thought about getting rid of the baby, but that lasted all of ten minutes when she contemplated how she would repay Spencer Tyson for his duplicity. It hadn't taken Jenah long to conclude that Spencer Tyson had no intention of leaving his wife despite the passionate declarations of love.

"It's not nice to harbor evil thoughts, Jenny." Her grandmother's warning came back to nag at her whenever she contemplated how she could repay Spencer for stringing her along. However, revenge would have to wait—wait until after their child was born. Then she would sue him for paternity and after DNA tests she wouldn't have to worry about providing for their son or daughter.

A quick glance over her shoulder revealed the man was no longer following her. She wouldn't have been out so late if she hadn't agreed to join her coworkers at a restaurant to celebrate their D.C. chief of staff's birthday. Slowing and breathing heavily through her open mouth, Jenah turned the corner. She hadn't gone more than half a dozen steps when a large dark figure sprang from the bushes and caught her around her throat. Then she felt a sharp pain in her side.

Going completely still, she stared numbly at the dark figure sprinting away from her. It wasn't until she heard the frantic barking that she realized the dog must have frightened the mugger.

"Are you all right, miss?"

Jenah stared at the elderly man with his dog straining on his leash. "I think so."

"He didn't get your bag, did he?"

Her heart was beating so hard that Jenah thought it was coming out of her chest. She tightened her grip on her cross-over bag. "No."

"Maybe you should call the police so they can be on the lookout for someone going around trying to mug women."

She shook her head. "It's okay. My building is right over there. Once inside I'll be safe. Thank goodness you were here with your dog."

"I walk Lady every night about this time."

Jenah wanted to tell the man that she'd made it a practice not to take public transportation late at night, but tonight had been the exception. It would not happen again. "Thank you again, and good night."

"We'll walk you to your building to make certain if that creep decides to come back."

She was given an escort to her building. Jenah unlocked the outer door, waving to her rescuer once she was safely inside the building. Not bothering to stop to see if she had mail, she walked to her first-floor apartment, unlocked the door and walked in and locked it behind her.

Her heart was still beating a little too fast and suddenly she felt faint. She managed to make it to the bathroom and sit on the commode when she felt a stabbing pain in her belly. Taking deep gulps of air, Jenah willed the pain to go away, but it intensified. She didn't need to look down to know she was bleeding. She was losing her baby. Somehow she managed to reach for a towel to soak up the blood, and holding it between her legs she made it to the telephone and dialed 911. Blood-soaked towels lay in the tub behind the shower curtain when paramedics wheeled her out of the apartment on a gurney.

Jenah surfaced from a dark hole to stare up at an unfamiliar face hovering over her. When she was able to focus she saw the IV taped to the back of her hand and heard the beeping sounds from the machine monitoring her vitals.

Her eyelids fluttered. "Where am I?"

The nurse gave her a comforting smile. "You're in a hospital, Ms. Morris. I'll let the doctor know you're awake."

Jenah placed a hand on her belly. "What about my baby?"

"The doctor will talk to you."

"I want you to tell me if my baby is okay!" she shouted. She hadn't realized she was still screaming until a doctor approached her bed, along with another nurse who injected something into the tube taped to her hand.

"Ms. Morris, my name is Dr. Warner. I'm sorry to tell you that you had a miscarriage. We have to perform a D & C. We also had to give you a unit of blood. We'll run some tests in the morning, and if everything looks good then you'll be able to go home. Meanwhile, is there anyone you want to call to let them know you're here."

She nodded. "Yes-s-s." Whatever they'd given her was making her very sleepy.

"Nurse Sharkey, please give Ms. Morris the phone so she can make a call."

The nurse adjusted the pillows behind Jenah's shoulders and back, permitting her to sit up while she tapped the buttons on the telephone. Everything appeared to be moving in slow motion when she listened to the prerecorded message. "Spencer, this is Jenah. Please call me on my cell tomorrow night. I have something very important to tell you. Don't... don't...forget. Call me...me back."

It was the last thing she remembered before she fell headlong into a comforting darkness that swallowed her whole.

"Are you sure you're going to be all right staying here alone?"

Jenah nodded as she flopped down on her bed. Spencer

hadn't called her back. He hadn't called the hospital, her cell or her home phone. She wanted to tell him he was free to go on with his life, and the only thing she wanted was for him to pick her up at the hospital and drive her home. In the end she had to call one of her coworkers and impose on her. Luckily, she hadn't told anyone she'd gotten pregnant, so that saved her from answering a lot of questions. She'd told Shaniece that she didn't know she had a fibroid until it ruptured.

"I'm good, Shaniece."

"What do you want me to tell them at work?"

"Don't tell them anything, because the nosy heifers don't need to know," she spat. "The only thing I'm worried about is whether the fibroid is malignant or benign. Tell Congresswoman Canton I should be back to work in a couple of days."

"She'll probably tell you to take the rest of the week off."

Jenah closed her eyes. She was still feeling effects of the tranquilizer they had given her to keep her calm. "I don't want to use up all my sick leave."

Shaniece stared at Jenah, realizing for the first time that she had two different-colored eyes. Jenah always styled her hair so that it hid her bright blue eye. "That's what sick leave is for. You take it when you're sick."

Jenah waved her hand and closed her eyes. She wanted her gone so she could cry for what had been and would never be again. "Thanks for coming to get me."

"I'm leaving, but I'll call you later to make sure you don't need anything. Don't you want me to leave you something to read?"

"Sure."

Reaching into her tote, Shaniece took out several tabloids and a copy of the *Washington Post*. "I read the paper, so you can keep it."

Jenah waited until she heard the self-locking door slam

behind Shaniece before she opened her eyes. She'd lied to the woman, but then Spencer had lied to her. Her life from the time she'd met Spencer Tyson that fateful election night had been one big lie. Whenever she didn't join her friends for after-work mixers she told them she had to meet her boyfriend who lived in Philly and was only in town on business for the night or the weekend. No one knew she'd been sleeping with a married man who'd put her up in a luxurious suite at the Victoria for their trysts. When she'd mentioned giving up her apartment to live in the residential hotel, Spencer had insisted she keep her apartment. Fortunately for her she had, or she would've found herself out on the street looking for someplace to live.

Reaching for the newspapers, she spied a tabloid that had come out of nowhere to challenge the other supermarket favorites. What she liked about the *Dish* was that it was devoted exclusively to Beltway gossip. The editor was more than clever. He or she was brilliant. Longtime insiders knew exactly who they were talking about, but because no names were mentioned the tittle-tattle had become hearsay.

Then there was the blog moderated by someone called the Insider. When Jenah had gone online to read the entries she felt as if they knew about her and Spencer, even though the blogger hadn't mentioned the occupation of the married man the aide was seeing after hours. When the Insider refused to identify the member of Congress the aide worked for but hinted at her breast size, Jenah knew for certain they were talking about her because she wore a 40DD.

She'd lost her baby, so there wouldn't be a paternity suit. However, there were other ways to make Spencer Tyson pay for messing her over.

Chapter Thirty-Two

Marisol sat in the middle of the bed with Wesley, her laptop turned at an angle where they both could view the monitor. She had completed floor plans for every room in the duplex; the last one was the living room.

She'd spent two weeks in Puerto Rico and Bryce hadn't returned any of her calls. Her initial concern for his well-being had become apathy. It'd taken her a while to conclude that if anything had happened to Bryce someone would've called her cell.

She pointed to a floor plan labeled Living Room. "From the entry hall, traffic should flow around the center love seat. These two chairs can be lightweight enough to move when entertaining," she said, pointing to symbols representing chairs.

Wesley leaned to his left, his shoulder pressing against Marisol's. "Why did you put a table behind the center love seat?"

"A dining-size table serves as a library table for display and may be used for impromptu meals when you want a view of the beach and ocean." Clicking the mouse, she dropped in a matching love seat. "I've arranged this one at a right-angle configuration to two conversation areas during a larger party." She clicked again, this time dragging a small table between two other chairs. "I added the small writing table that can be set up as a bar for parties. I know you said that your sisters plan to vacation here with their children, but there's always the possibility that the adults will want to do some entertaining."

"When we're all together we do a lot of entertaining. What are those circles on the tables?"

Marisol gave him a sidelong glance. "Those are decorative lamps. The one to the left of the right-angle love seat is a floor lamp. I placed them there to form a triangle of soft light for the evening hours."

He smiled. "Nice. What about a carpet?"

"I think you would do better with a room-size carpet because remember you're going to have to deal with sand being tracked inside the house. You can use a room-size carpet that should come to within eighteen to twenty-four inches of the walls. It's acceptable for furniture along the edges to sit partially off the carpet. You'll have to wait until we get back to D.C. to see the carpet samples."

"You make it look so simple."

Marisol saved the floor plan, then shut down the laptop. "It's simple because you can see it right in front of you. If I'd tried to explain it would be a muddled mess."

Wesley reached for the computer, placing it on the floor beside the bed. Then he eased Marisol down to the mattress, he turning on his side to lie beside her. "You are truly a renaissance woman. You're an incredible decorator and you cook as well as any TV chef."

Shifting, Marisol faced Wesley, their noses inches apart. "You probably thought I was going to give you ptomaine."

"No way. Not when my mouth was watering when you were making the *sofrito*."

"I have my *abuela* to thank for my cooking skills. She used to tease me that I would never get a husband if I didn't learn to cook. It was only when I was older that I realized I didn't need to learn to cook to get a husband when there were restaurants and caterers."

"If you hadn't become a decorator, what would you've been?"

"I don't know. I'd thought about becoming a nurse but I'm squeamish when it comes to blood."

"Where did you go to college?" Wesley asked.

"I completed my undergraduate work at the Pratt Institute School of Art and Design and I did my graduate work at Parsons New School for Design."

"Did you need an MFA?"

"I do if I decide I want to teach."

Wesley ran a forefinger down the length of her nose. "I admire you."

"Why?"

"You know exactly what you want to do with your life."

"And you don't?" she asked.

Long black lashes came down, concealing the intensity in Wesley's eyes. "No. I like being a politician but I don't like politics."

"That sounds like a contradiction."

He glanced up, impaling her with an intense stare. "It is." Wesley's expression changed. "How would you like to go swimming with me to celebrate our last day here?"

Marisol let out a groan. She'd spent her time designing

floor plans while Wesley had passed the time swimming and sunbathing. "I didn't bring a suit."

"Why don't you wear your bra and panties? I'm certain they cover more than some women who wear what could pass for a bikini."

"You're probably right. Go put on your suit and I'll look for a something that won't look too risqué. I'll meet you on the beach."

Waiting until Wesley walked out the bedroom, closing the door behind him Marisol left the bed and searched through her luggage for a bra and a pair of matching panties. Pulling on a black silk and lace ensemble, she skipped down the staircase, left through the rear door, smiling when she saw Wesley dive in under a wave. He'd spread out two large towels on the sand. Waving her hand, she caught his attention and raced into the clear green water to join him. Losing track of time, she and Wesley became children, swimming, floating and splashing each other in the warm water.

Unaccustomed to the strenuous activity, Marisol pleaded fatigue and collapsed facedown on the towel. She slipped the straps to her bra off her shoulders and unhooked the back to avoid tan lines.

"Why did you wimp out on me?" Wesley asked in her ear.

She peered at him through half-closed eyes. "It's been a while since I've swum in the ocean. It's going to take a while for me to build up stamina."

"Don't move. I'm going into the house to get sunblock for you."

Marisol wanted to tell Wesley she couldn't move if her life depended upon it. Resting her head on folded arms, she closed her eyes. The heat from the sun and the cooling breeze coming off the ocean lulled her into a state of total relaxation.

She hadn't realized she'd fallen asleep until she felt the cooling liquid on her back when Wesley slathered her with sunblock.

His impersonal touch changed when he rubbed the protective lotion along her inner thigh and down her legs. She was certain he could feel her trembling. "Wes."

Leaning down, Wesley pressed his mouth to her ear. "Don't worry, *querida*. I'm not going to do anything you don't want me to do."

Marisol swallowed the lump in her throat as she struggled to control the swell of foreign emotion that frightened her. "I want…" Her words trailed off when she met Wesley's hungry stare.

"What do you want?"

"I want you to make love to me."

"*¿Es cierto?*"

She smiled. "I'm very certain."

Marisol closed her eyes when Wesley removed her bra and panties. She'd just asked him to do something that no doubt would change her and her life forever.

If she had been completely honest with herself, Marisol would've acknowledged her attraction to Wesley Sheridan the moment he had walked into her home. She hadn't known what it was, but it was as if he could see through the facade she'd erected to pretend she was happy—indescribably happy. It wasn't that she didn't love her husband, but their relationship had been based on conditions: she wouldn't sleep with him until he committed to marriage.

The need for her to keep her business totally separate from Bryce's. Her need to maintain her independence at all costs. Her need to prove to her in-laws that she was worthy to become a McDonald. And she was tired. Exhausted and tired of fighting with Bryce to determine whether he was able to father a child.

She'd asked a man who wasn't her husband, a man who wasn't a friend but a client, to make love to her. Wesley may have planned to seduce her when he'd asked her to come away with him, but that no longer mattered. Looping her arms around Wesley's neck, she buried her face between his neck and shoulder when he moved over her.

"I can assure you there will be no turning back."

She smiled. "Did I ask you to turn back?"

Her bravado vanished when she found herself on her back, staring up at Wesley. The tropical sun had tanned his face until he was as dark as she was. Marisol's gaze did not waver when he pushed his trunks off his waist, down his hips and stepped out of them. Her eyes traveled from his face, down to his chest and still lower to his groin. He was fully aroused, his blood-engorged sex hanging heavily between muscled thighs.

Their gazes fused as she extended her arms. *"Venga, mi querido."*

Wesley couldn't believe he was going to make love to a woman who'd haunted him from the first time he saw her. Making love on the beach went beyond any- and everything he could've imagined. A mile of private beach guaranteed there wouldn't be any prying eyes.

Parting her legs with his knee, he guided his sex between her thighs, pushing gently until he was fully sheathed inside her moist warmth. Then he began to move. Thrusting, withdrawing over and over until the only thing in the world that mattered was the woman writhing under him. Without warning he reversed their position, cupping her hips as she sat astride him, her small, firm breasts bouncing as she came down on his erection. Watching his penis slide in and out of her body, the secretions from their lovemaking mingling with pubic hair.

Wesley reversed positions again, his hips slamming into hers until the dam broke and he completed himself inside her at the same time Marisol's screams echoed in his ear; the walls of her vagina held him in a vise before easing only to do it again over and over as she climaxed.

They lay together, joined and spent, while waiting for their breathing to return to a normal rhythm. The enormity of what they'd shared did not hit Wesley until he pulled out and lay on his back while staring up at the cloudless sky. It was the first time in his life he'd made love with a woman without using protection.

His anxiety subsided when he realized if Marisol had asked him to make love to her, then she had to be on birth control. She had waited for the last day of what had become a two-week fantasy vacation to let him make love to her. Even if it would become the only time at least he would be left with memories of their time together.

"Do you think we should go inside?" Her voice was low, sultry.

Wesley smiled. "No one's going to see us."

"How can you be so sure?"

"Everyone's stretch of beach is indicated by boundary markers. And no one trespasses or they're subject to a hefty fine."

"How much is the fine?"

"Five thousand for the first offense, and seventy-five hundred for the second."

"That's excessive, Wes."

"So is trespassing."

Marisol shifted until she lay on her side; she pressed her face to her lover's shoulder, resting one arm over his waist. "Flip me over once I'm done on this side."

Wesley cursed his luck. Marisol had waited hours before

they were to leave to return to the mainland to allow him to make love to her. He wondered if it was a deliberate move on her part so there would be no bonding.

They would return to D.C. to pick up the pieces of their lives as if the two weeks had been a dream. He'd deliberately kept his distance because she'd proved to be too much a temptation. She'd come to Puerto Rico to work, not have an affair. And she hadn't realized the scope of the project she'd taken on because there hadn't been time for her to visit with relatives. She had eleven rooms to decorate and twelve days in which to complete the task. If they hadn't shared meals, Wesley wouldn't have spent any time with her.

Marisol hadn't mentioned Bryce returning her calls, and he hadn't asked. What he didn't tell her was if Bryce didn't want his wife, then Wesley Sheridan was more than ready and willing to step in and replace him.

Chapter Thirty-Three

"Damn, girl, you are wearing the hell out of your vacation," Deanna remarked when Bethany's housekeeper led her into the back porch where Marisol and Bethany waited for her.

Marisol fluttered her lashes. "It was a working vacation."

Bethany patted the back of a chair. "Sit here, Deanna. I did ask our girlfriend how much work she got done, but she wouldn't tell me."

Marisol moved over to sit on a cushioned chair pulled up to the table Bethany had set with china, silver and crystal. "I completed floor plans for eleven rooms in twelve days. The other two days were for travel."

"Did you miss your honey bunny?" Bethany drawled.

Shaking out her napkin, Marisol placed it over her lap. "No."

"No?" Deanna and Bethany chorused.

"Why on earth not?" Bethany asked.

Marisol told her friends about calling Bryce and he not calling her back. "After the third day I said the hell with him.

If he's going to act like a jackass, then I'll treat him like one and ignore him."

Deanna stared at Marisol. She'd cut her hair in a becoming pixie style, while her face was tanned a deep tawny brown. "What did he say for himself when you got back?"

"He kissed me and asked if I'd had a good time."

"That's it?" Deanna asked.

Marisol lifted her tanned shoulders. "That's it."

Bethany picked up a bowl of salad, handing it to Marisol. "Did you have a fight before you left?"

"Nope. I know he didn't like me going away with a man."

"Especially if that man is Wesley Sheridan," Bethany crooned.

Deanna narrowed her eyes at their hostess. "What are you trying to say, Beth-Ann?"

"It's as plain as the nose on your face, Dee. Bryce is jealous of Wesley Sheridan."

Deanna trained her gaze on Marisol. "Have you given Bryce cause to be jealous?"

Marisol met Deanna's eyes. "No."

"Mrs. Paxton, there's someone at the door asking for you." The three women turned to look at the housekeeper standing at the entrance to the porch.

Bethany placed her napkin beside her plate. "Please excuse me."

Marisol waited until she and Deanna were alone to tell her that she'd slept with Wesley. "It was only once, and the day before we were leaving."

"But why?"

"I don't know. I suppose subliminally I was angry with Bryce and wanted to get back at him. Please don't tell me I was stupid and immature, because I've called myself that and a whole lot worse."

"Are you going to see him again?"

She nodded. "Yes, but not to sleep together."

"Be careful," Deanna whispered. "A love triangle usually ends badly."

"It was only one time, and I'm certain Wesley wouldn't do anything to jeopardize his political career."

"I hope you're right, Marisol. Sex can make people do crazy things." Deanna gave her friend a quick overview of what had happened at the Brandon-Phillips. "It happened so quickly I didn't have time to react. He'd barely taken a sip of his drink when he started gasping for breath. Some woman told me to get up and walk out and I didn't think twice. I never got to see what John looked like when he asked for my cell. He erased the number and it was over. I scoured every newspaper and online news story to see if there was anything written about Richard Douglas, but I found nothing."

"There has to be more to Richard Douglas than his wanting to blackmail you into sleeping with him for John to get that involved."

"Do you think John will tell you?"

Marisol shook her head. "No, and I'm not going to ask him. The maggot is gone and you'll never have to worry about him contacting you again."

"What did I miss?" Bethany asked as she entered the room.

Deanna smiled. "Marisol was telling me how much she enjoyed her stay in Puerto Rico," she lied smoothly.

Marisol gave Bethany a level stare. "I thought you told me you can't grow flowers. The ones here are beautiful."

"That's Mrs. Rodgers's handiwork. I spent all morning cooking, so y'all better eat up." The three friends dined on Southern fried chicken, collard greens, macaroni and cheese, fluffy, buttery biscuits, tossed salad and sweet tea.

"I've got to give it to you, Bethany," Marisol said,

swallowing a forkful of mac and cheese. "You can really cook."

Bethany raised her glass of iced tea. "Thank you very much." She set down her glass, leaned back in her chair and stared at Marisol, then Deanna. "I have something to tell you, Deanna."

"Well, what is it, Bethany?" Deanna asked when Bethany focused on the food on her plate.

"A source just told me they have information that Spencer was sleeping with a woman, got her pregnant, then paid someone to attack her so she lost her baby."

"Get the fuck outta here!" Marisol shouted.

Deanna couldn't say anything as she shook her head. "I don't believe it," she gasped once she'd recovered her voice.

Marisol threw her napkin on the table. "You're lying, Bethany."

The blonde closed her eyes. "Would you prefer to read about it in the *Dish* or hear it from me?"

Deanna slumped in her chair, unable to believe what she'd just heard. She and Spencer were making love around the clock to make a baby; meanwhile he'd had an extramarital affair where he'd gotten another woman pregnant.

"Who is your source?" she asked.

Bethany opened her eyes. "I can't tell you."

"What do you mean you can't tell me? I'd like to talk to *your* source before I confront Spencer."

"Try and understand that I'm a journalist, Dee. We don't have to reveal our sources even in a court of law."

"Cut the phony crap," Marisol snapped angrily. "Have you forgotten that we're your friends?"

Bethany chewed her lip. "I'll never forget that. Go home and tell Spencer what you know. Either he'll admit or deny it. But I'm going to warn you that the shit is about to hit the fan."

"Can you stop it?" Marisol asked. "Call in a favor, Bethany, and have them squash the story."

"I'll see what I can do."

Deanna ran a hand over her face. "When does the rag hit the newsstands?"

"Not until next Thursday."

"See if you can pull the story, Bethany. I'll talk to Spencer. Tell your source if the allegations are false, then be prepared for a helluva lawsuit. If this woman can't prove that Spencer paid someone to attack her, then she's going to jail for perjury."

Bethany nodded. "Go talk to your husband and I'll get in touch with my source. I'm so sorry about this, Deanna."

Rising, Deanna pushed back her chair and hugged Bethany. "Thank you for the heads-up."

Marisol also stood up. "I'm going to drop Deanna off at home." She hugged Bethany. "Thanks, friend."

Bethany sat at the table, knowing Mrs. Rodgers would show her friends out. It wasn't often Nathan Nelson left his hovel, but what he had learned he didn't trust to be said on an unsecured telephone line. Jenah Morris had contacted the editor of the *Dish* to out Spencer Tyson. Cheating on his wife wasn't a crime. But Bethany did overhear Spencer threaten Jenah that if she didn't get rid of the baby he would make her regret she ever drew breath.

She knew Nate wouldn't pull the story because it was something that would be talked about for a long time. And the bigger the scandal the more papers he sold. But Spencer wouldn't be the only casualty. The fallout would also affect Deanna. Bethany stood up and picked up the cordless receiver off a table, then closed the French doors. She dialed her husband's number, waiting until his personal assistant connected her.

"Damon, can you come home?" she asked as soon as she heard his voice.

"What's the matter, baby?"

"You need to come home—now!"

"I'll be there as soon as I can."

Bethany sat next to Damon in the sitting area of their bedroom, holding tightly to his hand. "You have to do something. If the story gets out, then Deanna's going to wind up as collateral damage."

Damon looked at the slender fingers entwined with his. He'd underestimated Jenah Morris. Hell hath no fury like a woman scorned. He exhaled an audible breath. "I'll call the editor and see what he wants if he's willing to kill the story. Ms. Morris is another matter."

"If Nathan does kill the story, there's no guarantee Jenah won't go to another paper."

"That's true, but perhaps I can make her an offer she can't refuse."

"Is it true Spencer paid someone to attack her?"

"I doubt it, Beth. I don't believe Spencer would jeopardize his license to practice law by putting out a hit on someone— especially his paramour." Damon kissed Bethany's hair. "I'm glad you called me. I'll try and get this straightened out before the end of the week."

She kissed his ear. "I'll walk you out."

Damon slipped into the back of the sedan, closing the partition between him and the driver. He punched speed dial. "I need you to go by Nathan Nelson's office and ask him how much he needs to retire in the Caribbean. I also want you to let the police know they're going to need a warrant to search Jenah Morris's apartment for a shipment of cocaine and counterfeit handbags. D-Day is Monday night."

He ended the call, not wanting to believe what he'd been drawn into. Deanna Tyson had protected his wife's reputation, and now it was his turn to protect her husband. Jenah had miscarried when she'd been injected with a drug used to precipitate labor, and she'd blamed her lover when he had nothing to do with it.

Damon knew it would be easier to cut a deal with the newspaper editor than it would be to deal with Tyson's spurned lover. He would set her up like she'd planned to set up her former lover. Ms. Morris had come to Washington as a wide-eyed aide to a popular Pennsylvania congresswoman who insiders had identified as one to watch closely, but unfortunately she hadn't followed the rules when sleeping with a married man: keep a low profile and never confront his wife.

Jenah would have a lot of time to reflect on her short-lived affair and her attempt to bring Spencer Tyson down after she was arrested and Mirandized.

Deanna averted her head when Spencer leaned over to kiss her, his mouth brushing her jaw. She hadn't been able to say a word during the drive from Falls Church, and when Marisol dropped her off she could only manage to mumble thank you.

"What's the matter, Dee?"

She patted the mattress. "Please sit down." Spencer sat on the side of the bed. "Instead of asking what the matter is, you should be asking what's wrong."

A frown creased his forehead. "Okay. What's wrong?"

"You are wrong, Spencer. You're wrong for lying to me, you're wrong for sleeping with other women, and you're doubly wrong for getting another woman pregnant while telling me—your wife—that you're still not ready to father a child."

Reaching under the duvet, Deanna pulled out the small automatic handgun. "Now the only thing that remains is where I shoot you."

Spencer stared at the registered handgun he'd kept in the house for protection. "Don't, Dee!"

"Don't what, Spencer? Don't shoot you? And why not?"

"Because we can talk about it."

"Not we. You. You're going to tell me about all the women you've *fucked* during our marriage and when you're done then I'll decide what I'm going to do with you."

Deanna couldn't believe she could sound so calm when all she wanted to do was cry. She'd come home and run up and down the staircase until she felt as if her heart was going to explode. Even when her lungs were burning, her leg muscles were hurting and her knees threatened not to support her body she'd continued to run up and then down. Then she stumbled into her bedroom, retrieved the handgun from a locked box in the walk-in closet and collapsed on the bed.

Numbed, it'd taken her hours to debate whether to shoot her unfaithful husband if he did lie to her. In the end she decided that he wasn't worth her losing her freedom, but hadn't bothered to put the gun back. One thing she did know was that she could never hurt Spencer Tyson the way his whore could. Outing him in the *Dish* would undo everything he'd struggled to achieve. And if the woman could prove her ex-lover was responsible for her losing her baby, then a judge and jury would decide Spencer's fate.

"I didn't mean to hurt you, baby."

Deanna palmed the handgun. "I don't want an apology. I just want the truth."

She'd asked for the truth, believing Spencer had slept with one, maybe two women, but when he told her about the other five, all of whom were married, Deanna felt like sliding off the safety and shooting her husband at point-blank range. But she couldn't—not now. Not when she suspected she was pregnant with his baby.

"I know I was wrong, but I'm not going to ask you to forgive me."

"What do you want?" she asked, staring at the man she thought she knew. He looked as if he'd been carved from stone.

"I want you to give me a chance to prove to you that I can be a faithful husband."

"Can you, Spencer?"

"I have been."

"I'm sure you have. But only when your ho told you she was *swole* the fuck up."

"Please don't talk like that, Dee."

"What! When did you become my daddy, Spencer, telling me what to say?"

"You know I can't stand it when you curse."

"And I can't stand a cheatin' ass husband."

"I told you I stopped."

"You're going to do more than stop, counselor. Your ho is 'bout to out you in next week's *Dish*. She's claiming you paid someone to mug her and she wound up losing her baby. Remember, you're not the only one in this baby-mama drama."

"How do you know all this?"

"I have my sources, Spencer. I know someone who's going to try and kill the story. Even if *he* does, you're still not off the hook, because I know too much about you."

Spencer's face flushed a deep red. "What are you going to do? Blackmail your husband?"

"Yes. I want you to write me a check for one point two mil for a property I want to buy in Reston. There's an eighteen-room abandoned farmhouse set on four acres of land I want to renovate and turn into a bed-and-breakfast."

"How long have you planned this?"

"Not as long as you've been whoring, Spencer."

"You're leaving me." His question was a statement.

"I'm starting up a new business, and because I'm hands-on I'll have to relocate from Alexandria to Reston. Whatever you decide to do is your business."

Resting his hand on Deanna's, Spencer moved it and picked up the gun. "Would you really have shot me?"

She gave him a direct stare. "I'd thought about it, then decided you're not worth me going to jail for. Fucking a man in *our* bed would be the ultimate payback."

"You do that and I *will* kill him."

Deanna shook her head. "No, you won't, Spencer, because then all your sordid affairs would be aired for all of D.C. to see. For you it's always been about image, ego and your ten-inch dick." Sliding off the bed, she walked out the bedroom, slamming the door behind her.

"Now we're even," Deanna whispered as she took the staircase to her third-floor office. She'd cheated once, while Spencer was a serial cheater. He'd claimed he'd stopped, but only time would tell if he could.

But for her it was time she turned a page in her life. She would buy the house and land in Reston, turn it into a B and B and hopefully raise her child in an environment away from the drama of the D.C. political scene.

Chapter Thirty-Four

"Mr. Tyson, I know you didn't want to be disturbed, but there's a Damon Paxton on the line for you."

Spencer's head popped up. He stared at the young woman who substituted for his executive assistant whenever she was out of the office. "Please patch him through." She closed the door and seconds later his phone rang. He picked up the receiver. "Paxton."

"Tyson. This will be the last time we'll discuss this. Make certain you watch the local news tonight."

"Why…" A click indicated Damon had hung up. The lobbyist's reference to *this* had to have been Jenah Morris. After Deanna's disclosure, Spencer had gotten his affairs in order. He'd given her the money she'd requested to buy the property in Reston and he'd drawn up his letter of resignation; he'd updated his will, leaving Deanna Tyson everything. If he was going to be named in a conspiracy, then he didn't want Jenah Morris to get one penny from him. He'd rather serve time than give her anything.

★ ★ ★

Deanna dropped the wand into the bathroom wastebasket, then washed her hands. What she'd suspected was confirmed. She was pregnant!

The joy she should've felt was missing. She still hadn't been able to process the reality of Spencer's cheating. If it had been one woman she knew she would've been more forgiving. But five or six! It would take her a long time, if ever, to recover from his duplicity, and Deanna knew she had to tell Spencer that he was going to become a father.

She walked into the kitchen to find him sitting on a stool at the cooking island, watching the local news. Their relationship was strained, both sharing a bed but sleeping with backs to each other.

She stopped when breaking news flashed across the screen. A woman, surrounded by police and agents with badges hanging from chains around their necks, was led out of an apartment building. The young woman had been under surveillance for trafficking in cocaine and counterfeit designer handbags. The reporter stated that more than half a kilo of cocaine, over a hundred thousand in cash and counterfeit bags worth half a million on the street were found in a closet in the D.C. apartment of an aide to Congresswoman Earline Canton.

"Oh, shit!" Spencer gasped.

Walking slowly into the kitchen, Deanna stared at Spencer. His hands were shaking. "She's the one, isn't she?"

Spencer jumped up as if someone had shocked him with an electrical rod. He met Deanna's eyes. He'd promised himself he was done with cheating, and he'd also promised himself he would never lie to Deanna again.

"Yes, she is."

"Did you know she was dealing drugs?"

He shook his head. "I never had a clue."

Crossing her arms under her breasts, Deanna rested a hip against the countertop. "You dodged a bullet, Spencer."

For the first time in his life Spencer Tyson was humbled as his eyes filled with tears. He'd been prepared to give up everything he'd worked to achieve when the news about his affair with Jenah Morris was made public. Deanna was right. He had dodged a bullet. He'd been given a second chance to become the husband she deserved.

Spencer knew Damon Paxton had something to do with Jenah Morris's fall from grace, and that meant he owed the man. "Yes, I did. I thought about you running a B and B and realized it would be nice to live in the country."

"What are you talking about?"

"I was thinking of putting this house on the market, handing in my resignation and becoming a country lawyer."

Deanna's eyebrows lifted. "Is that really what you want?"

He smiled. "I want whatever it is you want. I know you never really liked this house, but you compromised. Now it's time I do some compromising. Whatever you want, wherever you want to go, I'll be there for you."

"It's not so much about me anymore, Spencer."

"If not you, then who?"

"I'm pregnant."

Spencer felt his knees buckle, and held on to the edge of the countertop to maintain his balance. "Are you sure?"

Deanna nodded. "I just took the test."

Walking on shaking knees, Spencer folded Deanna to his chest. "I love you so much."

Anchoring her arms under his shoulders, she pressed her face to the column of his neck. "You're lucky I love you, too, because you're going to get another chance with me, Spencer Tyson."

Bending slightly, Spencer picked her and swung her around. Throwing back his head, he bellowed as if he'd lost his mind. "Yes!"

Bethany walked into Nathan Nelson's office and stopped suddenly when she saw dozens of cartons stacked along two of the four walls. There wasn't a piece of paper anywhere. "What's up, Nate?"

A clean-shaven Nathan held out his hand. He looked dapper wearing tan slacks, white shirt and navy blazer. Extensive dental work had restored his trademark smile. "Give me the netbook and flash drive and I'll tell you."

She handed him the canvas bag. "What brought on this transformation?"

Nate beckoned Bethany. "Come in and sit with me." He patted a corner of the desk. "I'm retiring," he said when she sat beside him.

"You are retired."

"I'm retiring again. This time for good."

"Where are you going?"

"I'm moving to a little bungalow on St. Thomas." Nate smiled when he saw Bethany's stunned expression. "I don't want to give up my American citizenship."

"Why, Nate?"

"When you asked me to kill the story on Spencer Tyson because his wife is your friend I knew it was time to stop ruining lives. I know you'd become a pariah when you married Damon, so when you told me how Deanna Tyson and Marisol McDonald saved not only you but your husband's reputation, I figured I owed you this one."

"How are you... Do you have enough money to live on in St. Thomas?"

"Believe it or not, I came across some bonds in a pile of

papers when I was looking for something and when I took them to the bank I couldn't believe what they were worth. So, the answer is yes. I have enough money to live a comfortable but humble life in the Caribbean."

Putting her arms around his neck, Bethany kissed his smooth check. "Don't forget to send me a card."

He kissed her back. "I won't. Now get out of here before the moving guys come. Everything in the boxes will be shredded and the computers will be disposed of. I know its polluting, but the flash drives will end up at the bottom of the ocean."

Bethany kissed her mentor again, then walked out of his office. Deanna had helped her and she'd gotten to return the favor. They were now BFFs.

Marisol made it to the bathroom in time to spill the contents of her stomach in the commode rather than on the floor. It was the second time that morning she hadn't been able to keep food down. It was Memorial Day weekend and she'd planned to spend it with her in-laws aboard the McDonald yacht.

She hadn't realized she was pregnant until the tenderness in her breasts continued beyond the end of her menses. When she'd gone to the doctor no one was more shocked than Marisol when the doctor told her she was pregnant. Her first impulse was to call Bryce, but she had decided to wait until he returned from California.

She brushed her teeth, rinsed her mouth with a minty wash and returned to the bedroom to dress for the day. She'd just slipped into a pair of jeans when Bryce walked into the bedroom. "Hey," she said, smiling. "You're back early." Marisol hadn't expected him until the next day.

Extending his arms, Bryce approached. "Hey yourself."

Ducking his head, he covered her mouth with his. "You taste good. I finished up early, so I decided to come back early."

"Did you eat?"

He nodded. "I came back first-class, so I had breakfast."

Marisol reached for the blouse she'd left on the bed. "I have some good news."

Bryce unbuttoned his shirt while Marisol buttoned her blouse. "What is it?"

A mysterious smile softened her lips. "We're going to have a baby."

What happened next would forever be imprinted on Marisol's memory. One moment she was standing in front of Bryce and within seconds she was on the carpet when he backhanded her across the face. His normally pleasant features were distorted, turning him into someone she didn't know or recognize.

"Whore!"

Marisol scrambled off the floor and launched herself at him, but he sidestepped her and she would've pitched forward face-first into the bedside table if she hadn't held on to the post on the canopy bed.

Eyes wide, she glared at him. "That's the first and last time you'll ever raise your hand to hit me."

"What are you going to do, chica? Gut me?"

"No, Bryce. I'm going to do one better. I'm leaving you."

"No, you're not."

"Watch me."

He grabbed her upper arm, holding her tight enough to leave a bruise. "You leave me and I will bury you. That baby in your belly can't be mine because I'm sterile. And I have a good idea whose it is. So if you don't want me to tell the world that Congressman Wesley Sheridan has been balling my wife, then you better keep your mouth shut and play the good little wife."

Marisol's mind was going into overdrive. She couldn't believe she'd been married to a man who'd concealed something so important as his inability to father a child. If the baby in her belly wasn't Bryce's then it had to be Wesley's.

"Okay, Bryce. You win."

His hand tightened, impeding blood flow. "You must really like him."

"Wrong, Bryce. I just don't want to ruin the man's political career. Now please let me go. I need to go out."

"Where are you going?"

"I have to look at some rugs for a client."

Bryce released her arm. "After I shower I'm going to try and get some sleep. We'll go out later tonight to celebrate."

Dream on, clown, Marisol mused as she finished dressing. If there was going to be any celebrating she would be the one doing it.

Marisol walked into small private hospital, asking to see a doctor because she was pregnant and her husband had assaulted her. The bruise on her left cheek and the swelling over her left eye and her upper left arm were examined and photographed.

Her next visit was to a local precinct where she filed a report that her husband had attacked her. She told the officer that she wanted to file an order of protection because she feared for her life and that of her unborn child.

Marisol stopped to eat because with the heat she'd begun to feel faint. Then she did what she'd promised herself she wouldn't do unless it had to do with business. She called Wesley. His phone rang three times and when she was ready to hang up he answered.

"*Hola.*"

"I have to see you."

"What's the matter?"

"I'll tell when I see you."

"Come on over."

Marisol was fortunate enough to find a parking space in front of Wesley's building. He was waiting when she got out of the car. A pair of oversize sunglasses had concealed most of the bruising on her face.

"Thanks for seeing me."

Wesley reached for her hand. "Why the frantic call?"

"I'll tell you inside."

Waiting until she was seated on a tall stool in Wesley's kitchen, sipping from a bottle of cold water, Marisol removed her glasses. She saw shock, fear, then rage in his eyes.

Wesley cradled her face. "What happened to you? Who did this to you?"

"My loving husband."

The natural color drained from Wesley's face. "That sonofabitch! I'll kill him!"

Marisol shook her head. "No, you won't. I went to the police and when he's cuffed, read his rights and locked up that will hurt him a lot more than a beating from you."

"You need to put some ice on your face."

Unbuttoning her blouse, Marisol slipped it off. "I'm going to need more."

Clapping a hand over his mouth, Wesley smothered a savage expletive. "Has he ever hit you before?"

"No."

"Why now?"

"Because I told him I'm pregnant."

"He doesn't want a baby?"

"He doesn't want another man's baby."

Wesley blinked once. "What aren't you telling me?"

"I didn't know Bryce was sterile until this morning."

"If it's not his baby then it has to be…mine." Marisol nodded. "Oh, shit, oh, shit," Wesley said over and over. He covered his mouth, then cradled the back of his head. "This is incredible. I want you to move in with me."

"Wrong, Wes. I can't move in with you."

"Why not?"

"What would it look like? I leave my husband to move in with the man he helped get elected. I've filed for an order of protection and soon as I have it I'm going back to the house to get my things. I'll move into a hotel until I find an apartment. Then I'm going to divorce Bryce McDonald."

"What about the baby, *querida?*"

"Don't worry, Wes. I'm not going to keep you from seeing your son or daughter."

"What about us?"

"Right now there is no us, Wesley. If you're willing to wait until I straighten out the mess I've made of my life I think there may be an us."

"You have to know that I'm in love with you."

She smiled. "No!"

"Yes, *querida.*"

"Come kiss me, then please bring me those ice packs."

Wesley kissed Marisol with a passion that communicated he would love and protect her with his life. She'd asked him to wait and he would, all because she was more than worth the wait.

Epilogue

A year later...

Bethany, Deanna and Marisol sat in the enclosed porch in Falls Church, Virginia, while Paige Paxton had volunteered to babysit Harper Tyson and Zara Sheridan.

Bethany had invited her friends to her home to tell them something she knew might destroy their friendship, but guilt had nagged at her like a toothache. She'd watched their expressions when she told them her involvement with *The Dish* and that she'd been the blogger known as the Insider.

"Even though I knew a lot of stuff about you guys I told my editor that I would never out any of you," she whispered.

"So, that's why you warned me about that woman outing Spencer," Deanna said accusingly.

"Think about it, Dee. If it hadn't been for me, then Spencer would've been ruined or in jail instead of that skank."

Marisol leaned forward, her eyes narrowing. "I find it to

be a little coincidental that drugs were found at her house days before the story was going to break."

Bethany sat stone-faced. "I know nothing about that."

"Yeah, you do," Deanna said. "There's no doubt you and Damon keep very few things from each other."

Shaking her head, Bethany drawled, "I ain't saying nothing."

Marisol winked at Bethany. "You did good, Barbie."

"I'll do even better when you and Wesley finally tie the knot."

"He proposed for the umpteenth time last night and I finally accepted." When she'd presented Bryce with divorce papers he hadn't contested it. He had also pled guilty to domestic assault and was placed on probation with a mandate he attend anger management counseling. Within a month of their divorce he'd remarried, and Marisol hoped he would tell this wife about his inability to father a child.

Deanna and Bethany stared at Marisol. "Have you set a date?" Deanna asked.

Marisol nodded. "Thanksgiving weekend. We're going to have a destination wedding. So everyone's invited to come down to Puerto Rico and hang out at the house. By that time it should be fully furnished. The adults can sleep upstairs while the kids can take over the first floor. It's going to be one big sleepover. Some of the relatives who don't live too far away will open their homes for the overflow."

"Do they speak English?" Bethany asked. "Because you know I can't understand a lick of Spanish."

Marisol rolled her eyes. "No, you didn't go there, Snowflake."

"You'll choke on that word once my son marries your daughter. Connor told me he's in love with her."

Marisol laughed. "Speaking of daughters, Paige asked if she can babysit Zara."

"You'll have to talk to Damon about that. Damon took her away on a father-daughter weekend last month and when they got back she'd changed so much that I thought she wasn't the same girl. I keep waiting for the other shoe to drop, but so far so good."

"Would you mind if she works with me once the B and B is up and running?" Deanna asked. "She could work the front desk during school holidays and recess."

"Now that she's come out of her shell, I'm certain she would love that."

A tapping on the door got everyone's attention. "Come in," Bethany called out.

Damon walked in, his gaze lingering on the two women who'd changed his wife's life. He'd done things he wasn't proud of but were necessary to protect her and her friends.

"We've fired up the grill and Wesley wants to know how you want your steaks."

Marisol stood up, the others following. "Tell Wes we're coming out."

Damon smiled. "The bar is open, so you're going to have to let me know what you want to drink."

Deanna and Marisol shared a look. They'd just stopped breast-feeding, so they were ready to get their drink on. They left the sunporch and walked to the rear of the house, where a large tent had been set up to ward off the damaging rays of the sun.

Damon had invited many of his associates and their wives, but none could compare to the three women who'd become the consummate D.C. wives.

★ ★ ★ ★ ★